GOTHIC RETURNS IN COLLINS, DICKENS, ZOLA, AND HITCHCOCK

List of Previous Publications

"Shopping for an 'I': Zola's *The Ladies' Paradise* and The Spectacle of Identity." *Excavatio* 14.1–2 (June 2001): 108–126, reprinted in *Writing the Feminine in Zola and Naturalist Fiction*. Ed. Anna Gural-Migdal. New York: Peter Lang, 2003. 449–470.

"*Villette* and the Perversions of Feminine Identity." *Gender Reconstructions: Pornography and perversions in literature and culture*. Eds. Cindy L. Carlson, Robert L. Mazzola, and Susan Bernardo. Aldershot: Ashgate, 2002. 53–75.

"Detecting Esther Summerson's Secrets: Dickens's Bleak House of Representation." *Victorian Literature and Culture* 25.2 (1997): 333–349.

"*Frankenstein* and Dis(re)membered Identity." *Journal of Narrative Technique* 24.3 (Fall 1994): 190–211.

GOTHIC RETURNS IN COLLINS, DICKENS, ZOLA, AND HITCHCOCK

Eleanor Salotto

palgrave
macmillan

GOTHIC RETURNS IN COLLINS, DICKENS, ZOLA, AND HITCHCOCK

© Eleanor Salotto, 2006.

First published in 2006 by
PALGRAVE MACMILLAN™
175 Fifth Avenue, New York, N.Y. 10010 and
Houndmills, Basingstoke, Hampshire, England RG21 6XS
Companies and representatives throughout the world.

PALGRAVE MACMILLAN is the global academic imprint of the Palgrave Macmillan division of St. Martin's Press, LLC and of Palgrave Macmillan Ltd. Macmillan® is a registered trademark in the United States, United Kingdom and other countries. Palgrave is a registered trademark in the European Union and other countries.

ISBN-13: 978–1–4039–7225–5
ISBN-10: 1–4039–7225–7

Library of Congress Cataloging-in-Publication Data

Gothic returns in Collins, Dickens, Zola, and Hitchcock / Eleanor Salotto.
p. cm.
Includes bibliographical references and index.
ISBN 1–4039–7225–7 (alk. paper)
1. Dead in literature 2. English fiction—19th century—History and criticism. 3. Literature and society—Great Britain—History—19th century. 4. Collins, Wilkie, 1824–1889—Criticism and interpretation. 5. Dickens, Charles, 1812–1870—Criticism and interpretation. 6. Hitchcock, Alfred, 1899—Criticism and interpretation. 7. Zola, Emile, 1840–1902—Criticism and interpretation. 8. Fiction—Technique. I. Title.

PR878.D37S25 2006
823'.8093548—dc22   2005057477

A catalogue record for this book is available from the British Library.

Design by Newgen Imaging Systems (P) Ltd., Chennai, India.

First edition: July 2006

10 9 8 7 6 5 4 3 2 1

Printed in the United States of America.

*To my father James Salotto who made
all things strange beautiful*

CONTENTS

Acknowledgments   ix

Introduction   1

1 Survival of the Unfittest: Collins's *The Haunted Hotel*
   and *The Woman in White*   13
   The Haunted Hotel and the Ghostly Feminine   13
   Gothic Fragments: Wordless Narration in
   The Woman in White   21

2 Phantasmagorical Narration in *Bleak House*   43

3 Shadowing the Dead: First Person Narration
   in *Our Mutual Friend*   61
   Drowning in Representation   62
   Postscript in Lieu of Preface: Writing Death   65
   Defacements and Live Burials: Narrating the Face   67
   First Person Narration: The Buried Text   75

4 Shopping for an "I": Zola's *The Ladies' Paradise* and
   the Spectacle of Identity   81

5 She's Not There: *Vertigo* and the Ghostly Feminine   101

6 Grave Narrations: Dickens's Later Writings   119
   Great Expectations and the Art of Gravetelling   119
   Narration as Resurrection: *A Tale of Two Cities*   133
   Wandering and Plotting: Dickens's Journalistic Writing   145

Conclusion   159

Notes   163

Works Cited   175

Index   183

ACKNOWLEDGMENTS

In the course of writing this book I have been inestimably indebted to the love, friendship, support, and conversation of many people. In the first stages of this book, Carol Bernstein and Diane Elam offered challenging positive critiques. I was extremely fortunate to have participated in an NEH Summer Seminar on Dickens at the University of California, Santa Cruz in the summer of 2004, led by John Bowen, and want to especially thank him for his intellectual vitality and rigor. The final chapter on Dickens and the novel emerged as a result of the seminar, and I am grateful for John's encouragement and support. The research for this book was supported generously by Sweet Briar College's Faculty Grants Program. *The Ladies' Paradise* and *Bleak House* chapters were published previously in different versions, and I am grateful to Peter Lang and *Victorian Literature and Culture*/Cambridge University Press respectively for permission to reprint.

This book could not have been written without the emotional support and encouragement of my family, particularly Arnold, Florence, and John Salotto. My life has benefited immensely from my colleagues at Sweet Briar College, particularly Lynn Laufenberg and Kate Chavigny. The courses I have taught at Sweet Briar College have been enormously helpful to my thinking regarding the gothic and narrative, and I wish to thank my students for their enthusiasm and questions. Thank you Mary and Mary Ann for all the stimulating conversations over dinner in Philadelphia, and finally thanks Tom for introducing me to the real London, a vibrant companion to the one of my imagination.

INTRODUCTION

In *Gothic Returns*, I take as my subject the literal and metaphorical returns of the dead in Wilkie Collins's *The Haunted Hotel* and *The Woman in White*; Charles Dickens's *Bleak House*, *Our Mutual Friend*, *Great Expectations*, *A Tale of Two Cities*, *The Uncommercial Traveller*, and *The Lazy Tour of Two Idle Apprentices*; Émile Zola's *The Ladies' Paradise*; and Alfred Hitchcock's *Vertigo*. I argue that these returns of the dead are a symptom of and a response to the influence of Darwin on the Victorian Novel, and that they situate plot and multiplot in a new relation. It is my contention that the Victorian novel internalized from Darwin a sense that origins are fundamentally uncertain, and in this way evolved as a field of narration in which multitudes of different stories vie for authority: the novel, if you will, as a survival of the fittest narrative. In this context, the returns of the dead, live burials, and other hauntings that constitute the multiplots of gothic fiction are evidence of the paradoxical survival of stories that have not in fact survived the novel's internal struggles. In *Our Mutual Friend*, The Postscript in lieu of Preface is one such return. In *The Haunted Hotel*, the incineration of a manuscript that reveals the identity of a murderer is another example in which one plot fails to exterminate another and is in turn haunted by it.

That manuscript in *The Haunted Hotel*, whose author is a woman, is also an opportunity to observe that these returns of the dead are typically inflected by gender and by a conspicuous association with categories like home, domesticity, and female subjectivity. In this connection, I argue that the female voice constitutes a particular species of return from the dead, a counter-narrative to a putatively "original" narrative of masculine desire. The Victorian novel performs the ghostly work of superimposition; there is no one identity but rather layers of identities. The multiplot then resembles the labyrinthine byways of gothic narratives. The ghostly dispersal of the female voice haunts the multiplot plenitude of my representative texts. In the interstices of the multiplots are the ghostly remainders of what has been repressed—the figure of woman.

In the penultimate chapter of *Gothic Returns*, I turn to Hitchcock's treatment of the ghostly and superimposition in *Vertigo* as an extension to my arguments about the meaning of the return of the dead in Victorian fiction. I argue that the Victorian novel provides Hitchcock with a formal vocabulary with which to consider gender, narrative, and the return from the dead in film, a twentieth-century repository of spectral narratives. The move that I make from Victorian literature to film links Victorian hauntings to the ghostly effects of projection on the screen, as well as to Hitchcock's obsession with the female body as a locus of masculine anxieties about gender. Through the vertigo shot, the film creates a visual representation of the gothic and the uncanny. Both are linked to Scottie's fear of falling and thus his association with the figure of woman. In *Vertigo* Madeleine becomes the figure for the return from the dead—she is resurrected in Judy and then transformed back into Madeleine. Woman in *Vertigo* embodies the figure of superimposition, covering over and substituting for Scottie's fears and desires.

In the final chapter, "Grave Narrations: Dickens's later writings," I return to Dickens to argue that he creates a gothic writing based on wandering, the multiplot, and double endings in *Great Expectations*, *A Tale of Two Cities*, *The Uncommercial Traveller*, and *The Lazy Tour of Two Idle Apprentices*. Dickens's obsession with the dead coming back keeps the impulse of narrative alive. Dickens narrates so as to avoid literal death, and he stages returns from the dead to spark the beginnings of narrative. In these later writings, Dickens obsessed with death, imagines a world peopled by ghosts whom in essence he has willed to return from the dead. Rather than these returns being negative, they inspire Dickens's imaginative vitality. These returns from the dead provide Dickens with an imaginative resource where he can stage death and resurrection.

Gothic Returns makes the claim that Victorian authors created a narrative mode to present repressive social practices and the effects of that repression whether in the form of live burials or spectral returns from the dead. Victorian gothic creates a spectral mode of narrative that depicts psychological studies of haunted characters, along with reproducing the technological. Much like the photograph, Victorian gothic creates a copy, but a copy with a difference. That copy produces multiple layers of hauntings.

Gothic Returns argues that the gothic served as a mode for cultural horror. It contends that specters haunt the so-called mainstream realistic novel. The realistic novel produces a mechanical imitation of character, but in reproducing men and women, there lurks the threat of a return, invoking the gothic. The mechanical image of representation cannot be put to rest and speaks in its own voice. The model for this return is Frankenstein's monster who embodies mechanical means of reproduction. And surely the Frankenstein monster presents the horror of live burial and a return from the dead in the sense that the true horror of the tale lies in the inability to separate the original, Frankenstein, from the copy or reflection, the Frankenstein creature. In reproducing the figure of woman in the representative texts I discuss, the respective authors and characters experience the created coming back to haunt the creator. The presence of ghosts and the uncanny in the Victorian novel signals an indeterminacy in representation. What is posited cannot rest on any definitive plane; rather, instability of interpretation and meaning undercuts the originary attempt to fix meaning or gender.

If narrative is predicated on origins and ownership, then the Victorian novel enacts the problems inherent in trying to postulate origins and ownership of the female body. That is, while Victorian women were socially and legally subservient, the narratives I discuss present a more ambiguous status for woman. Spectral presences hover over the attempt to figuratively bury women alive.

Moreover, Victorian gothic presents a parallel universe to the concept of the Victorian angel in the house. The Victorian novel focuses inordinately on the home and domesticity. The home is the site for the exploration of character interiority. But this home is haunted by the figure of woman. This space of the home is also closely aligned to the narrative home of first person narration. That is to say, the home becomes a spectral place for narrative representation. Thus, I am claiming that Victorian gothic actually charts a change in narrative representation focusing on the replica and the threat of the replica speaking back. If there is a ghost haunting the Victorian novel, then that ghost surely is the figure of woman who returns in a different guise from her original conception. The figure of woman was a problematic entity with several, and even contradictory, layers of signification.

The concept of origins obsessed the Victorians. I want to connect origins to narrative origins and the gothic novel's foregrounding of the origins of its narrative. For example, many gothic narratives are found manuscripts that the narrator of the tale unfolds to the reader. This predilection for origins points to fakery at the heart of the gothic. This fakery is founded on a fiction, a fiction that contains multiple layers of signification. Thus, origins are multiple and undefinable. And any attempt to certify the origins of woman is haunted by the return of a ghostly signifier that pulsates with contradictory layers of signification. What starts out as a live burial shifts to a return from the dead. All Victorian narrative in a sense entails a return to origins, whether to childhood or to a childhood home. This return is uncanny because it signals a return to the original home, the womb. Therefore, in returning to origins, one is confronted with the ghost of the feminine. The search for an original unity is disrupted by an origin that cannot be attained or fully articulated. The origin of species is indeed uncanny because it is not locatable. Therefore the Victorians' obsession with classification and order belies an original disunity. Darwin's *On the Origin of Species* actually prefigures Freud's essay on "The Uncanny." Both are inordinately fixated on origins: the former, with the origins of species, and the latter with the origins of horror that leads back to the originary home, the womb. Darwin argues for indeterminate origins for the species, and this indeterminacy surfaces in the novel in the form of specters that challenge an original model. Darwin posits that "a breed, like a dialect of a language, can hardly be said to have had a definite origin" (40).

Gothic narrative resembles Darwin's entangled bank; this metaphor for life rewrites a model of order and in its place fashions a world of chaos and transgression, a hybrid world. The last lines of Darwin's text present the metaphor of the entangled bank where Darwin imagines that "whilst this planet has gone cycling on according to the fixed law of gravity, from so simple a beginning endless forms most beautiful and most wonderful have been, and are being, evolved" (490). This last statement presents a succession of creatures, endless evolving into one another. This concluding image evokes the idea of a superimposed identity; that is to say, the endless forms he speaks of operate as ghosts flickering in and out of existence, presenting the idea that what is dead lives on. In this sense, Darwin's text is a gothic one in that the origins of species posit not one progenitor but a succession of ghostly indeterminate figures. What one considers home or the familiar as a basis of origins turns out to be filled with multiple reconstitutions of beings.

Thus, the home in Victorian gothic fiction bears the weight of a place that is haunted by the ruined structure of the domestic sphere. Home and its association with femininity and tranquility served as the site for the deployment of gender roles. The home turned into a haunted place because the dream of the stable home actually produced the unfamiliar or the monstrous. *Gothic Returns* shows that the domestic sphere in the Victorian period was a problematic concept because it ultimately brought to light multiple and contradictory layers of signification for the home and woman's place in it. What was supposed to be the locus for a sheltering from the outside world became a place full of ghosts, such as the fantastic home of Miss Havisham in Dickens's *Great Expectations.* The home represented a place of order, but the Victorian home also contained the spectral and haunting obsessions. The house became supernaturalized, and, in turn, I am claiming that narrative embodies the spectral through not only literal ghosts but also through layers of meaning that vie in the text. In Darwin's text what gets buried alive returns in a new form. This is the claim I am making for Victorian gothic. Victorian gothic announces that what was purportedly dead, either literal or figurative, is always in the process of appearing in a different guise. Therefore, the fixed subject position of the angel in the house evolves through the process of ghostly narration that refuses to locate woman in one particular place. Darwin creates a metaphor for death in life when he writes: "the great Tree of Life . . . fills with its dead and broken branches the crust of the earth, and covers the surface with its ever branching and beautiful ramifications" (130). This life in death I am aligning with a system of narratives that return and proliferate.

The move from British literature to Zola and France is in part influenced by *The Ladies' Paradise*'s insistence on the link between the gothic technologies created by the department store and Britain's fascination with the gothic as an outgrowth of the rise of technology, the rise of capitalism, and the development of the railroads. While Victorian gothic situated the gothic in the domestic sphere, *The Ladies' Paradise* locates the gothic in the new home—the department store. The home then becomes the site for the deployment of capitalism and technology. The home/department store transforms into a public space that incorporates the spectral residues of the private. In other words, the home becomes a space available for public viewing— one can learn to be "at home" by watching other displays of "being at home." Specters inhabit the home, a direct result of the ghostly residue of the spectacle. Interiority, no longer a private space, becomes peopled with others' images, ideas, and things. Interiority thus rests on a succession of images that one cannot claim as one's own. Thus, technology and the corporate structure of the department store form a new identity.

The department store creates a new model for identity, an identity that simply is a succession of ghostly images paraded in front of the spectator for confirmation and consolidation. Identity is no longer consolidated in one body but in a succession of bodies for consumption. Window shopping allows the viewer to enter the space of the display, encouraging identification with an entity outside oneself. This model for a new technological identity is located in the dummy, the figure who is dead/alive. The body thus becomes the site for the uncanny—is it dead or alive?

Too, the department store encapsulates the rapid technological accelerations provided by the railroad; that is to say, identity not only becomes spectral but it also becomes mechanized by the obsession with time. Identity then is not only transformed by space—the space of the department store—but by time, itself. The acceleration of time continually brought to the forefront the idea of a fragmentation of the self. If time fragments, then the self in time cannot be consolidated producing an uncanny feeling that one moves randomly through time and space.[1]

The uncanniness produced by rapid advances in technology involving space and time consolidates itself in the invention of the cinema. For the cinema is the mode *par excellence* for the spectral. Presenting a succession of images and a replication of character through the screen, the cinema as a mode is the apogee of the Victorian gothic. Fabricating a fabrication through the image and the screen, the cinema plays on presence and absence. Photography represents live burial, that is, it is uncanny in the sense that it recalls a fabricated return from the dead via the technology of the image. A technology of specters and shadows, the cinema embodies the mechanized and corporate self.

The body in cinema is the ghostly presence, and this is nowhere more evident than in the ultimate successor of Victorian gothic, Alfred Hitchcock's *Vertigo*, where Scottie falls in love with the ghostly Madeleine who mysteriously dies and returns from the dead. *Vertigo* is a meditation on the power of the cinema to coextensively kill the image and raise its ghost from the dead. In this sense, cinema is the perfect technology for live burial in that it is always involved in the in-between space of presence and absence—which is the place of desire. Desire in *Vertigo* becomes uncanny because it reflects a limbo-like space between the spectral and the real.

The lost object must be recuperated through the image—through the apparitional return from the dead. Too, the image guarantees an impersonation; that is, the image presents a ghostly figure with whom one can identify through inhabitation. But this illusionary model cannot hold, and we enter the phantasmagorical space of trickery or fakery. *Vertigo* simultaneously falls in love with the apparition of woman, but also points to her as a phantom illusion of Scottie's. He imaginatively kills her off so he can bring her back to life, but her ghostly presence also adds another layer of meaning to the film—she remains outside the scope of Scottie's representation of her. *Vertigo*'s true haunting engenders the phantoms of gender. Cinema provides the illusion of woman, but the image is full of ghostly presences that deny a univocal layer of interpretation. Scottie's story is layered over by Elster's, Madeleine's, and Judy's stories, all providing gothic excess. This gothic excess embodies a wish to preserve an originary model of desire, but the spectacle of the image of woman deconstructs that desire, revealing the fakery underlying this desire. Woman as ghostly figure is simply that, a figure of the imagination that haunts Scottie throughout the film. That she materializes so readily before him points to the power of the imagination to believe in the image one has created.

Criticism on the gothic has seen a resurgence in the past twenty years.[2] On the one hand, my study is concerned with social gothic; that is, the repressive social practices that engender the return of the repressed in Victorian fiction. On the other hand, I argue for the conjunction between the narrative and psychological dynamics of the gothic. Thus, the novel becomes the site for live burials; it turns into a ghostly narrative form. As the Victorian period progressed, the novel grew increasingly concerned with aberrant states of mind, such as we see in the portrayal of Miss Havisham in *Great Expectations* or in Dorian Gray in *The Picture of Dorian Gray*. The gothic, in a sense, becomes internalized, and the novel serves as the repository for obsession, fetishism, and displacement, in which repressed desires are figured. The Victorian novel becomes a phantom-like structure, where the representation of mind turns out to be an uncanny place, full of ghostly signifiers that cannot be articulated directly. Too, gothic narrative is obsessed with returns and the multiplot, which I argue is the narrative form in which to represent specters. That is, narratives proliferate much like an army of ghosts. Thus, the gothic participates in the creation of a new psychological reality where lack, absence, and psychological fragmentation inhere.

While this may seem to suggest a gloomy forecast, actually the live burials I am arguing about effect a reconstitution of identity where the subject encounters contradictory layers of signification. Out of this chaos arises indeterminacy—with the potential to challenge binary modes of thinking, particularly about gender. The ghost, populating the Victorian novel, in a sense, becomes the leftover, the excess in meaning. The ghost has a positive political role—in the Foucauldian sense that change can be effected through resisting the status quo. In making the domestic the source for the gothic,

Victorian novelists uncovered the form of oppression centered in the home. Part of the positive force of Victorian gothic is that in the home things never appear quite what they seem. Thus, the home for Lucy Snowe in *Villette* is inhabited by ghostly presences. Superimposition serves as the trope then for Victorian gothic; what appears on the surface is also subject to what lies beneath, and the two in the texts I discuss are always in conflict with one another. Victorian gothic replaces the haunted castle with a network of meanings, and live burial always suggests a story within a story.

Wilkie Collins's two texts *The Haunted Hotel* and *The Woman in White* both deal with the suppression of the female voice and the ghostly remainders of the narratives being haunted by that repression. Thus, while women's voices are buried in the text, they are resurrected by other forms of narration, such as the play text in *The Haunted Hotel* and Anne Catherick's dream text in *The Woman in White*. Thus, both narratives suggest that live burial of one's story in the text proper resurfaces in another text that then rewrites the main text. While the main text seems to have survived, actually the subtext through its terror and horror presents a struggle involving voices that will not die. Both texts capitalize on women's stories that lie just beyond the purported supremacy of the text proper. The true haunting in *The Haunted Hotel* entails the Countess's ghostly attempts to narrate her story in the form of a play. Her animated corpse reveals her difficulties in narrating her story; the dead-alive body becomes the symbol for the dead-alive story that she narrates. The ruin or fragment is important here; the text suggests that woman's story cannot be articulated fully in a narrative system that privileges survival of the fittest. But here the story articulates that survival of the fittest is simply a social construct to authorize a certain kind of power. The specter though undercuts the idea that what is killed off is dead. In fact, the specter and spectral narration continue to live on, in a sense more powerful than what has survived in the text.

"Gothic Fragments: Wordless Narration in *The Woman in White*" engenders a subtext to the logical detection posited by the legal discourse of Walter Hartright. This logical textual apparatus is haunted by the figure of woman in several ways. Anne Catherick presents the most unruly figure because literally her text cannot be interpreted under a survival of the fittest narrative—that is the fittest being the most rational. Laura's text is a graven image in the sense that Hartright writes her story, over her dead inert figurative body, literally while gazing at her portrait. Memorialization or narrative fixes women, but the text evokes specters that refuse to stay put.

"Phantasmagorical Narration in *Bleak House*" in effect presents the idea that the survival of the fittest narrative is a red herring; that is to say, each narrative cannot derive from clear-cut origins. Esther Summerson's narration is haunted precisely because in assuming her voice, Dickens comes face to face with the feminine. Whereas the two earlier texts present a descriptive view of woman's social position, in *Bleak House* Dickens channels the figure of woman in his portrayal of Esther Summerson. Now one could argue that authors do this all the time; they write in different voices and assume different identities. In *Bleak House* however, inhabitation of character produces a ghostly effect both in the narration of the story and in the text's obsession with ghosts, namely the ghost's walk. The confrontation with the feminine is particularly uncanny for Dickens in that he confronts a lack of difference. He goes home in this text to the domestic, but the domestic turns out to be a haunted place full of voices that have no definite origins.

"Shadowing the Dead: First Person Narration in *Our Mutual Friend*" links the figure of the corpse to first person narration and representation through the narrative mode of the multiplot. Thus, *Our Mutual Friend* brings to the forefront the uncanniness residing in figuring identity and telling the story of identity. This uneasiness is represented in the form of the novel—the multiplot that presents the structural hauntings of stories that proliferate. The multiplot calls forth the embedded story—in other words, something is being elided in the story. What lies behind the so-called plenitude of the multiplot is the figure of the corpse, the corpse of first-person narration that cannot be articulated until the middle of the text; and this story, full of confusion and meanderings, suggests the limits of representation of self and identity.

If the self is figured as a story told through third-person narration, then it operates as a form of the modern technology of narration at a step removed. Significantly, the text begins with the dispersal of the voice through the presentation of the corpse and third-person narration, and ends with the railroad in Dickens's Postscript in Lieu of Preface in which he recounts his near death by railway accident. This frame positions the novel as a kind of labyrinthine structure encased between two structures of dispersal.

"Shopping for an 'I:' *The Ladies' Paradise* and the Spectacle of Identity" moves the argument to France and shifts the focus somewhat to argue that technology and capitalism create a new form of identity centered on display and the copy. All of the items in the department store suggest fecundity, but they also summon the corpse of the dead woman, upon whom the store is literally constructed. Layers of representationality in the text simultaneously elevate and kill the female body. This doubleness surrounding the figure of woman sparks the uncanny. The image of the corpse serves as the ghostly remainder underlying the profusion of goods in the department store. The text is obsessed with describing and cataloging all of the items it offers for sale; this obsession underscores that woman cannot be fixed or contained. Lying underneath all the piles of words used to describe woman is the fear that she eludes comprehension.

"She's Not There: *Vertigo* and the Ghostly Feminine" links the motifs of live burials and returns from the dead in Victorian literature to the cinema, the media of specters. Film technology creates a phantom illusion of presence—that the image is really there in front of our eyes. The return from the dead in *Vertigo* underscores the rewriting of that image. In a sense, *Vertigo* is the most ghostly of the texts I discuss as film itself is a ghostly apparatus that presents illusions. The central paradox of the film is that Madeleine/Judy is never fully there—in the position which Scottie places her. She is always somewhere other. Thus, multiple ghosts structure the film.

Vertigo presents the cinema's illusionary crisis of seeing. That is, seeing is very much a field of ghosts and illusions, and seeing as a trope is centered on the figure of the woman. The vertigo shot famously zooms out and in presenting the vertiginous effect of Scottie's fear of heights. This formal aesthetic feature concretizes a failure in vision and in a forward trajectory of logical reasoning. Technology presents woman as the image *par excellence*; in *Vertigo*, however, hauntingly the nun speaks the last lines of the film: "I thought I heard voices." These voices of the nun—the no one—clash with Scottie's narrative of detection where he tries to find "an answer for everything." Voices and ghostly presences present an alternative reality to Scottie's logical detection. Scottie's vertigo is linked to his inability to place Madeleine/Judy in a perspective other than the apparitional image. Thus, the true vertigo in the film rests on the ghost woman who looks back and recasts her image. *Vertigo* presents the disjunction between woman as idea and woman as representation. This idea calls forth a limbo-like space teetering on the brink—where interpretation collapses into the vertiginous space of the vertigo shot, where the image is unstable.

"Grave Narrations: Dickens's later writings" posits that Dickens pioneered a new mode of narration—the multiplot. The multiplot novel continually restages death and rebirth through the dynamics of presenting new stories. Thus, stories are buried so that another story can continue. Structurally, Dickens uses the multiplot to stage repression in the texts, such as in *Great Expectations*, for example, where all of the adjacent plots bury the true story of Pip. Dickens also employs the multiplot to show the layering effects of a multitude of subjectivities, rather than a discrete one. Thus, superimposition of selves and stories precludes an originary identity. The network of narrative passageways that Dickens employs in his gothic stories and in the multiplot novels foregrounds wandering rather than arrival. As a representative for this wandering, Dickens calls forth the ghost who is homeless and who is animated by the desire to narrate. Narrating keeps the ghost alive and also Dickens the narrator.

Gothic Returns makes the claim that the novel after Darwin needed to tell a new story. Literary narrative replaced the scriptural word—narrative thus is a dynamic force that evolves and never dies. Narrative may be haunted by many voices, but these voices reconstitute narrative. In essence, nothing ever dies in narrative, but continually gets reworked into other stories. The returns that I argue for in my representative texts are all ghost-like; what is dead always returns through the return of the repressed, the multiplot, double endings, or stories that cannot seem to properly end. Rather than the terror usually associated with gothic stories, these texts create a gothic exuberance of the wandering ghost who narrates. Enlightenment seems to be the operative mode rather than fear or terror. The tortuous, fragmented narratives of the eighteenth-century gothic novel turn into a vibrant labyrinth of words and stories during the Victorian period.

CHAPTER 1

SURVIVAL OF THE UNFITTEST:
COLLINS'S *THE HAUNTED HOTEL*
AND *THE WOMAN IN WHITE*

THE HAUNTED HOTEL AND THE GHOSTLY FEMININE

Wilkie Collins's novella *The Haunted Hotel* offers a novel way to read the feminine voice in nineteenth-century British literature. I want to argue that when the female voice is repressed in the texts I discuss, whether structurally or thematically, that voice returns in some fashion. Therefore, we may say that one of the ghosts of the nineteenth-century British novel is the return of the repressed female voice. The gothic novel in its obsession with ghosts is always involved with flickerings from other worlds. These flickerings I locate in woman's speech that is buried alive but ultimately resurrected through attempts to get her story told. The gothic novel profoundly interested Collins because it allowed him to express the tensions between a rationalist discourse present in the realistic novel and an "irrational" discourse of the gothic that was more closely aligned both fictively and realistically with woman's legal and social position in nineteenth-century Britain.

In *The Haunted Hotel*, a dead body haunts the occupants of a hotel in Venice. The novella opens with the Countess Narona who is presented as an "enigma." The Countess marries Lord Montbarry but he dies soon after in Venice, and the Countess receives a huge sum of insurance money. The Countess Narona is reputed to have conspired with her brother and/or perhaps lover in having her husband killed and in exchanging his identity with his servant who is dying of consumption. Lord Montbarry is held a secret prisoner in the depths of the palace and is killed. His body is reduced to ashes with the exception of his head. The palace in Venice is later turned into a hotel, and the family and friends of the late Lord Montbarry have several encounters with his ghost. The dead man's head is buried in a secret passageway in the hotel room. Here is a description of the head of the dead man:

> The flesh of the face was gone. The shrivelled skin was darkened in hue, like the skin of an Egyptian mummy—except at the neck. There it was of a lighter colour; there it showed spots and splashes of the hue of that brown spot on the ceiling. . . . Thin remains of a discoloured moustache and whiskers, hanging over the upper lip, and over the hollows where the cheeks had once been, made the head just recognisable as the head of a man. Over all the features death and time had done their obliterating work. The eyelids were closed. The hair on the skull, discoloured like the hair on the face, had been burnt away in places. The bluish lips, parted in a fixed grin, showed the double row of teeth. (202–203)

This description of the ruined face of the Countess's husband parallels the buried and disfigured narrative of the Countess as she writes about the mysterious occurrences surrounding her husband's death in the form of a play that she hopes will be staged. The ruined face of the husband serves as the double for the ruined face of the narrative of the Countess. Her narrative within the text takes the form of a play, and at the ending of the novella, the new Lord Montbarry, the head of the family, consigns her manuscript to the fire. Thus, the story of the Countess is corrupted and co-opted. What is interesting is that we never know the "real" story. Is the Countess's play meant to be her confession or is her buried narrative meant to suggest that ghostly reverberations of her story hover over the text's rationalist discourse, calling into question notions about truth? The story then is gothic at the narrative level; that is to say, in its obfuscations and multiple embeddings, we travel through narrative labyrinths that refuse definitive meaning and closure.

Even though the narrative about the events that the Countess records in her play does not survive—it is thrown into the flames—still her voice haunts the text. Multiple stories vie for authority, and at the ending, her story is put to rest by the new Lord Montbarry. In Darwin's schema, her story does not survive, yet it remains powerful because of what it articulates about representation and power. Collins writes a story about the Countess's narrative and the difficulties in relating her story. Thus, narrative for the Countess is haunted. In this sense, the haunted hotel is a cover for the haunting occasioned by the Countess's writing. Even though the Countess's story is buried, it survives because the return of the story embeds multiple layers of meaning, and ultimately we are faced with a story that resists interpretation. The gothic is obsessed with the motif of live burial. Particularly gruesome instances appear in Charlotte Dacre's *Zofloya* and in Matthew Lewis's *The Monk*. One of the features of the gothic novel is the difficulty in getting the story told.[1] The narrative difficulties are aligned with the problem of narrating what lies just beyond language, which is most closely aligned with the language of terror or horror. I connect the thematic obsession with live burial to the burial of the female voice and the terrors that it occasions.[2]

Woman's speech in *The Haunted Hotel* is transgressive and must be contained by the narrative proper. Collins clearly aligns the gothic with the terrors of the female voice in that the Countess's confession cannot be spoken directly; it must be related in the form of a play. In the form of a play, the terror can be subdued and managed by the form of the gothic plot itself. Gothic stories do contain the unspeakable, the inconceivable, and the unnamable, but what would make the story even more terrifying is to have it told as a confession by the Countess.

Thus, *The Haunted Hotel* relates the Countess's terrible confrontation with narrating her story and having it heard. Her gothic plot involves writing a story only to have it buried alive. By burying her story, the new Lord Montbarry hopes to confine the terrors occasioned by a woman's collusion in killing her husband for his money. Collins's text foregrounds the gothic obsession with embedded stories—stories that proliferate like the labyrinthine passageways of the gothic castle. The most embedded story—the Countess's— reminds us that at the heart of the gothic lies the obsession with narrating and writing experience that is too terrible. Here the terror is a narrative one; it is almost as if the narrative itself becomes like the severed head of the Countess's late husband.

The introduction of the Countess signals the text's obsession with reading the female and how that is connected to managing the terrors she occasions. The text opens with the confrontation between the Countess and a medical man of science. The Countess asks the startling question: "I want to know, if you please, whether I am in danger of going mad?" (91). The doctor cannot explain her illness; he says to her: "You completely puzzle me" (92). There is something in the Countess that disturbs the Doctor; he can't quite put his finger on it. The narrator describes the effect the Countess has on the Doctor: "The startling contrast between the corpse-like pallor of her complexion and the over-powering life and light, the glittering metallic brightness in her large black eyes, held him literally spellbound" (90). To be held spellbound is to be in someone's power, and it is this effect of her eyes that most disturbs the Doctor.

The story then begins as a tale of the effect of a woman's look. What happens when the woman looks? Right from the beginning, the text positions the unruly woman as threatening. When the woman looks we are never far from the uncanny, because her look occasions what ought to have remained secret. Her look disturbs the binary opposition between man and woman and rational and irrational, thereby setting into play a discourse that is uncanny, neither here nor there, incapable of being categorized. This alignment with the uncanny is markedly observable when the Doctor cannot offer any medical aid to the Countess:

> Her wild black eyes looked upward, with an expression of despair so defiant and so horrible in its silent agony that the Doctor turned away his head, unable to endure the sight of it. The bare idea of taking any-thing from her—not money only, but anything even that she had touched—suddenly revolted him. (97)

The Countess calls to mind the figure of Medusa. She gazes at the Doctor; her gaze is fraught with the terror of disregarding the differ-ence on which the gaze is predicated.

One of the most unsettling things about the Countess is that she serves as the subject of gossip for the men at their club. "Every human creature, with the slightest claim to a place in society, knew the Countess Narona. An adventuress with a European reputation of the blackest possible colour—such was the general description of the woman with the deathlike complexion and the glittering eyes" (99). The tame woman in the text would be precisely the proper English woman Agnes Lockwood who in essence has no story to tell.

The Countess's threat lies not only in stories told about her, but also in her potential to tell stories. Her first question to the Doctor about whether she is mad creates the potential to unleash the unknown. And the fact that she has a story to tell leads to the idea of the Doctor being infected by her. "Had the woman left an infection of wickedness in the house, and had he caught it? (97). This fear of contagion is closely aligned with narrative; the gothic certainly does produce out-of-control narratives.

There is a way then that the text works to render the Countess into a corpse, an animated corpse that must be managed by counter-stories. Many of Collins's stories begin with the male fascination for and fear of the female. Think, for example, of Walter Hartright's gothic confronta-tion with Anne Catherick at the opening of *The Woman in White*. This encounter with the female I want to term gothic ambivalence. The confrontation with the female entails both beauty and terror in that it calls forth the sublime, but the negative as well as the positive sublime. Thomas Weiskel explains the sublime experience thus: The sublime moment occurs when the gazer is overwhelmed by something in the landscape. Weiskel argues that the positive sublime produces "death by plenitude," or "the abyss of idealism" leading to linguistic excess. The negative sublime, however, evokes alienation and terror resulting in a crisis or breakdown in language. He goes on to state, "We are reading along and suddenly occurs a text which exceeds comprehension, which seems to contain a residue of signifier which finds no reflected signified in our minds" (24). This description of the sublime is important for my argument because it allows for a connection between the sublime in nature and the feminine sublime in that woman provokes a feeling of terror, in her unleashing of the uncanny. The resulting feeling is one of unease, of disease, in fact, of the fear of contamination. The uncontained woman is not far from the idea of disease, the horror of which is that it cannot be contained. The model of rationality that the text tries to set up is haunted by the figure of the unruly woman.

Perhaps the uncanniest moment in the text is when the Countess writes her story in the form of a play. After several characters have stayed in the room occupied by the late Lord Montbarry at the hotel, they relate their tales of being haunted by someone or something. Mr. Francis Westwick, one of the deceased's brothers is most intrigued by the theatrical possibilities of the story as evidenced in the following:

> When his brother and sister first told him what their experience had been, he instantly declared that he would go to Venice in the interest of his theatre. The circumstances related to him contained invaluable hints for a ghost-drama. The title occurred to him in the railway: "The Haunted Hotel." (175)

The Countess wishes to tell her story and is motivated by many reasons. First, she thinks of money. "I always want money" (182), she exclaims. But this does not seem to be a fully satisfactory reason. She goes on to say to Mr. Westwick, "I am a living enigma—and you want to know the right reading of me" (183). Perhaps her motive then is to explain herself. But finally, we come to understand that she believes that transforming her life into narrative may lessen her terror. She relates:

> I am filled with presentiments which make this wicked life of mine one long terror to me. It doesn't matter, just now, what they are. Enough

> that they absolutely govern me—they drive me over land and sea at
> their own horrible will; they are in me, and torturing me, at this
> moment! . . . . [M]y resolution is to absorb this self-tormenting fancy
> of mine in the occupation that I have told you of already. (184)

The story that she tells of her husband's murder certainly partakes of
gothic machinations, but I want to focus on her narrative of the story
as participating in the gothic structure of indirection and secrets.

In telling her history in the form of a play, the Countess distances
herself from the original, perhaps suggesting that there will always be
a veil over narration. This distance from the original suggests that her
story is subject to distortions and gaps. Narrative itself then becomes
a sort of ghost; it is neither fact nor fiction, neither alive nor dead. It
is in the space of the precipice, or the border, on shaky ground, not in
a permanent place. This is the place of the uncanny. Not only does her
writing reveal a secret—that of her husband's death and its causes—
but it also uncovers the secret of writing a woman's life. Whatever the
real cannot postulate, the gothic fragment speaks. Instead of focusing
on her motives in the plot, she concentrates on the surface machinations
of the gothic plot employed to murder her husband. Her motives,
then, are hidden under a veil of language.

Woman's writing is very much aligned with the gothic in that both
have a secret; both exist outside the structures of language itself. The
Countess's play is marked by the fragment, by the missing part, by the
lacuna. She, herself, is figured as a corpse; "her face had fallen away to
mere skin and bone" (137). And her corpse-like face is likened to her
difficulties in bringing the narrative to life. In this regard, as I have
mentioned earlier, the Countess is associated with the dead rotting
face of her late husband. They have an uncanny encounter where the
Countess is forced to confront the dead face:

> Downward and downward the hideous apparition made its slow
> progress, until it stopped close over Agnes—stopped, and turned
> slowly, so that the face of it confronted the upturned face of the woman
> [the Countess] in the chair. . . . The closed eyelids opened slowly. The
> eyes revealed themselves, bright with the glassy film of death—and
> fixed their dreadful look on the woman in the chair. . . . [Agnes] saw
> the eyelids of the living woman open slowly like the eyelids of the
> dead. . . . (203)

This mutual gaze of terror confirms the connection between the dead
man and the Countess. Lord Montbarry's hideous face—a face in
ruins—aligns itself with the Countess's narrative in ruins. The

narrative in ruins is the result of her difficulties in articulating her story. The Lord's ghostly return from the dead, producing horror in the eyes of the guests at the hotel, evokes paralysis, in that the guests are rendered speechless. Similarly, the Countess in telling her narrative suffers from a kind of paralysis in articulation. Her story is left unfinished at the time of her death. As the narrator observes:

> Looking at the writing-table as he went out, Henry saw the sheet of paper on which the Countess had traced the last lines of writing. The characters were almost illegible. Henry could just distinguish the words, "First Act," and "Persons of the Drama." The lost wretch had been thinking of her Play to the last, and had begun it all over again! (230)

She obsessively returns to her writing; in fact, beginning all over again, as if one version is not enough to contain all the elements she wants. But the second version would also not be enough, and she would have to begin over again. In being doubly removed from language, the only thing her text can do is to endlessly go over ground already covered, all the while emitting ghostly remainders of secrets. Once the Countess creates a text, it is dead, so she must revive it by beginning it again. Gothic death in *The Haunted Hotel* returns in a different form—as a reconstitution of the original. When one seeks to return to origins, one finds not one but many.

The perpetual death of narrative as evidenced by closure and by the Countess's obsession with beginning her story anew parallels the position of the feminine—of being buried alive and returning from the dead. The return from the dead is the place of narrative, and narrative is a haunted text—forced to repeat. Narration then, at a step removed from the actual occurrence, acts as a screen. As the Countess struggles to tell her story, her narrative becomes a narrative in ruins:

> In one important respect, the later portion of the manuscript differed from the pages which he had just been reading. Signs of an overwrought brain showed themselves, here and there, as the outline of the play approached its end. The handwriting grew worse and worse. Some of the longer sentences were left unfinished. In the exchange of dialogue, questions and answers were not always attributed respectively to the right speaker. At certain intervals, the writer's failing intelligence seemed to recover itself for a while; only to relapse again, and to lose the thread of the narrative more hopelessly than ever. (234)

Henry attributes the failure of narrative to a failure caused by the Countess's approaching death. But perhaps the failure to narrate stems from her own horror in trying to narrate a story which if it were to be read correctly would reveal not only her secrets but the difficulties of storytelling for women who have a novel story to tell.

Reading her story simply as a ghost story undercuts the narrative ghosts that the Countess encounters as she tries to relate her story. That is to say, while multiple possible plots exist for her gothic ghost play, not that many would exist in a real woman's life. What is so haunting about her narration is that it occupies a limbo-like space, on the threshold of being real or not real. Her story thus is dead/alive: what mode does it occupy—a gothic narrative or a confession? Precisely, the hybrid nature of her story—the inability to categorize her story—is gothic. Gothic trappings inhabit the space of the Countess's mind—we cannot separate the generic conventions from the "real." The narrative is uncanny because we never know if we are in the real or in the realm of the fantastical gothic. Not only is she haunted by her story, but, we, as readers, also participate in the hauntings occasioned by the collapse of narrative. It is almost as if we are witnessing a gothic writing—one in ruins.

The Haunted Hotel also presents us with a multivoiced text that on the surface tries to contain the voice of the Countess, but her text, through its ghostly returns and circumlocutions, articulates the difficulties in getting the story told. The missing part of her text—the unfinished lines, the misattributions of speech—all point to a crisis in language that reflects the crisis of identity in the Countess. In losing the thread of her narrative, she questions and challenges the desire for an ending, which is after all the desire to see things neatly contained and wrapped up. Her story, partaking of the gothic and the melodrama, raises more questions than it provides answers. For instance, what really happened at the palace and who is the Countess? Her many names reveal her assumption of identities. Like a character in a play, she enacts many roles: that of Mrs. James, Lady Montbarry, and the Countess Narona.

The Countess occupies the position of the hysteric who has difficulty narrating her story. Her body as corpse reflects not only a body in ruins but also a narrative body in ruins. The burial of her story within a story—her play within the text of *The Haunted Hotel* itself—reflects a thematic concern with blocked narration. One cannot have direct access to the Countess's story. This blocked narration is a form of live burial, but the subtext returns to haunt the narrative proper through the frightening idea that the story can never be finished. The lack of closure of the Countess's story perhaps inspires the most dread, and that is why it has to be destroyed.

After the upheaval and disturbance caused by the Countess's narration, the new Lord Montbarry must restore the rational. He exclaims after consigning the manuscript to the flames:

> I won't believe anything that has happened. The supernatural influences that some of us felt when we first slept in this hotel—your loss of appetite, our sister's dreadful dreams, the smell that overpowered Francis, and the head that appeared to Agnes—I declare them all to be sheer delusions! I believe in nothing, nothing, nothing! (238)

The supernatural is equated with the manuscript of the Countess. Lord Montbarry thinks that by declaring the supernatural to be "nothing," then by magic he can will it away. What the text reveals, however, is that the figure of woman will continue to haunt in many different guises, through narrative, foremost. It is not so much that the hotel is haunted in the text, but rather that the Countess in the act of telling her story haunts the narrative through her ghostly attempts to narrate her story. Her animated corpse reveals that she will return to tell her story. Her narrative is a narrative in ruins in that it is disfigured by its literal destruction, but her story still exists in uncanny supplements to the contained narrative of rationality.

Gothic Fragments: Wordless Narration in *The Woman in White*

As we have seen, *The Haunted Hotel* highlights a woman's difficulties in narrating her story and her attempts to figure herself as a character in a gothic play, thereby ensuring that her story does indeed survive in a fictional form. In this story, however, narrative becomes the victim—the story must be thrown into the fire because of its transgressive potential. The Countess, never a victim in her own life, as she possibly colludes with her brother/lover in the murder of her husband, must be tamed through the destruction of her manuscript. Collins's text points to the subversive potential of what could happen when a woman narrates. The Countess's wanderings in her narrative announce the impossibility of fully reading woman and discovering any one truth about her.

The Woman in White, however, demonstrates the effects of what happens when there is no narrative for women's stories. What cannot be spoken in this text is gothic; the wordless speech of Anne Catherick and Laura Fairlie haunts the pages of the multiple narrators. The obsessive narration in the text proper masks what the women might say if they were afforded the possibility. Thus, their wordless speech becomes a gothic void that lies outside the text proper. Voices banished from the text, they become a ghostly presence; in between the void we glimpse the terror of what lies beyond language. In this sense, Laura and Anne are buried alive, neither alive nor dead in the system of narration the text sets up.

The Woman in White, however, continues the subversive gothic form of the wandering narrative that we saw in *The Haunted Hotel*. The structure of the tale—told in the form of many different narrators—privileges the open-endedness of narrative and the potentialities of being lost in the gothic byways of the multiplot. The gothic in this novel situates itself as a hybrid form—that is to say, the realist narrative mode of Walter Hartright's detective story continually conflicts with the gothic mode of the women in the text—namely Anne Catherick and Laura Fairlie. The two modes are superimposed upon one another—providing for a ghostly effect of a double narrative, neither here nor there. What cannot be incorporated directly in the realist narrative returns in gothic fragments of the missing parts of Anne and Laura's lives. We remember that Laura cannot remember what happens to her in the mental asylum. Hartright narrates: "At this point in her sad story there was a total blank. She had no impressions of the faintest kind to communicate—no idea whether one day, or more than one day, had passed—until she came to herself suddenly in a strange place, surrounded by women who were all unknown to her" (427). The device of the missing part of Laura's life suggests the terror of the unspeakable and the unnamable—her experience is too terrible to be narrated. But the missing part also suggests the possibility of a return. In this way the gothic elements deconstruct the realist mode of the detective story.

Walter Hartright, the detective figure in Wilke Collins's *The Woman in White*, explains his mode of detecting Sir Percival Glyde's secret: "[H]ere was the approach to the Secret, hidden deep under the surface of the apparently unpromising story which I had just heard" (472). That Collins's story explores the tension between depth and surface apprehensions of reality attests to the power he invests in the art of detection—to uncover that which lies underneath the surface.[3] One of the secrets to be unraveled pivots on the identity of Sir Percival. As we discover, he assumes the identity of a baron. Collins's fiction complicates our understanding of identity by having people take on false identities and by introducing doubles such as Laura Fairlie and Anne Catherick. Collins superimposes the detective plot that uncovers Sir Percival and Fosco's identity with the identity of woman in the text. In doing so, he points to the detective novel's failure to read woman. That is to say, logical detection represents an inadequate means to read the secrets of woman's identity. In place of truths about identity, Collins offers us the fiction of the undetected woman who remains a mystery.

Woman's identity is represented through the gothic plot. And this gothic surrounding of the woman prevents Walter Hartright from discovering what I want to claim is Collins's point—Walter fails to see the mystery right before his eyes. He sees the surface of Laura and Anne Catherick, but he accords them no depth. We, as readers, then must search for the clues Collins presents to unravel the secrets of woman's identity. Freud in "The Moses of Michelangelo" describes psychoanalysis as an inquiry "accustomed to divine secret and concealed things from despised or unnoticed features, from the rubbish-heap, as it were, of our observations" (*Standard Edition* 13:222). Hartright's obsession with uncovering the secrets of Sir Percival and Fosco's identities blinds him to the secret of woman in the text. Collins, in layering his story with multiple secrets, suggests the limits of the detective figure to apprehend a more complex view of reality that is encoded in the gothic plot.

Indeed, the structure of the text in its use of multiple narration privileges a layering of reality rather than a monolithic voice. This multiple voicing, or voicing over, dismantles the attempts of the detective to successfully solve the case.[4] The other voices contest and rewrite the straightforward narrative of logical detection. The multiple voices also point to a crisis in narrative. In the excess of the multiple narrations, we can discover the text's anxiety about what cannot be spoken. These other voices are most insistently heard in the interstices of the gothic plot.

The discourse of detection arises out of the nineteenth century's privileging of realism and rationality. But Collins is at pains to show the limits of realism in apprehending the core of identity, particularly woman's identity. Collins offers us mysteries or secrets about identity coded in the figure of woman. Woman in the text haunts the discourse of reason. And the secrets of woman's identity are associated with the gothic plot of buried secrets. The text creates a gothic form to encase woman's identity—and that gothic form is the labyrinth. On the one hand, the labyrinth calls forth the prison. Woman is enclosed in a set of structures: social, cultural, and narrative. On the other hand, the labyrinth evokes the gothic trope of wandering; woman in the text cannot be located clearly in one person or one story. Even though the text works to encase her in a structure of narrative where she is written about, she haunts the narrative by her refusal to stay put.

Anne and Laura are buried alive, but it is in this space that they paradoxically take on a life of their own, much like the wooden doll Olympia in Hoffmann's "The Sandman."

While Walter Hartright successfully discovers the secrets of Sir Percival Glyde and Count Fosco and restores Laura Fairlie to her "proper" identity, *The Woman in White* marks a failure in detection. Hartright's narrative is to a great extent informed by an impulse to cover up, to in fact be blind to the social inequalities the novel addresses. He smarts when he thinks of Laura's unjust treatment by Sir Percival, but in effect Collins doubles Hartright and Sir Percival in their treatment of Laura, as I shall show. Thus, Hartright is complicit in the crimes he seeks to detect.[5]

This failure of detection inextricably involves the identity of Laura Fairlie. The forward thrust of the story—the surface of the story—entails the restoration of Laura Fairlie to her rightful name. This is the logical part of the story. Collins's subtext, however, deals with another type of detection—the detection of woman's identity. The central problem the novel raises hinges on woman's identity in a culture where she does not exist—legally, socially, and politically. Collins makes clear the invisibility of women through his use of multiple narrators. The two women in white—Laura Fairlie and Anne Catherick—appear as figures in relief or in paintings where they are viewed and are not the viewers. In Walter Hartright's legal presentation of a mock trial, these pivotal figures are never afforded the opportunity to narrate their own stories. The two women in white become texts about which other persons speculate. They are rendered "illegitimate," outside the law of narrative practice, and Hartright takes great pains to link the law and narrative. Thus, Laura Fairlie and Anne Catherick suffer the fate of live burial; they are buried alive in reported narratives. Their lives are stories within stories, elucidating that there is something threatening about them that cannot be spoken. Hartright domesticates the detective story and becomes the patriarch who has complete control of the narrative and thus of these two women's identities.[6] Through narrative, he fills the vacuum that he has created for them.

We read the detective story to uncover its mysteries. The detective tale gives the reader pleasure as he or she gains knowledge by puzzling through the secrets afforded by the text. *The Woman in White*'s secrets pivot on the question of identity. Who is Sir Percival Glyde; who is Count Fosco; and what crimes have they effected? These secrets are disclosed to us by the detective handiwork of Walter Hartright. The question of the identities of Laura Fairlie and Anne Catherick, however, is not so simply resolved. The quest for origins, which I see as central to the detective story plot, reveals a cipher when it comes to Laura and Anne's identities. This cipher we can most readily discern in Collins's preoccupation with the category of knowledge in the text. Collins raises a philosophical question; namely, what is knowledge?[7] Is knowledge to be apprehended solely through logical means of detection? Or is knowledge a much more slippery category? That is to say, what is knowledge predicated on, and more important, what is its connection to power and interpretation or detection? Clearly, through the use of multiple narrators, Collins undercuts the forward logical thrust of Hartright's scheme. The multiple narrators introduce the element of diverse modes of detection and interpretation. Collins uses multiple narrators to render murky the question of truth or of one way to read knowledge or identity. Multiple positions uncover the limitations of logical thought by refusing to resolve contradictions. And particularly when it comes to the question of woman in the text, we cannot precisely discover her origins and identity under Hartright's system of detection.

In the center of the novel, four of the main characters discourse on crimes and their detection. Laura Fairlie maintains that "crimes cause their own detection" (232), that murder will be found out. Count Fosco replies: "The fool's crime is the crime that is found out; and the wise man's crime is the crime that is *not* found out" (232). He goes on to explain his view of the perfect crime:

> When the criminal is a resolute, educated, highly-intelligent man, the police in nine cases out of ten, lose. If the police win, you generally hear nothing. And on this tottering foundation you build up your comfortable moral maxim that Crime causes its own detection! Yes— all the crime *you* know of. And, what of the rest? (233)

Fosco believes that the wise criminal can elude the eye of the police; his secrets will be unreadable to the plodding police. This passage serves as a telling commentary on Walter Hartright and his secrets in the text. As we read the account of Hartright's battle to uncover the crimes committed by Fosco and Sir Percival, the text encourages readers to detect Hartright's secrets. As the detective story works to make its readers participate in the act of discovery—of who done it—Collins adds a new twist to the detective story. The detective becomes the figure to be detected. In a sense, then, he is the criminal who must be found out by the reader. In a text obsessed with detection, Hartright cannot exempt himself from being found out. And what exactly are his secrets and crimes?

Hartright would like to play the wise man. As detective, he uncovers the crimes of others, but his uncovering of crimes in the name of morality and truth is open to detection. In his presentation of the story, he is the savior who will restore order to the house of Fairlie; he will rid it of the stain of Sir Percival and Count Fosco. As the upholder of morality, he recasts himself as the knight figure who protects women. But as knight, he preserves hierarchy by condescending to Laura and Anne, rather than by envisioning equality. In the passage above, Fosco and Sir Percival believe themselves to be the wise men who can elude detection. Similarly, Hartright presents himself as beyond detection. In doing so, he becomes prey to his foolproof means of detection.

That is to say, he sees detection as a straightforward business of finding clues; for example, he discovers Sir Percival's identity from clues he gathers in the church registry. But detection, as Collins sees it, also involves a psychological detection that works against the detective's logical means. This psychological detection entails seeing below the surface level of reality to discover the secrets of identity. Thus, as against Hartright's mode of detection Collins sets up the much more difficult apprehension of character as something not given as in a clue, but something that must be apprehended intuitively. This means of discovering identity embodies contradictions and the by-ways of the gothic plot that has no definitive conclusion. Gothic identity thus is set up against logical identity, and the former introduces a counterpoint to reactionary systems such as the law and narrative that seek to enclose women in a neat category.

In seeking to find the "real" Laura Fairlie, Hartright at every step of the way misreads her; thus, he kills off her character in the name of detection. His scientific method of detection dehumanizes the woman whom he claims to have saved. Detection for him necessarily entails keeping woman in her proper place. Clearly, the women in the text must serve the needs of the plot, and that plot centers on Hartright as the detective figure who solves the mystery. Characterization for woman, then, is not possible in Hartright's scheme. In fact, Anne Catherick represents a threat that must be overcome. She first appears as an apparition, wandering the streets of London. This wayward female must be firmly encased in the plot of the detective story with the male hero as arbitrator.

Woman, however, remains a mystery to the reader who uncovers Collins's clues. Origins for her originate in a story told about her. The woman in white thus represents a blank page; she is known primarily by her silence, by her inability to narrate her own story, which equals a metaphorical and literal death. Her story within a story literally cannot be spoken. The figure of Scheherazade in *The Arabian Nights* remains alive as a result of her ability to narrate. She tells her captor story after story, night after night, and her listener, dazzled by her stories, spares her life. As the story of Scheherazade demonstrates, narration is inextricably bound to life, while the absence of narration signals death metaphorically and literally.[8] Traditionally, women have figured in stories as the object of the gaze, to be written about as idealized figures subject to a certain type of knowledge predicated on the legal and social codes of a particular culture. Collins claims that knowledge is in fact encoded in a set of beliefs or ideology. Further, he underscores the limitations of knowledge and thus the limitations of the detective story in that Walter Hartright never penetrates the secrets of Victorian woman's identity. He, like Oedipus, is blind to the central mystery the novel harbors.[9] Reading Laura Fairlie and Anne Catherick through a limited point of view, Hartright cannot enter into an empathetic identification with them.

Perhaps the success of a master detective resides in his ability to enter the mind of the criminal. In "The Purloined Letter," Poe's detective Dupin expresses that in many cases the police fail in their modes of detection because they "consider only their *own* ideas of ingenuity; and, in searching for anything hidden, advert only to the modes in which *they* would have hidden it" (292). Dupin here sets the stage for this ideal detective; that is, one who enters into the mind of the criminal to experience the world from his point of view. Detecting woman in the text becomes an impossibility for Hartright, because for him they are all material to be molded into his interpretation. While Hartright may enter the mind of the criminals Fosco and Sir Percival, he cannot view woman as a category with which he can engage in a dialogue. The multiple narrations speak to, challenge, and reinterpret one another's narration, but Hartright desires to present a monolithic account of detection.

Hartright's address to the reader will elucidate Collins's preoccupation with establishing his view in opposition to Hartright's, which is essentially a rationalist one.[10] Hartright's objective is "to present the truth always in its most direct and most intelligible aspect" (9).[11] Juxtaposed with this one universal truth, Collins presents multiple truths that upset Hartright's tidy world order. Of course, these multiple truths are encased in the narrative's presentation of multiple narrators. The story within a story destroys the idea of one definitive truthful story. The figure of the woman in white, unexplainable in the eyes of the law, remains outside the institution of narrative. As the law is an institution, narrative is also an institution controlled by the master narrator, Walter Hartright. He gathers all the evidence, abridges Marian's narrative, and in the last section of the novel assumes the role of omniscient narrator when he foregoes first-person testimonies and tells the story in his own words so that "the tangled web will be most speedily and most intelligibly unrolled" (414).[12]

Hartright tries to make his world knowable, but Collins takes great pains to undercut this view. At the center of Collins's story are the mystery of knowledge and the mystery of identity.[13] To be human is to be uncertain, and Hartright's attempts at rationalization reveal an overdetermined sense of trying to master what cannot be fully mastered.[14] Collins introduces irony into his portrayal of Hartright by showing his failure to see truly the characters of Anne Catherick and Laura Fairlie. Collins then may be said to have written a novel that is an anti-detective novel inasmuch as there are areas of knowledge that cannot be penetrated. P. D. James presents a similar picture of the multifarious ways of interpreting reality when she writes of her detective Dagliesh in *Death of an Expert Witness*:

> Before the case was finished Dagliesh would have received a dozen pictures of Lorrimer's personality, transferred like prints from other men's minds. From these amorphous and uncertain images he would create his own imaginings, superimposed and dominant, but essentially just as incomplete, just as distorted—as were the others—by his own preconceptions, his own personality. (75–76)

Hartright's way of reading and interpreting limits his way of seeing in the sense that his view is a distortion rather than a composite reflection of reality. Hartright wants a world where he reigns as the master narrator/detective, but as Collins suggests Hartright's world is a contingent one.

And what does Hartright see when he looks at Laura and Anne? He is a creative artist; he is a painter and teacher of drawing. Surely, the text ironizes Hartright's errors in perspective—that is to say, his inability to take in an entire picture and the meanings inherent beyond the surface. It is fitting, then, that Hartright teaches drawing. Further, his talents are transferred to the art of narrative where he adopts a methodical and rational way of apprehending identity or knowledge. In the opening of the story, Collins introduces his preoccupation with representation and ways of seeing. Hartright's role as a painting master entails teaching Marian and Laura perspective, thus to see. One day, Laura and Anne show their sketches to Hartright; as

Marian puts it: "the pupil's sketches must pass through the fiery ordeal of the master's judgment" (54). Then Marian proposes a carriage ride and continues:

> If we can only confuse him all through the drive, between Nature as it is, when he looks up at the view, and Nature as it is not, when he looks down again at our sketch-books, we shall drive him into the last desperate refuge of paying us compliments, and shall slip through his professional fingers with our pet feathers of vanity all unruffled. (54)

Marian's discourse on mimesis points ironically to Walter's misrepresentation of feminine identity. Lacking the skills of an artist, Laura and Marian corrupt Nature. Similarly, in his role as detective, Hartright is hampered by his literal rendering of Anne and Laura. Thus, as an artist, he copies them, but his copies suffer from his limited way of seeing. Material facts and a straightforward rendering of reality lead to misrepresentation. As master narrator, Hartright never quite understands that each rendering of character is a counterfeit. In addressing representation as a fakery, a forgery, so to speak, Collins opens up a space for multiple ways of seeing. For Collins, point of view, as evidenced in his use of multiple narrators, is predicated on contradiction and multiple ways of seeing.

To understand what Hartright does not see in relation to Anne and Laura, we must first examine Hartright's appraisal or reading of another woman, Marian. He is charmed and disconcerted by Marian's appearance; he praises her graceful figure, but is startled by her "ugliness." He goes on to explain:

> [T]o be charmed by the modest graces of action through which the symmetrical limbs betrayed their beauty when they moved, and then to be almost repelled by the masculine form and masculine look of the features in which the perfectly shaped figure ended—was to feel a sensation oddly akin to the helpless discomfort familiar to us all in sleep, when we recognize yet cannot reconcile the anomalies and contradictions of a dream. (35)

The latter part of Hartright's discourse is telling. He admits that the contradictions he sees in Marian's physical appearance render him extremely uncomfortable. She, in fact, poses an obstacle to his straightforward apprehension of reality. Hartright's way of seeing is to resolve contradictions. He sees reality in black and white; part of his discomfort lies in the fact that he compares his unease to a dream where the unconscious takes over, and all attempts at rational reading or interpretation fall by the wayside.[15]

When Hartright meets a woman in this text, we are never far from the uncanny. Thus, we might say that the textual apparatus that Hartright sets up is haunted by the figure of woman. The moments in which Hartright meets with Anne and Marian are marked by his being startled; the text presents us with two portraits of women that make Hartright uneasy. The third introduction of a woman figure, Laura Fairlie, satisfies him but only because he has constructed her image through drawing and narrative. It is interesting that he looks at her portrait while writing his narrative. "The water-colour drawing that I made of Laura Fairlie, at an after period, in the place and attitude in which I first saw her, lies on my desk while I write" (51). He writes in essence over her image, over her dead body. The text, in fact, is narrated retrospectively over two graves or corpses: Anne Catherick's and Laura Fairlie's graven water-color image. This fear of the woman must be managed by memorialization either through narrative or through the inscription on the grave. Anne, Marian, and Laura are particularly transgressive figures because, in effect, they have stories to tell.

In this connection the woman in white is like the figure of the nun in gothic stories. The nun in several gothic tales is the ghost of a female transgressor, for example, the Bleeding Nun in *The Monk*. She wanders because her story has not been fully resolved or heard. In this way, the female figures in *The Woman in White* are aligned with the transgressive nun; they may be buried alive, but they return. Anne Catherick sparks the entire narrative, Marian vies with Hartright as the detective figure, and Laura could narrate a story of madness—of her incarceration in the mental asylum. Laura through the image Walter draws of her is made canny; he needs this image as a talisman against the power of the uncanny as he writes his narrative. He writes of Laura within the domestic shrine containing her portrait.

When Hartright sees Laura or Anne, he is confronted with what he cannot logically explain. They then must be rendered into spectacles so he can look at them safely through narrative. The fact that they look alike is a cover for what so disturbs him about them. Their look or a returned look might produce a story out of his control. An interesting counterpart to Hartright is Mr. Fairlie who desires quiet in his life. In a sense, he wants no story, no complications of the plot, just as Hartright in his quest wants to resolve contradictions. Hartright's story is always already written and simply requires consensus. Mr. Fairlie in his disastrous handling of Laura's marriage settlement reasons: "Was it likely that a young woman of twenty-one would die before a man of forty-five, and die without children? On the other hand, in such a miserable world as this, was it possible to over-estimate the value of peace and quietness" (152). Hartright desires a story of his own making, where he can, in effect, control the outcome. He then may be said to short-circuit the narratives of Laura and Anne by interposing his detective plot on the course of the action. He wants for Laura and Anne the "peace and quietness" of not having a story to tell. He, in effect, co-opts their stories by not affording them the choice to narrate.

Walter's description of his unease in the passage quoted about Marian above is crucial for our understanding of woman's identity. Woman is like the sleep that Hartright describes in that she has the potential to disturb the logical processes of Hartright's mind. Marian's body and the woman in white's body produce sensations of terror. Both bodies embody contradictions that Hartright cannot tolerate. Contradiction for him would lead to a loss of identity that would, in effect, render him helpless.[16] The body of woman then must be put into an ordered and non-threatening place by the logical forces of the detective story. It is the aim of his narrative to make the woman in the text into the woman in white, into a legible creature whom he can control by his logical detection.[17] Thus, while the criminals in the text, Sir Percival Glyde and Count Fosco, usurp Laura and Anne's identities, another criminal exists in Walter Hartright.[18] I mean to suggest his criminality in the sense that he participates in a legal system, in a narrative system, and in a social system that renders woman into a cipher, a blank page on which he can write. At the close of Fosco's story, he relates: "With my vast resources in chemistry, I might have taken Lady Glyde's life. At immense personal sacrifice, I followed the dictates of my own ingenuity, my own humanity, my own caution, and took her identity instead" (612). Like Fosco, Hartright usurps Laura's identity by not allowing her access to narration. Marian says of Laura's impending marriage to Sir Percival:

> Before another month is over our heads she will be *his* Laura instead of mine! *His* Laura! I am as little able to realise the idea which those two words convey—my mind feels almost as dulled and stunned by it—as if writing of her marriage were like writing of her death. (185)

Clearly, Laura undergoes a symbolic death after her marriage to Sir Percival. Her identity is subsumed by her husband's; actually, her confinement in the mental institution represents the logical extension of her imprisonment in her marriage. In a sense, Laura is dead throughout the entire narrative. She, through the act of Walter's narration, becomes a memorial, an elegy, to his memory of her. Her name is an inscription on her tombstone—"Sacred to the Memory of Laura, Lady Glyde" (405). Hartright renders her dead by foreclosing her story. In effect, he treats her like a child whom he must protect. His contest with Count Fosco and Percival Glyde is a battle among men, and it is only as Laura's husband that he can achieve his purpose. "If I am to fight our cause with the Count, strong in the conscious-ness of Laura's safety, I must fight it for my Wife" (559). In effect, just as Hartright exorcises Fosco and Percival Glyde from the text through the machinations of the detective plot, he also exorcises Laura.[19]

In Collins's *The Law and the Lady*, he prefaces the novel with a note to the reader: "[T]he actions of human beings are not invariably gov-erned by the laws of pure reason." It is pure rationality that reduces woman to a blank.[20] While Hartright may align woman with the uncon-scious in that she is threatening to him and therefore he must re-present her in a logical detective narrative, Collins uses woman in the text to validate the unconscious. She is the mystery only insofar as she exists in a system that does not recognize her. In this system, she is veiled, inscrutable. Freud posed his famous question: what does a woman want? Collins's answer might be to suggest that woman will always be viewed as the unconscious or mysterious in a system that does not give her access to the conscious or rational; the rational and the conscious are embodied in cultural institutions such as the legal system and narrative.

The gothic elements in Collins's novel fissure Hartright's attempts to control reality through a logical narrative. It is important here to note that the gothic according to Hartright is a mode of terror; thus, he sees woman as a threat who might turn his world topsy-turvy. Collins though introduces what I want to term gothic *jouissance*; that is to say the gothic for Collins also suggests an excess in interpreta-tions of woman. It is no accident then that Collins aligns the gothic with the figure of woman. The gothic in its excess struggles to present the lapses and the gaps in all attempts to privilege a so-called rational world.[21] Hartright describes the apparition of the woman in white:

> There, in the middle of the broad, bright high-road—there, as if it had that moment sprung out of the earth or dropped from the heaven—stood the figure of a solitary Woman, dressed from head to foot in white garments, her face bent in grave inquiry on mine, her hand point-ing to the dark cloud over London, as I faced her. (23–24)

Her appearance causes a *frisson*. Hartright describes her as an appari-tion springing "from out of the earth or dropped from the heaven."

Clearly, she is unrecognizable; she does not fit into a knowable category in Hartright's mind. What Hartright sees is that which is always haunted by something else. She is the stuff of the imagination, the stuff of dark terror and the uncontainable.

In fact, she may be said to represent the uncanny that as Freud claims is "often and easily produced when the distinction between imagination and reality is effaced" ("The Uncanny" 244). This first appearance of the woman in white opens up a Pandora's box for Hartright that he must contain. Essentially, Hartright's detective project and ultimately his narrative project seek to validate what cannot be validated. This moment presents for Hartright an interpretation in ruins, for his attempts to read the woman in white founder. Woman arises out of chaos in that Hartright is suddenly confounded by the presence of the woman in white. The resulting narrative represses and contains the fear of this originary encounter with woman. He wants origins for woman to originate in a readable story, and his detective plot seeks to contain the gothic irrational element in woman's identity.

The appearance of the woman in white traumatizes Hartright. The text begins on a note of rupture. Anne gazes and eludes his control; this moment gets transformed into the sublime, of a crisis in interpretation that rests on how to read Anne. What is particularly uncanny about this moment is that Hartright is incapable of fully naming what inspires so much terror and dread in him. His reaction is overdetermined; his recognition of Anne's difference and non-difference produces a shock that upsets his neat binary distinctions. The sensation of terror that he feels is a kind of wordless sensation that reveals the sensation but fails to establish its originating cause. The sensation novel is thus linked to the uncanny in its inability to fully narrate the cause of the unease, even though as I have argued this cause is almost always a woman. The woman in white calls up the terror of the unnamable.

In the first appearance of the woman in white, Collins presents a tableau on the power of the gothic to disrupt the rational. The rest of the narrative tries to cover up this scene, in effect, repressing the terror.[22] This terror is recast by the means of condensation and displacement onto narrative. We might even argue that narrative represents Hartright's way of gaining control over his anxiety about the woman in white. If he can control her threat by narrating it out of existence, then his words cover over the originary scene of terror. Also, his uncanny sensation puts him into the position of the person without language, the person who screams to reflect terror, namely, the woman. He spends the remaining narrative trying to cover over this place of terror outside language, projecting his situation onto the women in the text whom he renders mute.

When Anne looks at him, she suggests the potential ruins of his tidy world. Collins describes her gaze as a "grave inquiry." It is this grave inquiry that leads to the death of Hartright's way of seeing. Her grave inquiry evokes an end-stop to Hartright's rationalist discourse. His discourse, in its tidiness, belies the terror that it just may come undone. As Foucault has maintained in *Madness and Civilization*, madness actually represents a crisis in reason. The detective plot and the gothic plot collide in this text. This collision produces superimposition suggesting a remainder that lurks in the background. David Punter writes of the Gothic as engaging with a "textual and psychic *chiaroscuro* where plain sight is continually menaced by flickerings from other worlds" (*Spectral Readings* 3). Within the detective text lie hidden secret passageways that throw shadows over the logical presentation of the story.

The woman in white does haunt the text, and her voice layers over Hartright's rationalist one. She embodies the gothic horror of what has been repressed. She, in effect, haunts the narrative because she remains outside the law and outside representation. In the passage quoted above, she gives a clue—her hand points to the "dark cloud over London" as if to illustrate Collins's critique of nineteenth-century society's system of beliefs and practices. The gothic may be read as a corrective to the social order, as a mode that undermines objective evidence and one logical way to read reality. Collins's gothic plot subverts all attempts at logical detection. The woman in white remains on the edges of the narrative, hiding and lurking, in effect, haunting the text.

The lack of her narrative actually produces another narrative: that of the hysteric who has difficulty narrating. Her narration is blocked; in effect, her narrative suffers from a live burial. But the ghostly remainders of her voice penetrate the rational detective discourse. When it is clear that Anne Catherick's identity has been exchanged with Laura's and that Anne is indeed the one in the grave, Walter exclaims: "So the ghostly figure which has haunted these pages as it haunted my life, goes down into the impenetrable Gloom. Like a Shadow she first came to me, in the loneliness of the night. Like a Shadow she passes away, in the loneliness of the dead" (555). But ghosts die a very long death, and I want to argue that her death does not guarantee her being put to rest. The narrative retains traces of her that have not been uncovered by the detective plot.

The instability of woman's identity must be presented through the gothic plot insofar as realism cannot contain what cannot be expressed logically. In this regard, the gothic is the mode for mutability, to express that which cannot be encoded in a tidy package. Perhaps what Hartright fails to detect is that as much as he uses the detective plot to construct a stable reality, it does not constitute a safety net to which he can cling. The figure of the nun in Charlotte Brontë's *Villette* presents a useful parallel to the gothic elements surrounding woman's identity in *The Woman in White*. The nun reveals that identity is a marker for instability and shifting points of view, as we find that she is not a ghost but the cross-dressed lover of one of the girls in the convent. Finally, the nun becomes a symbol for representation in the text, when Lucy Snowe tears up the effigy of the nun lying on her couch:

> In a moment, without exclamation, I had rushed on the haunted couch; nothing leaped out, or sprung, or stirred; all the movement was mine, so was all the life, the reality, the substance, the force; as my instinct felt. I tore her up—the incubus! I held her on high—the goblin! I shook her loose—the mystery! And down she fell—down all round me—down in shreds and fragments—and I trod upon her. (587)

The nun is all costume; her identity rests on the putting on of identity through the marker of clothing. This scene suggests that identity is a sign, and as a sign it can transform. The nun carries the burden of representation, which essentially separates substance from representation. She is shrouded in mystery, in stories told about her, particularly the legend of the nun who was buried alive in the garden "for some sin against her vow" (131). Her figure is overdetermined, when in reality the nun that haunts the Rue Fossette is a prop, an empty symbol. Brontë divests the nun of story and offers in its place a deshrouding of identity. The gothic in enshrouding woman in mystery actually recasts that mystery through a dismantling of story and symbol.

Anne Catherick, similarly, is encased in mystery, but that mystery is revealed through the limited vision of Walter Hartright. She has to be a mystery because literally Hartright cannot "see" her. The gothic then in this text undercuts Hartright's way of seeing; it undermines the clear-cut reality he privileges. Collins addresses through the gothic a reassessment of cultural ways of seeing woman. Walter sees Anne and Laura as a series of stories. They remain fixed symbols for him, thus incapable of transformation. Collins, however, in separating sign from symbol, sees the image of woman as a false one. If the nun figure in *Villette* is the ghost of representation, the turning of the sign into an empty relic, then Laura and Anne are the ruins of representation in Walter's scheme; thus, they, as the leftovers, haunt the system.

In *The Woman in White*, the scenes of the appearance of Anne Catherick turn on her inability to be represented or read definitively. If she were afforded the opportunity to narrate, she might upset Hartright's tidy narrative. When she does speak, it is always reported by another, as if to suggest that her discourse has to be filtered through an already existing one. Additionally, in labeling her mad, Walter casts her as the other, thereby privileging his rationalist discourse. To prop up his identity, he needs her to represent the opposite of him. She exists as a series of stories, the markers for identity or costuming. Underneath, she remains a mystery that cannot be decoded. Hartright associates her with secrets and mystery, claiming that "The way to the Secret lay through the mystery, hitherto impenetrable to all of us, of the woman in white" (455). Hartright sees her as white, as penetrable through his words, but she is unreadable. In presenting her speech, Hartright erects a *cordon sanitare* around her that effectively works to erase her agency through re-presentation.

But to complicate this argument on Hartright's attempts to contain the gothic, I want to posit that Anne Catherick's speech is heavily marked by dreams and their symbolism as if to suggest a corrective to a straightforward apprehension of reality. In a letter to Laura Fairlie, she recounts a dream in which she is the agent separating Laura from Sir Percival. The intent of the letter serves as a warning to Laura not to marry Percival. Anne dreams that Laura and Sir Percival are brought asunder by "two rays of light" that "pointed straight between you and that man. They widened and widened, thrusting you both asunder, one from the other" (80). These rays of light are actually Anne's tears that turn "into two rays of light which slanted nearer and nearer to the man standing at the altar with you, till they touched his breast" (79). In investing Anne's language with heavy symbolism, Collins suggests another level of reality. In doing so, Collins shows a leakage in a rationalist discourse predicated on binaries. In the story above, Anne imagines a counter-narrative to the one of marriage with herself as the agent of change. While Anne's imaginings are powerless to stop Laura from marrying Sir Percival, they offer a different reality in that Anne serves as the agent of change, a third agent upsetting the duality upon which gender rests in this text.

In contradistinction to the multidimensional reading of woman's identity in the text, the gothic elements coextensively portray the horrors of what happens when one's identity can be interchanged.[23] The woman in white thus becomes reduced to a gothic hall of mirrors. Looking into the mirror, she sees a duplicate image that is never properly hers.

When Laura meets Anne and converses with her, Laura explains to Marian:

> While I was looking at her, while she was very close to me, it came over my mind suddenly that we were like each other! Her face was pale and thin and weary—but the sight of it startled me, as if it had been the sight of my own face in the glass after a long illness. The discovery—I don't know why—gave me such a shock, that I was perfectly incapable of speaking to her for the moment. (277–278)

I read this passage as a reflection of woman's identity in nineteenth-century British literature. The nineteenth century was particularly obsessed with a quest for origins. From Wordsworth's *The Prelude*, to Dickens's *David Copperfield*, to Darwin's *On the Origin of Species*, nineteenth-century authors explored identity as an account of origins. But how might one formulate a narrative of woman's origins? What are they? One way to answer these questions is to say that when Laura Fairlie sees her double in Anne Catherick, Collins suggests that all women are double reflections—they have been reflected, so that when they see, they see an image that is like yet unlike them. When one lives in a legal and social system that co-opts one's identity, it is difficult to imagine what it is one sees when looking into the mirror. Part of the horror then of the woman in white is that she reflects women living in Collins's English society. Encasing Anne and Laura in the mental institution symbolically re-creates their lack of origins, in the sense that they originate from and in institutions.

In this gothic tale of terror, of the horror of a woman losing her identity, what cannot be known is transferred onto the body of woman. The woman in white then represents the spectacle of woman losing her identity, so that masculine identity can be all the more confirmed. In this romantic tale of terror, the contingencies of existence are mapped onto the figure of woman. The romantic tale of terror thus centers on the figure of the dead woman who consolidates identity for the male detective. Detection takes place at the site of the dead woman, whether this dead woman is literally or figuratively dead.[24]

The detective novel seeks to recoup the identity of the detective; Hartright is the monolithic figure in possession of the phallus. London is a terrifying place; the figure of woman in the appearance of the woman in white represents the mystery and fear that London embodies. When we first meet the woman in white, she points to London as if to suggest her relation to the nineteenth-century city as unknowable or unreadable. In Dickens's novels, the city in all of its lawlessness and byways represents the gothic terror of losing one's self as demonstrated, for example, in *Oliver Twist*. Through Hartright London is knowable.

By projecting his fears onto the body of a woman, Hartright can gain control. He reduces Laura to a medical case where, he, the detective, can explain the mystery of human personality. As we have seen, however, there are severe limitations to his mode of detection.

Woman's identity then is fixed irrevocably; paradoxically, it is in fact interchangeable. Hartright announces the fixity of men and women's identities in the opening sentence of the novel. "This is the story of what a Woman's patience can endure, and what a Man's resolution can achieve" (9). Clearly, in this one sentence, Collins reveals England's social codes; namely, men act and women appear. We are introduced then to a system that functions on categorical oppositions: man and woman and what kinds of behavior are required of each of them.

Perhaps we can better understand this idea of the fixity of woman's identity by studying the way in which Collins employs the motif of disguise. Count Fosco is a shifty character. We are told that his face has been altered so that he can elude death from the Italian secret society that he has betrayed. Sir Percival disguises himself as Sir Percival when he assumes a name that is not his. Disguise, for women, however, is another story. Disguise is predicated on having the power to alter one's identity. Thus, disguise is based on legal and narrative systems that recognize one as a subject *a priori*.

Disguise entails stepping out of one's character, in effect recognizing that identity is something that one puts on; one wears a face to the world. Disguise also involves an imaginative projection into another way of perceiving identity—to in fact appear as outside the self. Disguise is thus predicated on the irrational as against the rational that seeks to bind all oppositions. Disguise then presupposes a fluidity in identity. In Collins's later novel, *The Law and the Lady* (1875), Valeria, the detective figure, describes her transformed identity after the application of cosmetics.

> She [the chambermaid] came back with a box of paints and powders; and I said nothing to check her. I saw, in the glass, my skin take a false fairness, my cheeks a false colour, my eyes a false brightness—and I never shrank from it. . . . The transformation of my face was accomplished. (57)

Valeria's sense of identity as a masquerade is quite different from Laura and Anne's conception of identity in *The Woman in White*. This is due in part to Collins's divergent aims in both novels; but more fundamentally, the difference lies in Valeria's ascension to the position of narrator in *The Law and the Lady*. When one narrates one's life, one can get outside of character and become transformed into a masquerade.

In *The Law and the Lady*, Valeria describes entering the characters of others:

> I confess I have often fancied myself transformed into some other person, and have felt a certain pleasure in seeing myself in my new character. One of our first amusements as children (if we have any imagination at all) is to get out of our own characters, and to try the characters of other personages as a change—to be fairies, to be queens, to be any-thing, in short, but what we really are. (221)

Hartright's world of logic and detection presents a static story in con-tradistinction to one of imaginative fluidity. When Hartright is pursuing Sir Percival's secret and is in danger of being apprehended by Sir Percival's spies, he decides to assume no disguise, as he explains: "In my own character I had acted thus far—and in my own character I was resolved to continue to the end" (482). Similarly, Laura and Anne in *The Woman in White* are firmly stuck in their roles. They are granted no imaginative capabilities because of their inability to recast them-selves in language. The dictum of the novel might be: I narrate; there-fore, I am. But still the narrative proper is haunted by their gothic wanderings and ghostly reverberations as they move through plots told by people in different voices.

One may very well argue that Marian serves as the corrective to woman as cipher, as blank page to be written upon. Marian does keep her diary and faithfully records day-to-day events. She also protests against the unjust treatment of women. "Men! They are the enemies of our innocence and our peace—they drag us away from our parents' love and our sisters' friendship—they take us body and soul to them-selves, and fasten our helpless lives to theirs as they chain up a dog to his kennel" (181). She, in fact, takes on the role of the detective figure when she spies on Count Fosco and Sir Percival.

> A complete change in my dress was imperatively necessary, for many reasons. I took off my silk gown to begin with, because the slightest noise from it, on that still night, might have betrayed me. I next removed the white and cumbersome parts of my underclothing, and replaced them by a petticoat of dark flannel. Over this I put my black travelling cloak, and pulled the hood on to my head. (319)

Marian does transform herself, but the narrative contingency of Hartright's world brings her back to the social reality of the oppres-sion of women. Despite her resolution and strength, her narrative is cut short by the dictates of social prescriptions for women. Marian as much realizes this when she writes about Laura: "Who else is left to you? No father, no brother—no living creature but the helpless, useless woman who writes these sad lines" (194). Her narrative, however, is forceful and direct. Count Fosco admires her narrative skills when he comments: "These pages are amazing. The tact which I find here, the discretion, the rare courage, the wonderful power of memory, the accurate observation of character, the easy grace of style, the charming outbursts of womanly feeling, have all inexpressibly increased my admiration of this sublime creature, of this magnificent Marian" (336). It is interesting that Fosco writes this postscript to Marian's diary, in effect demonstrating that he has the power to write over her narrative.[25] Hartright possesses this power as he amends Marian's diary and finally subsumes her narrative voice under his when he tells the narrative in his own words in the final epoch of the story. In the name of truth, he presents his story as the master story. Thus, his role in the text is of the omniscient narrator who has complete control over his subjects. Marian may possess the ability to narrate her story, but that story is embedded in a series of stories that are judged by Walter Hartright. The drawing master maintains his superiority over the contingencies of life by imposing a narrative scheme on events.

But Collins does critique the notion of fixity, particularly the fixity of identity. The detective story pure and simple works to please the conscious mind, to in effect restore order after the murder that I read as an act of the unconscious. Thus, murder is outside the law, and the drive of the detective story is to return to a rational state of being. In *The Woman in White*, as I have been arguing, woman is murdered figuratively because she upsets the foundations of knowledge in that she is fundamentally unreadable in a system that is predicated on binary oppositions—where one category is raised above the other as maker and keeper of the law—namely, the masculine.

Collins merges the unconscious with the conscious or rational with the irrational which for him is necessary for an understanding of identity outside the law or narrative. Embracing contradictions leads to understanding but not to fully resolving mysteries. Pure rationality reduces women to disfigured human beings. When we allow the irrational to be subsumed by the rational, then we cripple individuals. When we can hold both types of thinking in our minds concurrently, when we can accept the irrational as a necessary component of life, only then can we accept men and women as equal and varied human beings.

At the ending of *The Woman in White*, order is restored, but underlying that order is the figure of woman—still not discovered or detected. She by her muteness haunts the narrative. In going beyond the realistic novel, however, Collins presents women who may not speak but who imaginatively remain in our minds as figures lacking a proper text to narrate. Through their muteness, their voices remain perpetually on the brink of disclosure. They haunt the text through their silent voices, poised ready for speech.

The limits of detection in Collins's *The Woman in White* address the inadequacies of privileging the rational over the irrational. The irrational for Collins is not simply a nightmare or an apparition that terrifies Hartright on the road to London. The irrational is the mystery in the formulation of an art that seeks to uncover the mystery at the core of identity, whether masculine or feminine. That the feminine remains a mystery in the text is a testament to Collins's perspicacious reading of woman's identity in nineteenth-century British society. But it is also a commentary on the master detector Hartright displacing the unknowable onto woman. She as against the rational must bear the weight of the mystery or the irrational that the rational-minded detective solves.[26] Collins points out that Walter Hartright's cover up of woman's identity is not the only solution to the riddle of woman's identity.

Chapter 2

Phantasmagorical Narration in *Bleak House*

While Collins presents us with texts in which women have difficulties narrating their stories resulting in the ghostly effects of the return from the dead of those muted voices, *Bleak House* suggests what might be the effect of storytelling that cannot be contained neatly in one person. The double narration introduces the ghostly production of the voice; the voice is no longer one, but is doubled. The double narration thus becomes the locus of haunting in that the ghostly production of the double narrative entails death and resurrection as each narrator stops and begins his or her portion of the narrative.

Dickens needed a narrative structure to showcase gothic narration, that is, a narrative in pieces where something other returns suggesting ambivalence and nonclosure. The spillage or leakage of one narrative into the other demonstrates that knowledge is haunted by a ghostly presence that lies outside one's consciousness. Thus, the double narration erects a haunted house in that it reflects the terror of another presence or voice lurking beyond consciousness.

Thus *Bleak House* returns to the issue of origins that we have been discussing and proposes the startling idea that narrative voices cannot be owned by the speaking voice. Dickens peoples his text with a magical lantern show of narrative personages: the anonymous narrator and Esther. In the place of voices that end or narratives that close, Dickens introduces narrative spillage and leakage, which provides a haunting effect. The last word of the text "supposing" leaves readers on the brink of the possibility of another narrative and another voice suggesting that what is done is never done. Origins do not originate and closure does not ensure closure. Both the double narration and the Chancery suit cannot be said to originate and to end—and along the way proliferate out of control.

In this uncanny narrative told by two different narrators, we are presented with the question of what would happen if narrative indeed were to become phantasmagorical. Dickens manufactures narrative as a ghost-producing technology of the revenant. That is to say, rather than presenting two divergent narratives, the text offers us a narrative filled with presences, with voices that speak to one another—a superimposition of voices, so to speak. We know from Terry Castle that in phantasmagorias "the figures were made to increase and decrease in size, to advance and retreat, dissolve, vanish, and pass into each other, in a manner then considered marvelous" ("Phantasmagoria" 30). It is my contention that the two narratives in *Bleak House* function as ghostly presences operating on one another. *Bleak House* is haunted by many ghosts, and narrative is one of them. That is to say, narrative can never be contained in one person; instead, it divides and proliferates. Narrative, itself, becomes ghostly; it is a phantom structure never to be confined simply to one voice. Rather, the double narrative presents a labyrinth of wandering voices.

The Chancery suit haunts several characters: most notably Richard Carstone, Gridley, and John Jarndynce's brother who blows his brains out. The Ghost's Walk is another means by which the novel is haunted by something or someone. Through Dickens's foregrounding of haunting, I want to explore how and why the text is haunted by the voices of the two narrators. We know that the conception of *Bleak House* is rife with the idea of Dickens's being haunted by his story. In fact, he wrote: "I feel the first shadows of a new story hovering in a ghostly way as they usually begin to do, when I have finished an old one" (quoted in Kaplan 286). Having just finished *David Copperfield*, Dickens feels inhabited by the ghosts of his new story. One of these ghosts involves Dickens's assumption of Esther Summerson's narrative voice. We also know that while Dickens was writing *Bleak House*, he experienced his "old nervous choking" (quoted in Kaplan 287). For Dickens, the act of narration produces a ghostly effect, and the voice of Esther in particular haunts the text, thereby causing his hysterical reaction of "nervous choking."

The question then becomes what is so haunting about Esther's narration? Her narration evokes the uncanny, and through its repetitions and returns mounts a critique of the institutionalization of her first person narrative. Many commentators have written extensively on the anonymous narrator's mordant critique of institutional practices, most notably the institution of the law. It is my argument that this critique crosses over to Esther's narration showing how the voice, particularly the feminine voice, has been institutionalized by narrative practices of first person female narrators. Much of the text centers on the motif of detection. The detective plot crosses over into Esther's narration thus deconstructing what lies underneath her writing.

In the preface to *Bleak House*, Dickens tells his readers that he has "purposely dwelt on the romantic side of familiar things" (xix). Esther Summerson's voice is the voice of fantasy, a romanticized version of the female voice. Esther's narration begins with the dramatic staging of her voice, with her imagining an audience—her doll. Before we discuss this moment, it is important to notice how Dickens leads up to the introduction of Esther's narration. In the first chapter, he introduces us to London and Chancery and the fog. The first chapter is magnificent in its announcement of the malaise occasioned by the Court of Chancery. The first chapter begins with and foregrounds the fragment: "London. Michelmas Term lately over, and the Lord Chancellor sitting in Lincoln's Inn Hall. Implacable November weather . . . . Fog everywhere" (1). The fragment calls attention to the fact that nothing in the text can be made into a coherent whole. It is almost as if words and narratives are haunted by the lack of origins. Thus, narration becomes a ruin, and the site of the ruin is London. In a spectacular move, then, as if to compensate for the dynamics of the fragment, Dickens announces his method in the text: he is obsessed with layering and accumulation,[1] and narrative is part of this piling up.

> Foot passengers, jostling one another's umbrellas, in a general infection of ill-temper, and losing their foot-hold at street corners, where tens of thousands of other foot passengers have been slipping and sliding since the day broke (if this day ever broke), adding new deposits to the crust upon crust of mud, sticking at those points tenaciously to the pavement, and accumulating at compound interest. (1)

All of this accumulation of text, of words, which we are conscious of in reading *Bleak House*, compensates for the irremediable lack of origins at the center of narration. David Punter, speaking of Dickens's use of the gothic in *Oliver Twist*, remarks: "Dickens prefers to build from one horror to another in an ascending series" (*The Literature of Terror* 218). In addition to the multiplot novel reflecting the demands of publishing of the day, it also foregrounds a concern with the profusion of words to counteract the instability of the death of origins, most noticeably announced by Charles Darwin in *On the Origin of Species*.

Confronted with an absence of origins or any reducible meaning, authors used the multiplot to people their stories with a profusion of voices—thus, the multiplot novel narrates in a hysterical way.

As Scheherazade wards off death by narrating a different story each night to the Sultan, the multiplot novel seeks to avoid the ending by compulsively staging other stories—recreating a kind of cinema of the imagination where stories merge into one another. Thus, the text seems to be haunted by what lies underneath the building of words— the house is in danger of ruin or decay. The passage quoted above focuses on the accumulation of deposits of mud. This city scene is in danger of falling apart. The passengers are "slipping and sliding," paralleling the text itself that is in danger of slipping and sliding with its accumulation of stories and voices. This layering of deposits creates a connection among the different stories and persons Dickens creates. And the layering calls forth the uncanny, which as David B. Morris claims is "a theory of terror" (307). Narrative becomes unmoored in this text; it wanders without a fixed marker.

When Dickens takes on the voice of Esther Summerson, he occupies the voice of another, a woman, which causes him to feel terror, the terror of the different, but also the terror of the same. The voice, then, in *Bleak House* evokes the uncanny, which as Freud describes is "that class of the frightening which leads back to what is known of old and long familiar" (220). Esther's voice occasions a collapse on Dickens's part in the text. In his layering of her voice—and here I mean the accumulation of Dickens, the anonymous narrator, and Esther, the character and her narrative voice—he sets up the idea of the substitute that evokes the uncanny. We keep wanting to ask ourselves—who is she as we are reading Esther's narration, and this question of who she is continually recalls to us how the text is forced to repeat (think of the establishment of the new Bleak House at the ending). The collapse announced by the opening chapter also leads to a breakdown in narration—of the impossibility of fully narrating the female voice. Rather than viewing the anonymous narrator's narration and Esther's narration as diametrically opposed, I propose a dialectic between the two.[2] In fact, the two become intertwined at points.

This lack of difference is terror producing for Dickens. On the one hand, he creates a romanticized version of a woman's life; on the other, that life returns to haunt him in its staging of difference. The staging of difference, therefore, turns out to be no difference at all. The two narrators are like a double exposure: doubly exposing that their voices are peopled by the presences of each other, denying categorical gender.

Dickens, obsessed with accumulation, introduces us to Lady Dedlock in the second chapter, who is notable for "shading her face with a hand-screen" (13). Lady Dedlock and Esther are very much connected, not only by their familial relation, but also through the idea of transgression. Lady Dedlock is the figure who walks, and her walking signals her transgression. Esther transgresses through the act of narration. The figure of woman is hidden, and importantly, the face is associated with the site of narration. Reading the face leads to uncovering the face, to telling a counter-story about the face.

And that story of the face is most clearly evidenced through the staging of Esther's identity in the chapter entitled "A Progress." Here are Esther's first spoken words:

> I have a great deal of difficulty in beginning to write my portion of these pages, for I know I am not clever. I always knew that. I can remember, when I was a very little girl indeed, I used to say to my doll, when we were alone together, 'Now, Dolly, I am not very clever, you know very well, and you must be patient with me, like a dear!' And so she used to sit propped up in a great arm-chair, with her beautiful complexion and rosy lips, staring at me—or not so much at me, I think, as at nothing—while I busily stitched away, and told her every one of my secrets. (15)

As Dickens conceptualizes Esther's voice, he gives her an audience—her doll. Thus, he foregrounds the dramatic performance of Esther—she performs for an audience and for him. The passage pivots on dialogue—the dialogue between Esther and her doll, suggesting that the two narrators, Esther and the anonymous narrator, speak to one another.

The moment of Esther's retrospective narration begins with a return, a return to her childhood where she recalls a scene of her speaking to her doll. This return signals the call to narration as a call to Lacan's formulation of the mirror stage, where one apprehends oneself as whole based on the mistaken notion that one's image and one's identity are coextensive. Instead of this joyful moment of self-recognition, however, the subject's conception of oneself is fraught with images of fragmentation. Many moments in nineteenth-century British novels recast the notion of an idealized identity as evidenced by looking into the mirror and seeing an ideal object of desire. Instead, the nineteenth-century novel's staging of identity entails the inability to apprehend an idealized identity. Think, for example, of *Frankenstein* where the look into the mirror images a monster and of *Great Expectations* which figures Pip as about to fall apart in the opening chapter. Pip on the marshes is a "small bundle of shivers growing afraid of it all and beginning to cry" (4). As if to compensate for this traumatic moment of origins, the nineteenth-century novel offers plenitude in the form of the multiplot novel. Also, at the place of origins, one finds the figure of the double as in the case of Esther and her doll and the anonymous narrator and Esther.

As we read Esther's narration, we glimpse a haunting effect of non-correspondence, which is most readily understood through Dickens's staging of Esther's looking into a metaphorical mirror and seeing her doll. The doll stares at her, but instead of Esther experiencing a sense of recognition, she feels a sense of nothingness. She says that her doll stares "not so much at me, I think, as at nothing." At the moment of the creation of Esther, she is there, but not there at the same time. This sense of being in two places at once—there and not there—produces haunting. Further, to complicate the argument, the moment that Dickens conceives of Esther, her voice talks back or talks over his narrating her voice. Esther is first and foremost an image, and it is the image that the text cannot quite get out of its memory. In many of the illustrations by Phiz, Esther's back is to the reader. The text seems to be haunted by the face of Esther; she is associated with the painting of her mother, and Jo confuses her with Lady Dedlock and Hortense.

These speculations on the face point to the fact that there is always something behind the face that is not revealed. Thus the face stands in for the act of narration. Face and narration become the same thing: they meet one another and at moments engage in hysterical moments of recognition. The text must endlessly stage its fascination with and hor-ror of the face. We begin with Esther's face—with her looking at her doll as the pivotal moment to evoke narration, and we end with her face—with her husband asking her if she "ever look[s] in the glass" (935).

This conjunction of the face and narration leads us to speculate on the secrets in the text. Just as Lady Dedlock is engaged in "shading her face with a hand-screen" (13), Esther's narration functions as a counterpoint to the text's obsession with the secrets of the other char-acters, especially Lady Dedlock and her secret. Bucket is engaged in literally finding Lady Dedlock and in detecting her secrets. We cannot take Esther's narration at face value; instead, we must uncover her secrets. It is almost as if Esther in her narration shades her face with a hand-screen. This shading of the face, this veil over the face, is a func-tion of haunting. One thinks that one might be getting a coherent narrative from Esther, but instead the text offers a ghostly articulation that is a function of Dickens's ambivalence in her portrayal. Again, we pose the question, is it her or isn't it her?

The uncanny informs Dickens's representation of Esther. The assumption of the first person feminine voice for Dickens produces a figure that is in-between. She is a character and a narrator but also an automaton with properties of being dead and alive at the same time. That is to say, the conception of her gets away from Dickens in the process of his writing and his assuming her voice and her taking on the voice. Does she represent the saccharine Victorian woman or does she represent something other, thus offering a haunting effect? Esther's representation in this text pivots on ambivalence, and this leads us to a consideration of Freud's essay on "The Uncanny."

In "The Uncanny" Freud spends a great deal of time on the definitions of the word uncanny and concludes that the "uncanny is that class of the frightening which leads back to what is known of old and long familiar" (220). Therefore, the uncanny does not simply represent something that is frightening or something that is completely outside our mode of perception; rather, the uncanny signifies something that is both known and unknown. We may read Freud's essay as an explanation of the idea of ambivalence itself, on the slippery quality of language that on the one hand asserts difference but then makes that difference ambiguous. He captures this ambiguity when he writes: "What interests us most in this long extract is to find that among its different shades of meaning the word 'heimlich' exhibits one which is identical with its opposite, 'unheimlich'. What is heimlich thus comes to be unheimlich" (224). Freud then concludes: "[H]eimlich is a word the meaning of which develops in the direction of ambivalence, until it finally coincides with its opposite, unheimlich" (226).

This shift to ambivalence informs Dickens's portrayal of Esther in *Bleak House*. He captures this ambivalence by introducing two narrators: the anonymous narrator and Esther. Both narrations occupy a space in-between, a space that is uncanny. Dickens places Esther in the home—in the house of Bleak House where she is given responsibility for the household keys. In conceptualizing Esther and her narration, Dickens goes home. And perhaps the injunction is simultaneously to go home and not to go home, because going home is fraught with many recognitions. Chief among these recognitions is that the return home is a return to the domestic, which is the stage of many Victorian novels. We should be at home in these novels, but there is something jarring about the home, which renders it coextensively familiar and strange. This going home is the site of the return to the feminine, with which in a sense all narratives must come to terms.

On the surface, the great quest for origins in the nineteenth-century novel charts a movement away from home; this is the great quest of the bildüngsroman. But nineteenth-century novels are haunted by the home which is very much tied to the idea of narration itself. This haunting encompasses repetition and inescapability. The uncanny would then seem to be about what is not dealt with in childhood and surfaces in repressed forms through one's life. The nineteenth-century novel returns obsessively to childhood to try to master through narrative what has been repressed—namely, the female body. Freud writes: "It often happens that neurotic men declare that they feel there is something uncanny about the female genital origins. This unheimlich place, however, is the entrance to the former Heim [home] of all human beings, to the place where each one of us lived once upon a time and in the beginning" (245). The return home in *Bleak House* is a return to a female habitation where one is confronted with ghosts of feminine presences. But it is important to note that this home is full of presences that deny one definitive site or being. In other words, Dickens channels the voice of Esther and in doing so sets up a narrative system that is peopled by ghosts: himself, the anonymous narrator, Esther the character, Esther the narrator, and the Victorian woman. The voice becomes detached from its owner; in this sense, it is ghostly.

Not only is Esther buried alive in the narrative home of *Bleak House*, but *Bleak House* also charts a gothic tale of Dickens's being buried alive in the impersonation of Esther Summerson. The uncanny operates in the space of this recognition, where language suffers from a kind of linguistic hysteria. Going home for Dickens, the spectral home of Esther's Bleak House, is a return to the ambiguous feminine, which is the site of the uncanny. The uncanny operates as a space without proper origins; we hear voices without proper attribution. In that sense, *Bleak House* embodies a phantom structure of each narration haunting the other. We are neither here nor there in each narration—this is what is particularly ghostly about reading the text of *Bleak House*. Rather than each narration setting up a dichotomy, each narration erects the category of no difference. The structure of superimposition, where one image overlays the other, layers *Bleak House*.

The return home—the return to the site of the feminine—is one where logical distinctions between categories break down. Going home is then fraught with terror and horror. Dickens relates this connection between going home and linguistic ruin in *Great Expectations* when Wemmick writes a note to Pip telling him not to go home because Magwitch has been discovered at Pip's premises. Pip goes to an Inn where he suffers a sleepless night forced to contemplate the words "DON'T GO HOME." He explains his distress:

> When at last I dozed, in sheer exhaustion of mind and body, it became a vast shadowy verb which I had to conjugate. Imperative mood, present

tense: Do not thou go home, let him not go home, let us not go home, do not ye or you go home, let not them go home. Then, potentially: I may not and I cannot go home; and I might not, could not, would not, and should not go home; until I felt that I was going distracted, and rolled over on the pillow, and looked at the staring rounds upon the wall again. (367–368)

Going home becomes a linguistic nightmare, and that linguistic nightmare aligns itself with the uncanny—with the recognition that language sparks the ghostly reminders of ambivalence or the terror of what cannot be known and represented directly. Just as Pip is estranged from his narrative in *Great Expectations*, which is reflected in his inability to return home, Dickens cannot fully situate Esther in the home. He as well as she ghost walks.

Perhaps Dickens suffered from his choking fits during the conception of *Bleak House* because in telling the story of Esther, he returns home to the site of the feminine. That which is feminine should have remained a secret. Instead, Esther's narration brings to light what has been repressed. Freud details Schelling's explanation of the uncanny thus: " 'Unheimlich' is the name for everything that ought to have remained . . . secret and hidden but has come to light" (224). It is as if Dickens places us in the secure home of the angel in the house only to have Esther destabilize that house through her spectral homeliness. Undoubtedly, this is a haunted house. It is only in the familiar that Dickens can show the operations of the strange.

Freud's reading of E.T.A. Hoffmann's "The Sandman" presents a lens with which to read Dickens's return home to the site of feminine narration in *Bleak House*. Freud reads that text as a primer on castration anxiety. He argues: "A study of dreams, phantasies and myths has taught us that anxiety about one's eyes, the fear of going blind, is often enough a substitute for the dread of being castrated" ("The Uncanny" 231). Freud stages his own repression in his text by discounting the presence of the feminine in Hoffmann's text. The feminine, however, will return as evidenced in the following passage:

As I was walking, one hot summer afternoon, through the deserted streets of a provincial town in Italy which was unknown to me, I found myself in a quarter of whose character I could not long remain in doubt. Nothing but painted women were to be seen at the windows of the small houses, and I hastened to leave the narrow street at the next turning. But after having wandered about for a time without enquiring my way, I suddenly found myself back in the same street, where my presence was now beginning to excite attention. I hurried away once more, only to arrive by another *détour* at the same place yet a third time. Now, however, a feeling overcame me which I can only describe as uncanny, and I was glad enough to find myself back at the piazza I had left a short while before, without any further voyages of discovery. ("The Uncanny" 237)

Freud's meanderings lead him to the site of the uncanny, the prostitute, whose body serves as the marker for the familiar and the strange. He obsessively returns to this place, impelled by an inescapable compulsion to repeat. The passage recalls the uncanny sense of difference that Freud experiences as he walks the streets. Perhaps, he feels the sense of difference breaking down because he, along with the prostitutes, is walking the streets. Here we have evidence of the uncanny marking a sense of being fatefully compelled to return to the site of the feminine. Instead of difference in the portrayal of Esther, *Bleak House* proposes a model of recognition, which is terrifying. But this model of recognition in turn sets up the uncanny and the haunting effect of the narrative.

The text also recalls the dead and the undead in its portrayal of Esther. Thus, she resembles her doll, an inanimate object that produces an uncanny effect. She resembles the inanimate creature, Olympia, created by Professor Spalanzani in Hoffmann's "The Sandman." Nathaniel observes her through an opening of a curtain and describes her as "tall, very slim, perfectly proportioned and gorgeously dressed. . . . her eyes had in general something fixed and staring about them, I could almost say she was sightless, as if she was sleeping with her eyes open. It made me feel quite uncanny, and I crept softly away into the neighbouring lecture-room. I afterwards learned that the figure I had seen was Spalanzani's daughter Olympia, whom, incredibly and reprehensibly, he keeps locked up so that no one may come near her" (99). This passage is significant in several regards: first, Nathaniel observes her through a curtain, through a lens which suggests there is something blocking or impeding his view. He views her in effect at a second remove. Second, the sight of her calls forth the uncanny in Nathaniel. Perhaps Hoffmann foregrounds the dynamics of representation: one imagines a perfect lifeless female who is locked up, encased in a field of representation that performs an idealized version of femininity. Esther partakes of this lifeless representation immured as she is in the bleak house of representation in *Bleak House*. Dickens animates his doll, Esther; he raises her from the dead. But the uncanny doll reveals that she is neither living nor dead. Thus, this inanimate creature also comes to life in her narration producing the uncanny.

She comes to life in her refusal to occupy fully her position in the house. Her writing is like a ghost writing. She says: "It seems so curious to me to be obliged to write all this about myself! As if this narrative were the narrative of *my* life! But my little body will soon fall into the background now" (26). Esther simultaneously realizes that this narrative is not the narrative of her life, that, in effect, she writes a script divorced from her body. She deports herself as the little body in the background, but the self-reflexivity of her text posits another identity—an imposter identity.[3]

A pivotal moment appears at the ending of "The Sandman" when Nathaniel realizes that Olympia is a lifeless doll.

> The professor had hold of a female figure by the shoulders, the Italian Coppola had it by the feet, and transformed with rage they were tearing and tugging at it for its possession. Nathaniel recoiled in terror as he recognized the figure as Olympia; flaring into a furious rage, he went to rescue his beloved, but at that moment Coppola, turning with terrible force, wrenched the figure from the professor's hands and dealt him a fearful blow with it, so that he tumbled backwards to the table, on which retorts, bottles and glass cylinders were standing, and collapsed on to it—the glassware was shattered into a thousand pieces. Then Coppola threw the figure over his shoulder and, laughing shrilly, ran quickly down the staircase, so that the feet of the figure hanging down repulsively behind him thumped and clattered woodenly against the stairs. Nathaniel stood numb with horror. He had seen all too clearly that Olympia's deathly-white face possessed no eyes: where the eyes should have been there were only pits of blackness—she was a lifeless doll! (119–120)

Olympia turns out to be lifeless—but the representation of her makes her simultaneously lifeless and alive, thus evoking the uncanny. Hoffmann constructs a lifeless doll for his story only to have her pulled apart at the story's end and shown for what she is—a figure. In *Bleak House*, Dickens simultaneously creates Esther as a lifeless doll, but she undoes that representation by her resurrection from the dead. In imagining a lifeless woman in *Bleak House*, Dickens confronts the image of the terror of representation. Thus, the text cannot uphold singularly the image of the angel in the house. Dickens may have started out constructing Esther as a lifeless doll, but that doll simultaneously remains dead and undead. Her image in effect images the constructed nature of representation, and her deconstruction of the image calls to mind a destabilization of the figure.

Narrating the story of *Bleak House* leads Dickens back to a house, a haunted house whose occupant seems familiar and strange at the same time. We should be at home the most in Esther's narration, but we are not. This sense of dis-ease is readily observable in the text's positioning of the resemblance between Esther and her mother. Here, I want to focus on Lady Dedlock's painting and the unease it causes in Mr. Guppy. During Guppy's tour of Chesney Wold, he sees a portrait of Lady Dedlock and exclaims: "Blest! . . . if I can ever have seen her. Yet I know her!" (91). This scene serves as an inset piece for the gaze and its relation to the face. This gaze suggests that the face cannot stay in one place. Identity, thus, does not rest in one name, in Esther Summerson, but occupies multiple places at the same time. The face then would seem comparable to the multiplot novel in its incessant wandering from one story to another. Here faces transmute into one another. The narrative in its repetitions of the face and its multiplications of the face leads to multiplicity, to the many names that Esther occupies in the text. "This was the beginning of my being called Old Woman, and Little Old Woman, and Cobweb, and Mrs. Shipton, and Mother Hubbard, and Dame Durden, and so many names of that sort, that my own name soon became quite lost among them" (102). This inability of identity to stay in its proper place makes the narrative uncanny, and positions the face as a trope of representation, where the act of writing and copying necessarily leads to other figures and to a certain self-reflexivity about the nature of first person narration. Looking into the mirror of Esther, Dickens sees, in effect, some remnant and revenant of himself.

This gaze at the face returns us to Lacan's mirror stage where the self apprehends an idealized version of him/herself through the coalescing of the body through the idealized image of the mother. To tell a story in this text is to return to the site of the mother. It is the mother who enables narrative to proceed. The connection between the face and narrative coalesces in the scene where Esther gazes at her mother: "But why her face should be, in a confused way, like a broken glass to me, in which I saw scraps of old remembrances; and why I should be so fluttered and troubled . . ., by having casually met her eyes; I could not think" (263). The face inspires "scraps of old remembrances." Thus, narrative would seem to be fragmentary and broken just as the child's inner state is one of fragmentation and disunity. That the glass is broken suggests that the self through time is a function of the uncanny. That is to say, a coherent narrative cannot inhere; rather, narrative pivots on the scrap or the fragment. Now one could argue that this is the position of the orphan in the text, and that this position is anomalous. However, John Jarndyce makes the observation that "the universe . . . makes rather an indifferent parent" (75).

Origins, then, may be irrecoverable, and this stares Dickens in the face through the course of his narrating *Bleak House*. Origins lead back to the home, and the home is full of ambivalence, particularly surrounding the figure of the mother. The narrative is not only haunted by its return home to the feminine, but also by the mother figure herself who is the stand-in for ghostly unrecoverable origins.

As Esther later gazes at her mother, she tells us that "there arose before my mind innumerable pictures of myself" (268). To tell a story then is to consort with the dead, the "innumerable pictures." To tell a story always entails a return, and that return involves a doubling or a layering of apprehension. This doubling we see markedly through Esther and her mother. The double confirms that identity cannot stay in one place. As Julian Wolfreys points out: the double is the "figure of haunting *par excellence*. It is itself not only itself but already other than itself, every instance of doubling being the singular instance of the 'ghost like manifestation', irreducible to the general law of doubling on which the signifier plays" (*Victorian Hauntings* 15).

Esther is haunted by her mother through the act of remembrance which calls up those "innumerable pictures" of herself. Thus, narration participates in this haunting, in the difference that obtains between the thought and the narration. Perhaps what Dickens finds so haunting about Esther's narration is that the representation in its very layerings becomes too ghostly. When Dickens adopts the voice of Esther Summerson, he looks into the mirror and consorts with the terrifying idea that to embody feminine narration is to enter the world of the other—upsetting binary distinctions. In creating Esther Summerson, Dickens engenders a figure who comes back to haunt him—threatening his masculine identity.

To further the argument on the double, the ambivalence occasioned by the formulation of the double figure provides us with a feminist reading of the double. As Freud points out in "The Uncanny," the double "was originally an insurance against the destruction of the ego," but the double also announces "the uncanny harbinger of death" (235). The encounter with the double is the encounter with the same, and this produces the uncanny where difference was supposed to reside. *Bleak House* shows that repetition or sameness resides everywhere. The text then remains uncanny because it is unable to consolidate differences and show the boundaries between two separate distinct worlds, most notably the worlds of the anonymous narrator and Esther. Sir Leicester Dedlock, announcing his conservative views about a member of the middle class becoming a member of Parliament, laments that it is a "remarkable example of the confusion into which the present age has fallen; of the obliteration of landmarks, the opening of floodgates, and the uprooting of distinctions" (413–414).

Structurally, we see the concept of the double appearing in the Ghost's Walk. Significantly, this passage occurs in the same chapter where Guppy visits Chesney Wold and sees the portrait of Lady Dedlock and thinks he has seen the resemblance somewhere. Immediately following his unease occasioned by the uncanniness of the portrait, the housekeeper, Mrs. Rouncewell, narrates the story of the Ghost's Walk. We learn that in ancient times, Sir Morbury Dedlock's lady committed an act of sedition, was rendered lame by her husband, and loved to walk upon the terrace. Her dying words are "I will die here where I have walked. And I will walk here, though I am in my grave. I will walk here, until the pride of this house is humbled. And when calamity, or when disgrace is coming to it, let the Dedlocks listen for my step" (94)! This Lady's story is aligned with transgression, and her story connects her to Lady Dedlock and Esther. Transgression is very much linked to the former Lady's dis-ease, with her unwillingness to stay still. Lady Dedlock's transgression is figured through her walking, particularly her last walk to London to die at the grave of her former lover, Captain Hawdon. Wandering becomes a trope for the inability to stay in one body and in one narrative.

After Lady Dedlock tells Esther that she is her mother, Esther walks over to Chesney Wold and performs the walk of the ghost:

> The way was paved here, like the terrace overhead, and my footsteps, from being noiseless, made an echoing sound upon the flags. Stopping to look at nothing, but seeing all I did see as I went, I was passing quickly on, and in a few moments should have passed the lighted window, when my echoing footsteps brought it suddenly into my mind that there was a dreadful truth in the legend of the Ghost's Walk; that it was I, who was to bring calamity upon the stately house; and that my warning feet were haunting it even then. Seized with an augmented terror of myself which turned me cold, I ran from myself and everything. (542)

The gothic trapping of the Ghost's Walk is the figure for Esther's narration. For Esther too transgresses the rules of the house—the rules of narration. If we apprehend Esther's narration as a meta-narrative, as a kind of live burial, a story within the story of Dickens and the anonymous narrator's narration, then we can see that this being buried alive calls for a return from the dead—to the undead.[4] The echoes of the Ghost's Walk relate that all has not been put to rest—that Esther's voice will be heard in conjunction with the other voices. In a sense,

Esther does bring calamity upon the house by writing with a differ-ence. She copies the story of the angel in the house, but the copy strays from the original. Unlike the law copiers who copy documents, Esther writes a covert document, a forged document, so to speak. Her narration falls in line with Krook's efforts of learning to read and write. "He then produced singly, and rubbed out singly, the letters forming the words BLEAK HOUSE" (59).

Once Esther starts to copy, that copy becomes erased by difference. In a sense, Esther's narration is uncanny because she brings to light what should have remained secret. This sense of nonconformity causes her to feel terror. In the passage above, she feels terror of her-self. This terror is related to her narrative walking or wandering away from the prescribed path. Coextensively, this terror we can see in other places in Dickens's narrative; it is as if the narrative itself is threatened with presence and absence, with echoes and reverberations that it cannot reconcile.

This terror arises in part from the many connections the text makes between disparate characters. We continually get the sense of one world superimposed on another world: one thinks of the connection between the horror of Tom-all-Alone's and Chesney Wold and Bleak House. Dickens makes this connection clear when the anonymous narrator asks:

> What connection can there be, between the place in Lincolnshire, the house in town, the Mercury in powder, and the whereabout of Jo the outlaw with the broom, who had that distinct ray of light upon him when he swept the churchyard-step? What connection can there have been between many people in the innumerable histories of this world, who, from opposite sides of great gulfs, have, nevertheless, been very curiously brought together! (230)

The connection between one person and another recalls Darwin's *On the Origin of Species* where he relates: "It is a truly wonderful fact—the wonder of which we are apt to overlook from familiarity—that all animals and all plants throughout all time and space should be related to each other" (128). That origins are varied and multiple sug-gests a world of correspondences that relates to the narrative world of Esther and the anonymous narrator.

The narrative is haunted by these correspondences; everything leads back to something or someone. The text continually wanders to repress these correspondences. Here I want to draw a connection between Jo and the injunction given to him to "move on" and Esther who in a sense occupies a similar position. Her moving on the line of her plot paradoxically leads her further and further from the plot in which she is placed. She is forced to move on; her narrative, as I have argued earlier, is very much connected to the idea of walking. As I have also stated, it is as if Esther occupies a haunted castle where she is confined and forced to narrate her story; simultaneously, she breaks out of the castle and reveals a series of hidden passageways.

The secrets of Esther's narration are most readily observable in her face: with the way the text locates her face as the site for her identity. As discussed earlier, much is made of Esther's face, and her face is clearly identified with the act of narration. Her face enables her to create pictures of the world. It is as if narration arises from her coherent beautiful face. What are we to make of the fact that Esther's face is scarred? The scars mark the return of the uncanny—they are the signifiers of what ought to have remained secret. The scars signal an eruption, not only on the face, but on the narrative body as well. The scars signify a return of the repressed: the disease occasioned in the narrative body forced to occupy a position not of its own choosing, so to speak. The scars form the excess of what cannot be narrated in the narrative proper. In this sense, they are a hysterical symptom.[5] And the scars are most gothic; they haunt the project of narrating a coherent story of feminine identity given the limitations imposed by the institutions Esther encounters.

In this regard, the scars take on a social critique. Not only do they mark a disjunction in Esther's psyche and narrative, but they also signal a rift in the social body that is Victorian England. In this way, Esther's scars are associated with the spontaneous combustion of Krook; it is as if the text must break out of all of the stories and personages and stage an uncanny event where Krook combusts. But traces of his body are found in all of the stories and personages. At the very center of *Bleak House*, the text must explode. But still remnants of Krook remain. The effects of Krook's spontaneous combustion are explained by the narrator: "A thick yellow liquor defiles them [Guppy and Weevel], which is offensive to the touch and sight and more offensive to the smell. A stagnant, sickening oil, with some natural repulsion in it, that makes them both shudder" (477).

Krook's remains produce terror; the remainder of Esther's story similarly evokes horror at what cannot be stated directly but must return in another form. During Esther's illness, she experiences many terrors, most notably:

> Dare I hint at that worse time when, strung together somewhere in great black space, there was a flaming necklace, or ring, or starry circle

of some kind, of which *I* was one of the beads! And when my only prayer was to be taken off from the rest, and when it was such inexplicable agony and misery to be a part of the dreadful thing? (515)

This passage self-reflexively returns to being on a line of narratives about women. Esther is forced to occupy a narrative space that reveals her dis-ease. The string of beads we may read as being on a narrative course. Esther wishes to be in a narrative not bound by time and history, which, of course, is an impossibility. Her text, therefore, is haunted by the cosmological trauma of being in time. And being in time produces a trauma associated with narrative—she endlessly repeats a story that is never properly hers.

Soon after this passage, Esther looks into the mirror, and again we want to answer the question, what does Esther see when she looks into the mirror? Is it her; is it not her?

My hair had not been cut off, though it had been in danger more than once. It was long and thick. I let it down, and shook it out, and went up to the glass upon the dressing-table. There was a little muslin curtain drawn across it. I drew it back: and stood for a moment looking through such a veil of my own hair, that I could see nothing else. (530)

The scene pivots on the staging of identity. She draws a curtain from the mirror, and her face is hidden by the veil of her hair, preventing her full access to the image. The veil suggests a blocking force, the veil of language so to speak. But the veil also reveals a space from which to hide. We remember that Lady Dedlock several times in the text shades her face with a hand-screen; in this sense, the veil suggests the counterfeit. The veil signals that there is always something lurking beyond the visual space of representation, producing a haunting effect.

The text ends on a note of repetition; another bleak house is reconstructed for Esther. The text takes us back to the beginning; in other words, the text is fated to repeat what has not been mastered. Dickens is haunted by the figure of Esther. He cannot quite fully narrate her story. Through all of its repetitions, we hear remainders of what the text cannot master. The traumas of Esther—narratological, psychological, and cosmological—are heard through the other voices, the other stories that are related to her story in some fashion. It is almost as if Esther's text is in danger of spontaneously combusting through its searching for a narrative of its own. It is significant that we never fully get Lady Dedlock's story. Bucket, the detective, finds out the basic details of her love for Captain Hawdon and the birth of her illegitimate child, Esther. But, none of the details are filled in. The mother then returns to haunt the text, in the form of the Ghost's Walk, but also in the text's never quite getting over the loss of the mother. This loss of the mother is very much tied to the text's obsession with the face, with narrating a story of desire that never ends.

Dickens's wish to capture Esther through narrative is coextensive with Esther's desire to create a story of her own. Both are haunted by their projects. As Dickens returns home to the search for Esther's narration, he is haunted by the narrative home he has created for woman. This voice is most insistently heard overlaying Esther's narration in *Bleak House*. It is as if the search for the mother is the real secret of *Bleak House*, not the mother of the house, but the transgressive mother who pushes the limits of narrative space. Perhaps the text is haunted because it cannot quite articulate and get past the sin of the mother—illegitimacy—which positions her in the in-between space of the uncanny—alive but dead to institutions that pivot on the law of the father who only can legitimate the feminine position. Similarly, Dickens, the creator of Esther's narrative, creates a legitimate daughter who moves into the space of illegitimacy as she unleashes her narrative secrets.

Esther's text ends on a note of supposition. The text cannot quite get rid of its uncanny returns, but we have Esther always wishing to narrate her dis-ease. Perhaps this is the strength of *Bleak House*; Esther narrates, but she creates a different text, one that is not fully contained. Dickens cannot quite get out of his text; the voice of Esther will keep on supposing. We hear this voice superimposed over the voice of Dickens. This is what makes the text haunting—in the place of one voice we have multiple voices all presenting the reader with remainders and layers of stories. The narrative itself is one long Ghost's Walk, in that it is an echo of the original. Like haunted houses in gothic tales, *Bleak House*'s narrative reveals a ghostly hall of mirrors.

CHAPTER 3

SHADOWING THE DEAD: FIRST
PERSON NARRATION IN
OUR MUTUAL FRIEND

In the previous chapters, we have focused on the difficulties women face in narrating their stories. *Bleak House* confronts head-on the problems in women's narration by introducing the double narrative which deconstructs a unified speaking subject and thus gendered identity. Rather than two gendered narrators, we are presented with the ghostly signifiers of gendered narration, and these ghostly presences wander at will and indiscriminately. *Our Mutual Friend* presents a problem of a different order: the novel is haunted by the specter of first person narration. The narrative home is haunted by the question of how to reproduce the voice of the "I." In the novel's return to origins—to the face of the dead man on the boat in the opening chapter—it is confronted with the point of unattainable origin. To compensate for this haunting effect, the novel deploys the multiplot. It is as if the multiplot novel has run amok in its attempt to wander away from first person narration. The proliferation and contagion of plots and characters point to a covering over of first person narration. In trying to present the unrepresentable, the text creates the multiplot. Whatever first person narration cannot speak, third person narration covers over. In this way, Dickens creates gothic writing—the ruin and decay of first person narration.

First person narration is buried alive within the plenitude of the multiplot novel. This burial reflects the difficulties in telling a story of the self, and in this, Dickens's last finished novel, it reveals an estrangement from the "I" that we see in *Great Expectations* where Pip is shadowed by his former self in his retrospective narration of his life story. In *Our Mutual Friend*, the self becomes a technological self, a spectacle not to be looked at up close, but at a remove—it is as if Dickens creates the self as the object of the gaze. The new technological age produced a dispersal of the voice in that it cannot be directly owned by the speaking voice. The self is a series of reproductions, shadows, and specters existing in a realm of the dead. Technology in this novel resurrects the self by manufacturing images of the face in the form of the posters advertising the dead men on the wall of the Hexam's house. The face then becomes the site for narration where it cannot narrate directly but serves as the locus for other stories and plots. The face and subjectivity are manufactured and sold announcing that capitalism engenders an alienation from the self.

DROWNING IN REPRESENTATION

In *Our Mutual Friend*, Gaffer Hexam makes a living by dragging the Thames River for corpses. In his house, he keeps posters of these "drowned people starting out and receding by turns" (211).[1] These images announce the novel's obsession with identity and representation. The novel begins with the corpse of a dead man; the novel cannot quite get over this originary trauma—of the absence and lack of coherence in identification. These images of dead men on posters, without proper identities, signal that the novel is very much obsessed with the limits of representation in forming identities. The images of drowned men forecast the inability of the self to narrate a coherent story. They are *memento moris* without proper burials; consequently, the self is a figure always coming back to haunt in some way. The death of representation informs this last finished Dickens novel. Dickens conceives of identity as uncanny; the dead corpse will haunt what follows in the divergent plots. We might say that narration is founded on a corpse. The novel is able to move forward precisely because it has a story to tell about this dead figure, but the image of the dead man encompasses a story of disfigurement and lack.[2]

In setting up the novel in this way, Dickens challenges Victorian conceptions of domesticity—the uncanny will haunt the project of domesticity. In fact, the domestic will always be haunted by what has been repressed, namely the false idea of the self that is predicated on rationality and wholeness. In this novel, the dead body forecasts the ways in which the self has always been a figure, subject to representation, an image on a poster given animation only by someone breathing life into it. The specter of this corpse alerts us to the fact that representation is about reanimation—it deals with figuration and disfiguration.[3]

The novel is obsessed with the tropes of figuration and disfiguration, and this leads to the startling claim that in writing a novel with this focus, Dickens self-reflexively comments on the fact that perhaps the Victorian model of the self—one concerned with the domestic and with rationality—is simply not an adequate one. The disfigurement of the body in the opening chapter of *Our Mutual Friend* is superimposed onto the subsequent multiplots.[4] The result is that of profound unsettlement. It is as if the text is haunted by the image of the dead man—it cannot put his body to rest. As I will argue, the text seeks to bury the dead man, but he keeps resurfacing. This body of the dead man serves as the joker in the pack—he upsets the binaries at the foundation of the Victorian world order. The dead body is part of the realm of the unexplainable in that it represents what we cannot know and consequently what we cannot represent directly.

It is as if this story is so full of fragments and lacunae that the text must compensate in some way by burying the dead man in the interstices of the multiplot. In this way, the novel partakes of the gothic, in its insistence on the difficulties surrounding the telling of the story of the dead man. The novel seeks every way it can through the function of the multiplot to escape the trauma occasioned by the horror of the dead man. The novel's labyrinthine narrative structure leads it further and further from the origins of the tale. Thus, the gothic novel's difficulty in getting the story told can be related to live burial of first person narration in this text. It does not appear until the middle of the novel in the form of John Harmon's soliloquy narrating the events of his supposed murder.

In this way, the novel challenges modes of representation, particularly Victorian feminine representation. If the self is foremost a figure and is disfigured by representation; and further if the uncanny surfaces to haunt the domestic sphere, then the novel may be said to operate by a ghostly effect of superimposition. That is to say, in the interstices of the multiplots are the ghostly remainders of what has been repressed in the text—the figure of the dead man.[5] Thus, in any attempt at representation there is a remainder, a missing part. It is almost as if Dickens, the great master plotter, in this novel conceives of narration as founded on a lacuna; whose site is the disfigured corpse. This disjunction profoundly changes our apprehension of Victorian conceptions of identity, particularly feminine identity which cannot be fully represented because it is always something other, bypassing and lying underneath the surface text of representation.

Perhaps it should come as no surprise that Dickens's last finished novel *Our Mutual Friend* obsessively returns to first person narration. Up to this point, Dickens employed a first person narrator three times: in *Bleak House, David Copperfield*, and *Great Expectations*. He returns to it again in *Our Mutual Friend*, but in a roundabout way when in the middle of the novel, he has John Harmon try to articulate his story involving his near murder and his assumption of a false identity. Dickens is haunted by the specter of first person narration. One of the dust heaps of the novel is the ghostly remainder of telling the story of the "I." Dickens uses third person narration to convey the plenitude of his fictional world; simultaneously, however, first person narration encompasses a story of loss, death, and decomposition.[6] Thus, first person narration hovers as a ghostly effect—it haunts by figuring a story of uncanniness surrounding the telling of the story of identity.

Dickens begins the novel with a corpse; subsequently, characters figure stories about this dead man. The ghostly dispersal of the voice haunts the multiplot plenitude of the text.[7] If the self is figured as a story told, then the novel inaugurates the modern technology of narration at a step removed. Significantly, we begin with the dispersal of the voice and end with Dickens's account of his near death by railway accident in his Postscript in Lieu of Preface. The railroad emblematizes the dispersal of time and space in Victorian Britain, thus paralleling the dispersal of the voice in the novel. This frame positions the novel as a kind of labyrinth encased between two structures of dispersal—first person narration and the emergent technology of the railroad.

As the omniscient narrator takes us through the byways of plot, he articulates the text's fictional world. Coextensively, the text disarticulates a composite fictional body and thus a composite subject through its use of first person narration. An analogy will make my point clearer. During the course of the narration, Mr. Venus, the master articulator of the human skeleton, puts together a body; analogously, he, like the narrator, pieces together bodies from disparate elements to make a whole. As the skeleton grows, so does the novel. But the novel is haunted by the decaying corpse presented in the opening pages. On the one hand, narration affirms the plenitude of the Dickensian world; on the other, it marks that narrating the "I" is riddled with missteps, mistaken identities, and death. The multiplot novel then substitutes for first person narration—for the subject who cannot express himself directly. On the one hand, the multiplot novel is like Darwin's entangled bank with its ever branching and beautiful ramifications; on the other hand, the multiplot novel's traumatic moment of origins centers on the dead body and the inability of language to fully represent subjectivity.

POSTSCRIPT IN LIEU OF PREFACE: WRITING DEATH

That Dickens writes a postscript signals he cannot properly get out of his text; that this postscript involves a writing about death, Dickens's near-death by railway accident, suggests Dickens is haunted by death—he has to obsessively narrate to, in effect, stop looking death in the face. In fact, death for Dickens also would seem to embody the fear of being buried alive in that he has so many more stories to tell. An after writing also means that the text proper has not gotten it all—Dickens must step in again as the storyteller to go over ground already covered; this is an uncanny effect. It is almost as if the text must obsessively repeat the death that it seeks to cover over. After writing suggests that there will always be something missing, that one must in effect try again.

The novel begins with a death and ends with the near death of the author, as Dickens narrates his near death by railway accident. The Postscript thus is an after writing: it traces the story of an almost dead man: Dickens himself. Death surfaces in the novel as the fear of not being able to narrate. This is discernible on several different levels: first, death haunts the narrative in that language is a fall into death, and second, in spite of this, the novel must work obsessively to cover over death by telling different stories. The Postscript, a writing after, works backwards in time to delay a kind of murdering. The author in telling of his near death postpones the end of the novel proper. Dickens in the Postscript reminds the reader of his role as a storyteller: parting company with his readers can take place only at his literal death.

> I remember with devout thankfulness that I can never be much nearer parting company with my readers for ever, than I was then, until there shall be written against my life, the two words with which I have this day closed this book:—The End. (894)

The Postscript dismantles the idea of an ending, and instead takes the reader back to a beginning, to the act of the birth of story telling. Is it not another attempt to plot, to begin the telling of another story? In fact, the ending of *Our Mutual Friend* does not move toward closure but toward an anxiety that the text be able to go on and on. Death for

Dickens would result in the *frisson* of the blank page. The Postscript in Lieu of Preface then articulates a notion of the next installment or a future volume, implying that there is always more to tell, and perhaps, more important, that the narrative body can never contain the voice of its author in any definitive meaning or frame. Because of the multiplot novel's impulse to keep narrating, the ending then stands as a non-ending. In this connection, note Dickens's public readings that he insisted on performing even though they may have resulted in his death. Narration becomes in the life and in the text an obsession: one literally cannot stop until one dies.

Paradoxically, the Postscript reads as if it were an obituary—a lament for the death of Dickens as narrator in the text, as well as his near death by railway accident. And in Dickens's autobiographical relation, the "I" resurfaces as if to concurrently suggest that all it can relate concerns death. Thus, the Postscript in Lieu of Preface is also a kind of grave telling. The novel begins with death and ends with death, which through desire it always seeks to avoid. In the Postscript in Lieu of Preface, Dickens comes face to face with the idea of narrative as obituary—of narrative as being one long march toward death. Narrative as obituary conjoins Dickens the author, John Harmon, and the corpse. Representation becomes inextricably tied with telling and retelling to avoid closure. We are brought back full circle to the opening: how to tell the story of the self when it is in danger of short-circuiting through death, the death of language. The railway accident then gives rise to what is most frightening in the text: not being able to relate the story of the "I."

The figure of Bradley Headstone conjoins the dialectic between death and repetition, in effect, narrative as a means to ward off death or closure. After Bradley Headstone's attempted murder of Eugene Wrayburn, the narrator reports that

> Bradley toiled on, chained heavily to the idea of his hatred and his vengeance, and thinking how he might have satiated both in many better ways than the way he had taken. The instrument might have been better, the spot and the hour might have been better chosen. To batter a man down from behind in the dark, on the brink of a river, was well enough, but he ought to have been instantly disabled, whereas he had turned and seized his assailant; and so, to end it before chance-help came, and to be rid of him, he had been hurriedly thrown backward into the river before the life was fully beaten out of him. Now if it could be done again, it must not be so done. Supposing his head had been held down under water for a while. Supposing the first blow had been truer. Supposing he had been shot. Supposing he had been strangled.

Suppose this way, that way, the other way. Suppose anything but getting unchained from the one idea, for that was inexorably impossible. . . . But as he heard his classes, he was always doing the deed and doing it better. (777)

In the realm of possible fictional worlds, the multiplot novel redoes the deed over and over again in its recombinations and retelling of stories. Bradley Headstone, an inscription on a grave, is what the novelist continually works against. While Headstone represents a final inscription, he, in fact, wishes to alter the plot into which he has fallen: in the repetition of the word "suppose," he wants his deed to be repeated over and over until it is conclusive. After the deed is done, he continually reworks the plot over and over again. Each plot line dies in the text, but the next plot line resuscitates the narrative. Consequently, the multiplot novel stages live burials and returns from the dead. In this way, narratives die but only so that they can proliferate all the more.

Bradley Headstone's musings on doing the deed better in his head align him with the master plotter Dickens, whose narrative is one long supposition—in effect, the multiplot in this Victorian novel replicates the labyrinthine byways of gothic narratives. Thus, Headstone and Dickens are locked in the fatal embrace of narrative as a way to ward off death. Narrative then is coextensively a talisman to ward off death, but also its subject is only ever death.

What is the deed that is being repeated in *Our Mutual Friend*? As I have argued, plot diverges from the opening story as if to avoid confronting the story of the "I." Paradoxically, as plot moves further and further away from what it seeks to repress, it is continually brought back to the scene of the crime, and that scene involves a gazing at the "I" and seeing disfigurement and fragmentation. Desire then works dialectically: first as a movement toward plenitude that is immanent in the multiplot novel, and second as an impulse toward remembrance (or the act of narration) that is fraught with decomposition and disarticulation.

DEFACEMENTS AND LIVE BURIALS: NARRATING THE FACE

Images of dead men haunt the novel. Looking into Gaffer Hexam's house, Eugene Wrayburn sees the "bills upon the wall respecting the drowned people starting out and receding by turns" (211). These remainders of the dead posit narration as an act of memorialization—with a live burial and the subsequent ghostly remainder of a flickering image. The novel begins with the deployment of the gaze pivoting on the face and the body. As Gaffer watches the river for dead bodies, Lizzie gazes at her father's face. Lizzie's gaze is full of "dread or horror" (44). Her look involves not only glimpses of her father's face, but at one point it flickers and reveals "a slant of light from the setting sun glanc[ing] into the bottom of the boat, and, touching a rotten stain there which bore some resemblance to the outline of a muffled human form, coloured it as though with diluted blood" (44). Through this description, the text presents a lexicon of dilution. The first glimpse we have of a body is simply an outline. Lizzie sees this outline through a slant of light, and the sun glances. She sees a rotten stain that resembles the outline of a human form. What she sees, she glimpses through a filter: she does not see the body but sees an outline. She does see blood, but the blood is diluted. Dickens shrouds the body in mystery, in half-glimpsed light, as if to suggest the impossibility of reading it.

The text begins with the uncanny, with the decaying face of the dead man causing Lizzie to feel dread and horror. The corpse, in a condition of rupture, disjunction, and fragmentation, inspires these feelings. The text stages its version of Lacan's mirror stage. In the opening chapter, Dickens foregrounds looking—Gaffer and Lizzie gaze at each other. But there is avoidance in this look, and it shifts to the body of the dead man. To look into the mirror is to look into the face of death. And this seems to encapsulate the dread and horror that Lizzie experiences—the terror of the unspeakable and thereby the unnamable. This scene is so traumatic that the text—through the operation of the multiplot—must continually seek to evade it. In Lacan's mirror stage, the self mistakenly assumes that the idealized image it sees is coextensive with itself. Lacan points out that underneath this illusion is the body in pieces (*corps morcélé*). The body in pieces actually aligns itself with the image of the corpse because the body in pieces is neither alive nor dead; it is a fragment of something other. This idea is brought to fruition most notably in *Frankenstein*. Similarly, the multiplot novel is like the idealized body image in that it tells a story of plenitude through its divergent plot lines. Underneath this image, however, exist the fragmented body of the dead man and the fragmented story of first person narration.

The dead body impels narration in the text. In the second chapter, Mortimer Lightwood relates the story of the Man from Somewhere to the guests at the Veneerings. The novel begins with a dead body and is haunted by this death. This body is linked throughout the novel with narration; the dead body propels narration, reading, and interpretation. Perhaps Dickens suggests that one of the dust heaps in the novel is that of first person narration; the telling of the "I" can only ever be presented by another.

The central problem for *Our Mutual Friend* entails representing the "I." The buried mystery of the novel, the figure in the boat—the stand-in for John Harmon—is the relation of the "I." And that face in the figure of John Harmon will tell the story of the "I" in the very center of the book. John Harmon's story involves mistaken identity, misrepresented identity, delay, and murder. As we shall see, his story of identity is told through the dynamics of repression and delay. The question of identity in the text is coextensively implicated in the question of narrative. And delay finds itself embedded in the aesthetics of the multiplot novel. Dickens articulates that identity is always already mistaken, and that mistakenness finds itself aligned with the desire in the novel to move away from the scene of the crime, for the scene of the crime involves, in a sense, articulating identity only to find that once one articulates it, it is murdered. The text is haunted by the figure of John Harmon, of the figure supposed to be the dead man on the boat, but as the text will play out, he turns out in effect to be a dead man in his articulation of first person narration. Much like Bella Wilfer who complains of the Secretary that she "couldn't get rid of a haunting Secretary, stump—stump—stumping overhead in the dark, like a Ghost" (257), the novel cannot quite get rid of the substitutions and misrecognitions for the "I."

It is no wonder then that the novel begins with a scene involving the aftermath of a crime: the murder of John Harmon/George Radfoot. The trope of the face figures predominately in the opening chapter entitled "On the Look Out." What does it signify that the novel opens with the search for bodies, and what do the several gazes (Lizzie's and Gaffer Hexam's) relate about reading the face? Dickens clearly associates murder with the face. It is as if the act of reading the face or narrating a story about the face aligns itself with a crime, in that the act of narration mutilates or corrupts the face. "Sartre claimed that in order to narrate one's life one must become one's own obituary" (quoted in Brooks, *Reading for the Plot* 33).

Dickens sets up an atmosphere of mystery, darkness, inscrutability, and terror surrounding the body on the boat; thereby demonstrating that one may be on the look out, but reading the face is an impossibility. The opening chapter announces the problematics of autobiographical inscription—the inability of the face to construct a face—the self can only ever be someone else which, in fact, represents the position of John Harmon in the text. The narrator describes the figure in the boat:

> What he [Gaffer Hexam] had in tow, lunged itself at him sometimes in an
> awful manner when the boat was checked, and sometimes seemed to try

to wrench itself away, though for the most part it followed submissively. A neophyte might have fancied that the ripples passing over it were dreadfully like faint changes of expression on a sightless face. . . . (47)

The figure in the boat points to the problematics of narration as epitaph. The face registers a site of terror in that the act of looking never quite yields what one had intended. Of course, this opening scene is reminiscent of the creation scene in *Frankenstein*, where Frankenstein gives life to his creature and then runs away in horror. In *Our Mutual Friend*'s scene of creation, which announces the problematics of identity to its readers, Dickens reveals that self-figuration is a disfiguration entailing deviation in that one represses to avoid fully facing the figure. This repression is played out in the novel through the dynamics of the multiplot. The obsession with the detour serves as a means to avoid looking at the face.

But what about the figure must be repressed? The disfigured corpse becomes the emblem for Dickens's treatise on identity. Self-relating will lead to disfiguring, murder, and mistaken identity. *Our Mutual Friend* begins with a murder that sets up the forward impulse of the novel, but this death also sets up the function of desire—the desire to embody the speaking "I" which in effect will turn out to be a murdering, for the "I" murders the moment it begins to speak. Coextensively, the text begins with the desire to give life to the drowned man through narration.

We might thus speak of *Our Mutual Friend* as articulating a philosophical argument about identity and representation. "Narrative," in Tzvetan Todorov's words, "equals life; absence of narrative, death" (74), but Dickens's novel deals with the idea that once one begins to articulate, one occupies the figure of the dead man on the boat. The obsession with telling the story haunts the narrative; in this way, narration substitutes for lack or death. Thus, the novel in its opening passages comes to an impasse with regards to narrating the face, or the site of the "I." The opening forecasts a lack of origins; more succinctly, who is the man behind the face and for what or for whom do Lizzie and Gaffer Hexam search? The text suggests that the man from Somewhere, or the Man from Nowhere, as the body is later referred to in the text, figures a face without an identity.

To avoid this lack, the novel must avert its gaze from this scene of identity and move on to other plots. The multiplot novel in its progression from scene to scene images the fragmented body; coextensively, it moves on to avoid the scene of the fragmented body. Thus, the multiplot novel by breaking the story line into multiple fragments announces what cannot be said in the story proper about identity rupture. While the first chapter pivots on the de-animated face, the multiplots move toward reanimation as if to evade the dead corpse. The multiplot novel suggests that the "I" does not achieve wholeness; rather, it is subject to another story, another interpretation, and another identity. Plot is inextricably linked to the scene of the crime of the first chapter. Plot then becomes the secret in that it serves as the locus for the misunderstanding of the "I." And that misunderstanding is tied to the subject's evasions, secrets, and puzzlements—in effect, its scheming not to reveal what cannot be revealed and what must be avoided— death. Plot then becomes the site for the paradoxical secrets and unfold- ings of identity in the text. At the same time, the novel is obsessed with the construction of plot as if to move away from the construction of character that reifies the construction of fragmentary images.

Perhaps *Our Mutual Friend* offers its most startling critique of the notion of character in its insistence on focusing on the multiplot. The encyclopedic quality of the multiplot novel serves as its disguise in avoiding the "I." But paradoxically, it is in the articulation of the face that it encounters the impasse of self-construction. The multiplot also might be seen as a labyrinthine narrative structure that seeks to avoid the first moment of uncanny excess as evidenced in the opening chap- ter. The multiplot transcends this moment by staging a live burial through the story within a story.

In a sense, then, the novel concerns itself with transference, with the movement from story to story to resist disclosure which would mean facing the death of the figure in the boat. The paradox the novel advances is this: as the novel moves forward, it is continually brought back to the scene of the crime, to, in fact, a relation of the "I." Death implies an inability to narrate, but always already embodied in the concept of narration is the idea of death. Lacan posits that "the symbol manifests itself first of all as the murder of the thing, and this death con- stitutes in the subject the eternalization of his desire" (*Écrits* 104). The corpse posits the death of the subject vis-à-vis his or her position in lan- guage. In other words, the subject's "radical ex-centricity to itself" (*Écrits* 171), as Lacan phrases it. My point can be made clearer by an analysis of the title of the text. Our mutual friend describes Boffin's epithet for John Harmon. The title announces that naming becomes substitution, in fact becomes an epithet. First person narration approaches epithet in that a series of substitutions stand in for the "I." In fact, desire embodies all that the subject can ever do—cover over the telling of the "I." Language serves as the means of articulating the blots and stains of the remnants of translating identity into language.

This covering over of the telling of the "I" is most clearly observable in the text's obsession with storytelling, particularly stories of identity. Embedded in the novel are stories that characters relate to one another. This anxiety about narrating the "I" points to what might be the scene of the crime in the novel: self-narration is representation, a figure removed from the self, as image. This idea is announced when Eugene Wrayburn describes himself as a riddle in answering Mortimer Lightwood's questions "What is to come of it? What are your doing? Where are you going" with

> "[B]elieve me, I would answer them instantly if I could. But to enable me to do so, I must first have found out the troublesome conundrum long abandoned. Here it is. Eugene Wrayburn." Tapping his forehead and breast. "Riddle-me, riddle-me-ree, perhaps you can't tell me what this may be?—No, upon my life I can't. I give it up!" (349)

In speaking of the self as a riddle, Eugene points to the figural quality of the "I"; it is a story. In other words, an image takes the place of subjectivity. The subject is a textual one; in figuring the self, the self disfigures. Self-relation becomes deviation, the subject of a riddle that cannot be answered. Additionally, a riddle positions the subject as a figure to be made out, to be discerned by a series of words. And as the novel shows, this riddling leads to narration whose dynamics embody evasion and disguise.

What particularly gives tension to this novel is its movement forward, its obsessive focus on moving forward—on becoming—and its being brought backwards by the very impetus that propels it forward. Thus, the novel charts a dialectic of the life and death instincts which leads to internal contradictions. This formulation is reminiscent of *Beyond the Pleasure Principle* where Freud postulates about the death and life instincts:

> For a long time, perhaps, living substance was thus being constantly created afresh and easily dying, till decisive external influences altered in such a way as to oblige the still surviving substance to diverge ever more widely from its original course of life and to make ever more complicated *détours* before reaching its aim of death. These circuitous paths to death, faithfully kept to by the conservative instincts, would thus present us to-day with the picture of the phenomena of life. (32–33)

Freud describes a struggle between the two instincts: one that results in a continual battle between quiescence and dynamism. This tension

Peter Brooks has developed into a narrative model for plot—the divergence from quiescence is the motor drive of plot and animates the story. Brooks elaborates: "Between these two moments of quiescence [beginning and ending], plot itself stands as a kind of divergence or deviance, a postponement in the discharge which leads back to the inanimate" (*Reading for the Plot* 103).

Plot in *Our Mutual Friend* obsessively focuses on the postponement or the detour, and the goal is to precisely avoid the ending—there is no goal of quiescence. Rather, the impulse is to avoid quiescence which would mean a final death. The prevalence of multiple endings in the nineteenth-century novel as evidenced in *Villette* and *Great Expectations* attests to Brontë's and Dickens's inability to stop narrating desire. The nineteenth century was obsessed with the detour to ward off death—to in fact forestall representation's inability to posit full meaning.[8] What better way to do this than to never stop narrating desire? Brooks conceives of plot as being "a kind of arabesque or squiggle toward the end" (104). Rather, I would argue that plot for Dickens moves outside of a dynamics of beginning and ending and into a realm of inexhaustibility of narrative as narrative.

Perhaps this point can be made clearer if we return to the text for one of its many exegeses of narrative. At the Lammle's breakfast party, Mortimer Lightwood is being rather coy about relating the story of the Man from Somewhere, and Eugene admonishes him: "It's like . . . the children's narrative."

> I'll tell you a story
> Of Jack a Manory
> And now my story's begun;
> I'll tell you another
> Of Jack and his brother,
> And now my story is done. (470–471)

The emphasis on storytelling and on the digressions inherent in narrating various different stories works against a desire for the ending, for any desire for coherence, for, in effect, the mapping of a life in narrative. It is as if Dickens posits that a life cannot be contained because of the presence of desire or delay. The ending for Brooks is the moment when tension is released. He writes: "The desire of the text (the desire of reading) is hence desire for the end, but desire for the end reached only through the at least minimally complicated detour,

the intentional deviance, in tension, which is the plot of narrative"
(*Reading for the Plot* 104). Rather, I argue that the multiplot novel as
evidenced in *Our Mutual Friend* is subject to the forces of displacement and condensation. Plot thus cannot be bound in the final
coherence of an ending.[9]

The multiplot novel rehearses the dynamics of desire that can never
be contained in the text. This pleasure in the text is the pleasure of the
complicated detour, and Eugene Wrayburn's description of his
engagement of Bradley Headstone in the pleasures of the chase provides
a model for plot:

> Having made sure of his watching me, I tempt him on, all over
> London. One night I go east, another night north, in a few nights I go
> all round the compass. Sometimes I walk; sometimes I proceed in cabs,
> draining the pocket of the schoolmaster who then follows in cabs.
> I study and get up abstruse No Thoroughfares in the course of the day.
> With Venetian mystery I seek those No Thoroughfares at night, glide
> into them by means of dark courts, tempt the schoolmaster to follow,
> turn suddenly, and catch him before he can retreat . . . Thus I enjoy the
> pleasures of the chase, and derive great benefit from the healthful
> exercise. (606)

Eugene's discourse on the "the pleasures of the chase" is comparable
to the pleasures of the most complicated detours of the multiplot
novel. The detour then becomes a means of seduction (Eugene
tempts Headstone). Like a master plotter, Eugene even studies his
routes in advance and plots out "abstruse No Thoroughfares." The
activity of walking propels the two characters forward through a
textual journey of desire and open-endedness. The multiplicity of
routes and byways attests to the going off the line of an uninterrupted
process toward the end.[10] Similarly, the pleasure of the masterplotter,
Dickens, is evident as he takes the reader along the byways of his text.
Multiplot, then, erupts into *jouissance*. The motility of the plot dis-
rupts the linear order of the "conventional" plot line; and the multiplot's desire to attain potential infinity, its wish to avoid closure, is
where the eruption of *jouissance* can be heard in the blank spaces
between each plot.[11] Mortimer Lightwood articulates the desire in the
plot for its continuation when he replies in response to a question
about the man from somewhere, "I must postpone the reply for one
moment, or we shall have an anti-climax" (472).

The desire in the text to continue narrating demonstrates that plots
cannot be sutured in the form of a definitive closure. Endings
represent scenes within scenes and lead to an excess of meaning.

Brooks argues that

> The very possibility of meaning plotted through sequence and through
> time depends on the anticipated structuring force of the ending: the
> interminable would be the meaningless, and the lack of ending would
> jeopardize the beginning. We read the incidents of narration as "promises
> and annunciations" of final coherence, that metaphor that may be
> reached through the chain of metonymies. (*Reading for the Plot* 93–94)

But the interminable informs the multiplot novel. The multiplot novel
is engaged in a struggle with death—with the death of the subject and
the death of the storyteller Dickens at the conclusion of the novel.
Dickens as narrator cannot rightly get out of his text. Like Scherazade
in *The Arabian Nights*, his function is to keep on narrating to avoid a
literal death.

FIRST PERSON NARRATION: THE BURIED TEXT

Thus, we recognize deviance as a means of pleasure, but also as a
means of avoidance. Working its way back in narrative to the man
from Somewhere, the man from Nowhere, to the man with several
names (John Rokesmith, Julius Handford, and George Radfoot), to
the epithet man (our mutual friend), the novel is haunted by the
figure in the boat and the lack he reifies. The novel in midcourse
returns to the scene of its own evasion and works out a theory of narrative plots based on fragmentation, mistaken identity, and deviation.
The "I" in the opening chapter of *Our Mutual Friend* is an inscription
on a grave. In *Beyond the Pleasure Principle*, Freud posits that the
compulsion to repeat stems from not being able to remember an inci-
dent as a past event. He tells us that the neurotic "is obliged to *repeat*
the repressed material as contemporary experience instead of, as the
physician would prefer to see, *remembering* it as something belonging
to the past" (12). This function to repeat can also be seen as a function of plot. As Peter Brooks puts it, "Narrative always makes the
implicit claim to be in a state of repetition, as a going over again of a
ground already covered . . . as the detective retraces the tracks of the
criminal" (*Reading for the Plot* 97).

At the center of the novel, John Harmon returns to the scene
of the crime in the opening chapter—the murdering of "his" body and
his subsequent assumption of a false identity. This return to the scene
of the crime announces the buried text—first person narration—in
that this return stages the relation of the "I" and the death inherent in

that representation. The novel in fact restages the story of the "I" in a very strange way. All of a sudden in a novel recounted by a third person narrator, John Harmon, a.k.a. John Rokesmith, Julius Handford, the man from somewhere, the man from nowhere, George Radfoot, and our mutual friend, resurfaces to tell his story, in effect, redoing the deed or the story of the "I" over and over again.[12] John Harmon is introduced as a character in the opening chapters, then he becomes a story told (the man from somewhere (57)), and finally he becomes a text that he relates himself. What this tells us about first person narration is that the subject is foremost a textual self that is other the moment it begins to narrate or even at the moment it begins to achieve the status as an image.[13]

Mr. Boffin says of John Harmon, "An invaluable man is Rokesmith . . . But I can't quite make him out" (362). As the opening chapter "On the Look Out" makes clear in its deployment of the gaze and of the disfigurement and decomposition of the subject, identity can never be found out. To figure identity is to plot, to tell a different and multiple story. Dickens uses John Harmon to tell his story of the "I" in the middle of the text to suggest that John Harmon's story revolves around the intricacies of plot or articulation rather than around final coherence or understanding of the self. Several critics point to the awkwardness of the introduction of first person narration in the middle of the text.[14] What I would suggest, however, is that this stylistic disharmony actually adds to the linguistic mystery of the "I" in the novel. The stylistic disjunction of the introduction of the solil-oquy or interior monologue in the midst of third person narration recalls a lacuna that the text cannot quite find a way to surmount other than by breaking its narrative trajectory and introducing an aberration. As it introduces self-narration, the text engages in an internal break-down, so to speak, to prepare readers for the narrative disjunctions that follow in the text proper of John Harmon's story.

Additionally, the attempt to explain or narrate the self actually leads to more mysteries about the self. We, for instance, are never sure what really happened the night of the murder. Was Riderhood in on the plot to murder George Radfoot? This aura of mystery is crucial for an understanding of the linguistic puzzles that the novel introduces. Harmon's narration is more about the discursiveness of plot, with moving on from one point to another without an attempt at an apparent logic. Harmon's narration then becomes one of the many riddles in the novel, similar to Eugene Wrayburn's formulation of self-articulation when he asks: "Riddle-me-riddle-me-ree, p'raps you can't tell me what this may be?" and then replies "No. Upon my life, I can't" (339).

In titling the chapter, "Solo and Duett," Dickens alludes to the idea that one's story is always already told. First person narration documents a struggle with an other, a third person narrator, so to speak. The linguistic mystery of the novel turns precisely on appropriating the speech of a dead man. Dickens mixes the voices of the narrator and John Harmon thereby complicating the articulation of identity. Bakhtin writes that

> Language is not a neutral medium that passes freely and easily into the private property of the speaker's intentions; it is populated— overpopulated—with the intentions of others. Expropriating it, forcing it to submit to one's own intentions and accents, is a difficult and complicated process. (294)

The third person narrator relates about John Harmon:

> He tried a new direction, but made nothing of it; walls, dark doorways, flights of stairs and rooms, were too abundant. And, like most people so puzzled, he again and again described a circle, and found himself at the point from which he had begun. "This is like what I have read in narratives of escape from prison," said he, "where the little track of the fugitives in the night always seems to take the shape of the great round world, on which they wander; as if it were a secret law." (421–422)

John Harmon is confused as he moves through a maze of streets, finding himself back in the place from where he had begun, which in a sense is the function of narrative in this text—to go over ground already covered. It is important that Harmon relates his figuring out of where he is to a prison escape because in telling the story of himself, he is always already figured in a narrative of containment and secrecy that cannot be penetrated. Harmon's first person narration is a layer of formal and rhetorical enclosure in a text that is obsessed with storytelling.

Third person narration gives way to first person immediately following this scene: first person narration is the medium through which Harmon expresses his ex-centricity to himself. The first words he speaks are "I have no clue to the scene of my death" (422). These words are crucial for an understanding of the dislocation of the "I" from itself. His purported death, which, of course, the reader by now knows is a lie, serves also as another kind of death—the murdering of the "I" by transforming it into an image.[15] Third person narration must transfer to first person narration the act of ventriloquating the self.

First person narration in this text arises out of nowhere. The man from somewhere and simultaneously the man from nowhere assumes a voice and begins to speak of the "I," but this "I" quickly becomes speech in another person's language. It is as if third person narration wishes to give over to first the means with which to articulate the self, but narration is doubly suspect because first person narration yields quite similar results as if one were, in fact, speaking in the third person. We witness in these scenes a specter figure rehearsing the scene of the "I" that always seems out of place dislocated from the first person voice of which it speaks. The man from somewhere in other persons' third person accounts (one recalls Mortimer Lightwood's story) actually becomes a man from nowhere in his own account.

At every turn in his narration, Harmon expresses his ex-centricity to his narrative self. He relates: "I saw a figure like myself lying dressed in my clothes on a bed" (426), and "I cannot possibly express it to myself without using the word I. But it was not I. There was no such thing as I, within my knowledge" (426). Now, one could argue forcefully that Harmon's puzzlement arises from his being drugged, effecting his identity confusion. But Harmon's monologue on his confusion about the "I" announces Dickens's method of the plotting of the "I." It is not to be figured out; it will remain a secret—not only to readers but to the articulating "I" behind the narration.[16] Thus, John Harmon's narration takes the form of the multiplot novel itself: it is full of detours and secrets to avoid the lack that posits no center. Desire propels the next plot. Narrating by its very premise will resort to twists and turns to avoid the contemplation of the figure embodying lack and death.

This relation of first person narration involves an extreme dislocation. Thus, evasion becomes a way to avoid looking into the mirror of the self and seeing an other. The multiplot novel may then be a means to cover over the dislocation and disjunction in any attempt to narrate the self. The impulse to narrate exists as a way to master this unease. As John Harmon tells himself: "Don't evade it, John Harmon; don't evade it; think it out" (423). But at the same time, the competing impulse is to bury himself alive when he says about revealing his true identity: "Cover him, crush him, keep him down!" (435).

Narration functions in *Our Mutual Friend* as a means to evade death, to cover over an earlier state of things as evidenced in the grisly scene of the face or the site of the "I" in the opening scene. Narration thus becomes epithet; to relate the story of oneself means to relate the story of an image, a fictional other, who will necessarily be disfigured in the telling. The multiplot novel moves on and on so as to avoid being brought back to death, but as we have seen, the figure of the "I" does resurface in the novel. That figure tries again to relate the "I," but is brought to an impasse by the means with which Harmon has to tell his tale—namely, first person narration that is always already another telling. The story, however, must go on, and the novel charts its obsession with storytelling. Freud tells us that the aim of all life is death; however, the multiplot novel insists that the aim of all life is in the detour. Ultimately, the multiplot novel attests to the contradiction inherent in the play between the life and death instincts. That is to say, the simultaneous impulse in the text toward articulation and disarticulation. This paradox announces an articulation of ambiguity—the denial of the closure of plot and the denial of closure of the individual. The inability to suture desire or to reign it in points to no determinate image of the narrative body or subject.

CHAPTER 4

SHOPPING FOR AN "I": ZOLA'S
THE LADIES' PARADISE AND THE
SPECTACLE OF IDENTITY

As we move to France and the latter part of the nineteenth century, images of identity become buried even more under the cover of technology and capitalistic progress. That is, the self turns into a spectacle of dispersal. As we have seen in Dickens's *Our Mutual Friend*, the self is a buried text of images that resurfaces in changed forms in the novel through the dynamics of the multiplot and through buried first person narration. While Dickens's novel focuses on drowning by death through representation and the consequent transforming of the self into an image, Zola advances the change in novelistic representation by conceiving of the self as pure spectacle.

In *The Ladies' Paradise*, identity is linked to consumerism, and this shifting signifier of the self is located primarily in the obsessive description that is a hallmark of this novel. Trying to describe woman is gothic in that through the words employed to depict her and the department store Zola buries her, but the obsessive description illustrates that she cannot be named or put to rest. In this sense woman turns into a series of images that refuse identification. That she is embedded in a series of words suggests the difficulty in telling the story of woman. Written onto the body of women is a labyrinth of words that collapses in its excessiveness.

In the descriptions, she is linked to the *flaneur*, the figure who walks the streets of Paris, taking in the spectacle of the moving images the city has to offer. In fact, the department store prefigures the

emerging cinema in that it offers through its displays of dummies and
models ghostly scenes of the performance of identity. These props of
selfhood offer a phantasmagorical spectacle of specters of identity.
Rapid technological acceleration engenders a self that is fleeting and
phantom-like.

Zola stages the department store as the site of the feminine: on the
one hand the store owners create a series of labyrinths to entrap
women, making them victims of consumption. On the other hand,
the department store takes on the aspect of the haunted castle in
gothic novels in that it becomes a space where phantoms of gender
walk. The department store transforms into a haunted space taking on
a life of its own. The department store stages identity as a figure—its
costuming entails dummies and props. The department store becomes
the locus for the dead—for the dead figure and for the replica. In this
way, the department store houses the uncanny where women are rendered lifeless, but paradoxically they return from the dead making any
attempt to define them futile. She may be buried alive underneath
the store, as the store owner's first wife is, but her ruin announces the
residue of the spectral that cannot be encoded. Thus, the store itself is
paradoxically a beautiful fantasy erected on a ruin. In this way, it is
always in danger of collapse.

In *The Ladies' Paradise*, the body of woman figures obsessively.
Zola creates an elaborate story about this body by linking it to the
items in the department store. He imbues the items in the store with
images of the female and female sexuality to generate desire for goods.
Everywhere we find women and their bodies put on display—women
in fact become the prime signifiers for consumer goods. Alongside
this narrative of the exploited female body is another narrative of the
female body—that which embodies decay and death. The store is
founded on the dead body of a woman—the original owner Madame
Hédouin. Also, the dead body of Geneviève, the daughter of one of
the small shop owners, haunts the narrative of progress that the store
encapsulates. These images of women as corpses provide a strong
counterpoint to the images of life that the goods evoke. The text
operates on the motif of superimposition—simultaneously elevating
and killing the female body. This doubleness surrounding the figure
of woman sparks the uncanny.

On the one hand, the sublime excesses of the descriptions of
women serve as a paean to her power; on the other hand, the text
seems to collapse in its excessive piling up of images to represent
women. The text through all of its various descriptions of women tries
to animate them, but the corpse serves to remind us of the ruin of

representation. This image of the corpse—suggesting the impossibility of representing women—haunts this narrative of capitalistic progress. Capitalism engenders a gothic double that returns to haunt the narrative of progress; in this way, the decaying body of woman figures as the return of the repressed.

The department store creates an identity for woman in late nineteenth-century Paris. Zola uses the department store as an icon for woman, reflecting the broad political, social, and technological changes in France in the latter part of the nineteenth century. Woman's identity rests on the cult of the spectacle: the image of woman gazing at a fantasy image. But there are fissures in this fantasy image, and the department store disturbs the unitary image of woman. One may argue that commercialization further encases woman in a static image; she actually buys a created image that she consumes. Thus, woman in the store is exploited.[1] But the novel takes pains to turn this categorical reading topsy-turvy. As the department store operates as a maze to confuse women and render them helpless before the profusion of items, so too women's identity in the novel figures as a maze, not reducible to closure or completion.[2]

Accoutrements standing in for the woman abound in the department store. The store, representative of woman in the text, continually changes its look. Mouret, the store's owner, mounts elaborate and intricate displays to shock and woo women in order to engender desire for the exotic and unusual. This commodity culture paradoxically produces a transformative and progressive identity for woman. As I will argue, the mania in the text to prescribe images for the woman actually conceals a desire to be in her place. The objects in the store that render woman into an object for consumption translate into a displaced desire for her. And Zola's love plot—or the desire for a happy ending—encapsulates the capitalist success story of a rags-to-riches heroine and the department store workers' need to consume fictions of their own. But the plot of woman and the love plot converge to reveal the constructed and artificial nature of woman's identity and the plots into which she is placed.

The profusion of items in the department store represents a change in conceptions of identity for women. Jacques Lacan elaborates a notion of identity that moves metonymically on the signifying chain, mimicking desire, for that which cannot be possessed. Lacan proposes that signification always refers back to another meaning when he states: "Its [signification's] origin cannot be grasped at the level at which it usually assures itself of the redundancy proper to it, for it always proves to be in excess over the things that it leaves floating within it" (*Écrits* 126). The department store operates as the signifier for the breaking up of the discrete identity of the individual. In other words, woman in the department store cannot be reduced to one definable meaning. Walking the department store, woman receives glimpses of meaning, fragments of a possible self. Desire for goods and their consumption suggests the possibility of moving outside one's proper identity. The world of Zola's novel and the culture of capitalism take as their cultural repository of meaning the department store, and the store offers a way to challenge and reinterpret the cultural sign of woman.

One of the ways that the text accomplishes this reinterpretation is through the department store's reconstruction of the notion of time and the self existing in time. If we view a person's movement through time as a kind of cultural narrative that places him or her in a meaningful and coherent narrative, then the department store in its deployment of departments and the cult of the spectacle begins to chip away at the notion of a discrete identity in time. Much like the *flaneur*, who in his walking apprehends identity through a series of fragmentary moments, woman in the department store reflects a narrative in which a series of moments are not unified.[3]

In this reclassification of the signifier through time, we have the possibility for the creation of new potential signifieds for woman. This potentiality is embedded in the spectacle in nineteenth-century French society; the spectacle promises a movement outside the self. When Denise Baudu first arrives in Paris, the sight of the department store arrests her: "On arriving in the Place Gaillon, the young girl stopped short, astonished" (5). As Zola makes clear, the spectacle arises out of capital culture in nineteenth-century society. The store presents itself as the object of the gaze, and Denise is captivated. The spectacle made so popular in nineteenth-century society (as a marker of the spectacle, we witness the spectacular success of the Crystal Palace in England and the cult of the *flaneur* in France) actually produced a change in conceptions of identity.

The spectacle engenders desire for the other, essentially a desire to be what one is not. The spectacle then makes identity into something that one moves toward, not something which one is.[4] The spectacle recalls Lacan's mirror stage where he postulates that it inaugurates identity in that identity is based on an idealized image one has of oneself. He elaborates: "The jubilatory assumption of the image in the mirror shows the truly imaginary nature of the Ego" (*Écrits* 15). The fragmented subject pulses underneath the idealized image. The notion of the self is a visual one that guarantees a coherent image as

Lacan makes clear when he writes:

> [I]n the scopic field, the gaze is outside; I am looked at, that is to say, I am a picture. This is the function that is found at the heart of the institution of the subject in the visible. What determines me, at the most profound level, in the visible, is the gaze that is outside. It is through the gaze that I enter life and it is from the gaze that I receive its effects. Hence it comes about that the gaze is the instrument through which light is embodied and through which . . . I am photo-graphed. (*The Four Fundamental Concepts of Psycho-analysis* 106)

As the passage demonstrates, the subject sees itself through the other as a spectacle. To conceive of oneself as an image, in Lacan's words, "I am photo-graphed," is to accede to the notion that one is a series of images that moves, rather than remaining static and closed. The photograph coextensively suggests the remnants of something lying underneath the self. The spectral informs any attempt at categorizing the self in that there is always another possibility lying underneath the surface presentation of the self. The self then truly becomes a moving picture in time.

The department store makes possible the display of a fantastical projection of identity. The store presents to its customers staged scenes of identity in which they are available for public display. One sees oneself as an object to be viewed, thus allowing for a performative view of identity. Zola writes of the performance Denise has to put on. "It happened that the next day she had to play the part of the well-dressed girl. Some well-known customers came in, and Madame Aurélie called her several times in order that she should show off the new styles. And whilst she was posing there, with the stiff graces of a fashion-plate, she was thinking of Pépé's board and lodging" (112). Identity in the department store is something one puts on; it becomes a fictional way to represent the self. Zola employs the department store as a marker to represent a novel view of character and thereby masculine and feminine representations in fiction.

Across the Channel, Charles Dickens in his public readings of his own fiction put on display his re-enactment of the fictional lives of his characters. Dickens, through the profusion of his characters, privileges character as spectacle. In the famous painting, "Dickens's Dream," by Robert William Buss, painted in 1870, Dickens's characters are on display. They appear as in a parade, arising out of his imagination. The characters become a crowd; in other words, identity is mobile as in the crowds in the London or Paris streets.[5] Identity also does not guarantee ownership; one can move freely into one person's identity or the next. Identity then becomes something that is transferable because in the realm of the fantasy of the department store, one can switch identities at will. Identity has turned into something to be imagined; in this sense, the body is inhabited by a ghostly parade of selves.

The department store stages the spectacular spectacle of viewing. Looking through the window of the department store prepares the viewer to see identity as a succession of images. Identity moves through space, whereas before the advent of the department store and the cult of the spectacle, identity spatially was more fixed. So too the development of the railroad produced a new conception of the visual in time. The development of the railroad aligns itself with the technology of the cinema in that both register time as a succession of fleeting images. The view of identity I am suggesting is embodied in the figure of the model or the dummy that Zola describes.

> The well-rounded neck and graceful figures of the dummies exaggerated the slimness of the waist, the absent head being replaced by a large price-ticket pinned on the neck; whilst the mirrors, cleverly arranged on each side of the window, reflected and multiplied the forms without end, peopling the street with these beautiful women for sale, each bearing a price in big figures in the place of a head. (8)

At first glance, the dummy forms in *The Ladies' Paradise* present a negative view of woman without a head, and thus without a brain. Looking for identity yields to looking at the symbol of desire—namely capital. This desire for an image is ever changing and exchangeable.

Zola's use of the dummy intimates that what lies behind the image of woman is a stand-in that can never fully capture her. The dummy is the gothic prop *par excellence*—it is a fake image, an artificial construction. In essence, it is a spectral presence. The mirror in the passage reflects and multiplies the figure of the dummy. This image creates a new picture of identity in nineteenth-century society. It makes identity into replications, into desire for an image, which always already begins as an image, as we have seen in Lacan's mirror stage. This view of identity may suggest that underneath the figure of woman lies a prop, a stand-in that undercuts the image of woman as immanent presence. The dummy puts us in the realm of the ghostly— for the dummy is neither alive nor dead. The dummy exists in the liminal space of there and not there, suggesting that the representation of woman is simultaneously a spectacle and spectral; thus, bodily forms are ghosts. Furthermore, identity is something to be viewed and corroborated by the masses suggesting its fictional nature. This new view of identity is most readily gleaned through a reading of the love plot of Denise and Mouret, as I shall argue subsequently.

In her introduction to the novel, Kristin Ross has observed that the department store is the main character (x–xi). In making the department store the central character in the novel, Zola adds to our apprehension of identity. The store in its plurality suggests that identity cannot remain in one frame—it continually moves on a chain of meaning. To give the store the characteristics of character is to suggest that character in consumer culture becomes a text that can be changed. The subtitle of *The Ladies' Paradise*, "a realistic novel," figures an ironic way to read identity. Identity is no longer realistic in commodity culture in that it becomes a desire for the fantasy image. Through the juxtaposition of the fantastical and the real, the text produces an uncanny view of woman that is contradictory. Zola through the use of "fantasies" of identity offers a "realistic" view of how to read identity. That is to say, identity is a series of signs that can never be reduced to one meaning.[6] Clothing as the signifier for woman veils the notion of a discrete character.

To give a face to a thing is paradoxically to say as Paul de Man has shown in "Autobiography as De-facement" that words produce tropological substitutions for things. To personify a thing recalls to us that in our use of language we try to give a face to inanimate things; thus we are always confronted with our attempts to give a name to something. Zola personifies the department store's provisions several times in the text, and these items are meant to stand in for the woman.

> The silk department was like a great chamber of love, hung with white by the caprice of some snowy maiden wishing to show off her spotless whiteness. All the milky tones of an adored person were there, from the velvet of the hips, to the fine silk of the thighs and the shining satin of the bosom. Pieces of velvet hung from the columns, silk and satins stood out, on this white creamy ground, in draperies of a metallic and porcelain-like whiteness: and falling in arches were also poult and gros grain silks, light foulards, and surahs, which varied from the heavy white of a Norwegian blond to the transparent white, warmed by the sun, of an Italian or a Spanish beauty. (366)

The trope of personification suggests that the air has been taken out of what we know identity to be; that is to say, personification highlights the limitations of taking on a persona. To take on an identity is to assume a persona of successive images. The figure of Coppelia in Hoffmann's "The Sandman" demonstrates that the wooden doll is the figure for identity—it is an image created and then taken apart by Coppelius. At the ending of the tale, he drags the figure of the dummy down the steps, and parts of her body break off. Similarly, personification of the goods in *The Ladies' Paradise* shows that woman functions in a system of language that names, controls, and defines her. But through personification, Zola demonstrates that woman has the power to remake the image. Using a thing to figure woman, Zola presents woman as presentation, capable of representing herself. We remember that Lacan points out the "illusion that the signifier answers to the function of representing the signified" (*Écrits* 150).

The store's history demonstrates a way of refiguring woman. Zola relates that Madame Hédouin inherited the store from her family, and after becoming a widow she married Mouret. When Madame Hédouin dies, Mouret inherits the entire business. When she looks at the portrait of Madame Hédouin, Denise thinks of stories she has heard: "The idea of this woman who had met her death amidst the foundations came back to her" (28). The store is literally founded on the body of a woman, "whose blood has helped to cement the stones of the house" (52). One could very well argue that this history is one of woman's oppression, that the store itself traffics in women, thus replicating the masculine traffic in woman.[7] Even though I find some aspects of this argument seductive for an understanding of woman's position in nineteenth-century society, my argument turns on a more complex reading of identity. I want to posit another reading of Zola's configuration of the tale of woman. The live burial of Madame Hédouin is resurrected in the store's inability to figure woman. Through all the profusion of words used to describe her, the novel stages the animation of the female body. The death of Madame Hédouin and the erection of the store mark the death of the old image of woman; thus, the store fabricates a new image of woman.

The death of Mouret's wife inaugurates the new age of the department store. The store thus becomes the spectacle of the cultural apparatus of femininity. And with Madame Hédouin dies an old age; in its place, an age of capitalism and the resulting fluidity in woman's identity emerges. Denise listens to Madame Hédouin's story as if listening to "a fairy tale" (22). If fairy tales point to embedded tales of cultural ways of being, then the embedded story in Madame Hédouin's tale seems to be one of sacrifice and redemption. And that redemption is writ large upon the sign of the store: "The Ladies' Paradise." Paradise here is foreign to a woman's life of domesticity and adherence to a prescribed identity. It is worthwhile in this context to point out that none of the illustrations depicts the department store itself; instead, we are offered depictions of the characters. The Ladies' Paradise is a place to be imagined. The story of Madame Hédouin, a corpse upon which the store is erected, makes possible the image of woman to live on in a different story, a story of display and theatricality.

At the same time, the representation of the body of Geneviève, the daughter of one of the small shop owners, signals the return of the repressed female desire. Her body haunts the narrative of progress offered by the store. Her body as corpse marks the death of the old way of doing business. Zola offers us a double geography of the advent of capitalism. In essence Paris is two cities in one: the world of the department store is superimposed onto the world of the old shop owners. This double geography evokes ghosts. In the interstices of all of the words used to describe the objects in the store, we find the ghostly remainder of the body of Geneviève. It is significant that the new model of capitalism is infused with images of life, while the old way of doing business is associated with degeneration and decay. This degeneration and decay is figured onto the body of woman—the body of Geneviève.

> And there she lay, so very thin, under the bed-clothes, that one hardly suspected the form and existence of a human body. Her skinny arms, consumed by a burning fever, were in a perpetual movement of anxious, unconscious searching; whilst her black hair seemed thicker still, and to be eating up her poor face with its voracious vitality, that face in which was agonising the final degenerateness of a family sprung up in the shade, in this cellar of old commercial Paris. (324)

The body of Geneviève signals the gothic corpse of representation. Her body encodes what the main plot concerning the fantasy ideal of woman cannot say about her. Capitalism's destruction of the small shop owners parallels its domination over women by turning them into consumers. Thus, consumerism figuratively murders woman. But another way to read the decaying body of Geneviève is that it represents the decay in the representation of woman: the old ways of figuring woman as a stable signifier collapse.

The store founded on the literal dead body of woman comes to stand in for the figure of woman. Zola remarks of the store: "Was it not an astonishing creation? It was causing a revolution in the market, transforming Paris, for it was made of woman's flesh and blood" (68). The store is fleshed out with the accoutrements of woman's pleasure, and this pleasure is readily observable in the store's displays. Mouret creates a display for one of the store's sales:

> And the marvel, the altar of this religion of white was, above the silk counter, in the great hall, a tent formed of white curtains, which fell from the glazed roof. The muslin, the gauze, the lace flowed in light ripples, whilst very richly embroidered tulles, and pieces of oriental silk striped with silver, served as a background to this giant decoration, which partook of the tabernacle and the alcove. It made one think of a broad white bed, awaiting in its virginal immensity the white princess, as in the legend, she who was to come one day, all powerful, with the bride's white veil. (353)

The thread of illusion, adduced from the passage, leads to a speculation on masculine and feminine identity. Zola employs the department store to traffic in illusions, and his use of metaphor and embedded stories of a princess in his description of the bed above alludes to the textual inscription of masculine and feminine identity.[8] That is to say, identity represents a changing text of signifiers that has as its central backdrop the department store and its changing face.

Zola's language overturns neat categorizations of the masculine and feminine creating a novel understanding of gender in late nineteenth-century French society. At first glance, as already pointed out, the novel represents woman as a pawn in the capitalist system of exchange. The store is a place where Mouret imagines himself as "lord and master of the conquered city" (64). Further, Zola goes on to explain Mouret's trafficking in woman.

> And if woman reigned in their shops like a queen, cajoled, flattered, overwhelmed with attentions, she was an amorous one, on whom her subjects traffic, and who pays with a drop of her blood each fresh caprice. Through the very gracefulness of his gallantry, Mouret thus allowed to appear the brutality of a Jew, selling woman by the pound. He raised a temple to her, had her covered with incense by a legion of shopmen, created the rite of a new religion, thinking of nothing but her, continually seeking to imagine more powerful seductions; and, behind her back, when he had emptied her purse and shattered her nerves, he was full of the secret scorn of a man to whom a woman had just been stupid enough to yield herself. (69–70)

This scene casts Mouret as the seducer of woman who uses her for his own gain and then feels contempt for her. Underneath his worship lies his contempt for her and a wish to demonstrate his supremacy. But Zola does not stop there; the text juxtaposes contradictory views of masculine and feminine relations. It is almost as if the text itself uncannily stages its ambivalence about gender relations through a spectacular economy of the spectral.

The text reveals an ambivalent and ambiguous portrayal of gender reflecting the nineteenth century's ambivalence about and obsession with the emerging new woman who clamored for changes in every aspect of society from reform in divorce laws to advocating for the power to vote. This ambivalence lies at the very heart of the notion of a department store for women. For the department store brought women into the public sphere while at the same time exploited their desires.

Laura Mulvey in her groundbreaking "Visual Pleasure and Narrative Cinema" provides a way to understand representational meanings in patriarchal culture when she posits:

> Woman . . . stands in patriarchal culture as signifier for the male other, bound by a symbolic order in which man can live out his fantasies and obsessions through linguistic command and by imposing them on the silent image of woman still tied to her place as bearer of meaning, not maker of meaning. (29)

While I find Mulvey's argument productive for a framework in which to understand woman's oppression, it is my intention to try to get beyond binary oppositions that reinforce inscribed meanings of masculinity and femininity. Mary Ann Doane presents a similar argument to Mulvey's when she writes of the "female appetite for the image, an appetite sustained by the commodity fetishism which supports capitalism. And the ultimate commodity . . . is the body adorned for the gaze" (198). Again Doane presents a convincing argument, but Zola's text mounts its own resistance to woman as passive spectacle and instead presents us with plurality of meanings to inscribe woman.[9]

One of the ways that the text reinscribes the meaning of woman is by its obsession with objects that stand in for the woman. The text presents to us woman as a commodity through a series of objects meant to adorn her. The obsessive piling up of images to describe the objects in the department store and consequently to depict woman reveals the inability to fix her. The text through its anxious use of metaphor desires to animate woman; paradoxically, this use of metaphor as a stand-in for the woman uncovers the impossibility of fully representing her. The edifice that Mouret builds—the department store—and the images that Zola constructs to embody woman all in a sense collapse revealing a lack at the center of the text. Lying underneath all the piles of words used to describe woman is the fear that she eludes comprehension.

Coextensively, the profusion of images for the woman uncovers a fascination with her. The obsession with woman and with all the objects that are displayed in *The Ladies' Paradise* reveals a wish simultaneously to make woman into a fetish object so as to ward off the threat of castration,[10] but also, and more important, to occupy her shoes, so to speak. This fascination in the text to dress woman, to provide her with all the different items that go into making her into an identifiably read woman, actually is colored by identification. The spectacle encourages identification by imaginatively allowing viewers of either gender to enter the space of the window display. Additionally, the department store serves as the site of the feminine that in patriarchal culture has been cast aside in favor of masculine erections. The department store and by association woman come to figure as the object that is invested psychically with a power that cannot be denied.

To dress woman in the text means to participate in the undressing of binary notions of the masculine and feminine. That is to say, dressing woman becomes a way to imaginatively recreate a scenario where masculine and feminine meet. It is almost as if the text's focus on women reveals that which haunts the societal erection of male supremacy—the feminine. The store serves as a *memento mori*, that is to say, a continual reminder of the sacrifice of woman's flesh and blood to a masculine economy. As Zola points out, the erection of the store rests on the literal body of Madame Hédouin. The *memento mori* of the store then brings man's desire into play for something that has been lost, namely the feminine.[11]

All of the language of mastery and control masks the desire to inhabit the position of the feminine. The text simply cannot rid itself of woman and her significations, as Zola makes clear in the following passage: "And at this last moment, amidst this over-warmed air, the women reigned supreme. They had taken the whole place by storm, camping there as in a conquered country, like an invading horde installed amongst the overhauling of the goods. The salesmen, deafened, knocked up, were now nothing but their slaves, of whom they disposed with a sovereign's tyranny" (236). One could argue that women have become slaves to fashion and that their power is ultimately empty, but to read the passage categorically is to deny woman's potential for disorder and disruption. The women in the passage take the "place by storm." If we read the passage as one that overturns and upsets gender identification, then we can uncover the text's preoccupation with questioning gender categories.

Dress has always functioned as the covering and the marker for gender identity, in that dress accentuates femininity and masculinity. Anne Hollander argues that "the mirror remains a picture, inextricable from the representational style of its moment" (416). One in a sense is read as masculine or feminine by virtue of his or her dress. Chinese opera, drag, kabuki, and Elizabethan theater all play out this idea in their acting out and performing gender through an elaborate system of dress and gestures. Zola's text of commercialism has at its core the element of fascination that strives to produce endless vistas of possibility. Desire in the text, which is ultimately a desire for the other, moves from object to object without resting on one fixed meaning. Desire for embodiment is simply an illusion. Thus the passage about the dummies as already analyzed above represents the wish for clothing to embody the figure as a cover for what was not there to begin with.

Therefore, beneath the image of woman, nothing is there but the images used to describe her. All is illusion and word play as commercialism takes up the image of woman as image to be seduced and taken in, but the image proves to rest on an inability to fully embody woman. The department store then becomes the site for the absent woman, the woman who can never fully occupy the text of the displays of her. Zola reports:

> And the stuffs became animated in this passionate atmosphere: the laces fluttered, drooped, and concealed the depths of the shop with a troubling air of mystery; even the lengths of cloth, thick and heavy, exhaled a tempting odour, while the cloaks threw out their folds over the dummies, which assumed a soul, and the great velvet mantle particularly, expanded, supple and warm, as if on real fleshly shoulders, with a heaving of the bosom and a trembling of the hips. (16–17)

What is woman? The passage indicates that she is stuffs: laces, cloaks, and mantles. The stuffs of identity? The department store then becomes the sign for the taking on of identity through a series of goods: what makes the woman is a commercial machine that turns her out.

As I have stated previously, these accoutrements surrounding the woman reflect desire for her. The profusion of objects that the store offers its clientele may be understood as traces of desire. And we know from Lacan that lack and the resultant desire stem from the separation from the loved one, namely the mother. Language, according to Lacan, reflects this desire in its search for the ultimate object of desire, which, of course, can never be fulfilled. I am suggesting here that the store, with all of its signs for the woman, with its textual apparatus for the woman, underscores nineteenth-century culture's desire to embody woman, to, in effect, recreate her in an image of fantasy and desire. To be this image of fantasy and desire would recapture the fantasy of the mirror stage where the child conceives an image of himself or herself based on the idealized figure of the mother or the idealized figure of the subject in the mirror. All of the heaped up objects in the store serve as a means of displacement or rather as a way to manage the loss of the loved object, which is the mother. But, as we have seen, all of the objects underscore the need to cover over what perhaps might not be there to begin with: the illusion of femininity protects and cements the power of the masculine "I."

Woman in patriarchal culture is particularly associated with desire. Her body has been subjected to and scrutinized by the male gaze, thereby denying her agency. But this subjection of woman also figures a desire to be in her place. Looking may involve power and control, as Freud has noted, but it also entails feelings of loss.[12] Woman as object retains her power because she simply cannot be captured or read. The frenetic activity in the store reflects a longing and desire, and all of the things represent stand-ins for what cannot be represented. Elizabeth Grosz explains Jacques Lacan's depiction of woman as the unconscious: "[A]re women, not, partly, the unconscious? That is, is there not in what has been historically constituted as the 'unconscious', some censored, repressed element of the feminine" (171). The fixation with the objects in the store signals a desire to embody the feminine. The desire for the image of the woman is fraught with the loss of ever capturing that image. The objects serve then to manage and control the anxiety of the masculine subject. Zola describes a display of silks:

> At first stood out the light satins and tender silks, the satins *à la Reine* and Renaissance, with the pearly tones of spring water; light silks, transparent as crystals—Nile-green, Indian-azure, May-rose, and Danube-blue. Then came the stronger fabrics: marvellous satins, duchess silks, warm tints, rolling in great waves; and right at the bottom, as in a fountain-basin, reposed the heavy stuffs, the figured silks, the damasks, brocades, and lovely silvered silks in the midst of a deep bed of velvet of every sort—black, white, and coloured—skillfully disposed on silk and satin grounds, hollowing out with their medley of colours a still lake in which the reflex of the sky seemed to be dancing. The women, pale with desire, bent over as if to look at themselves. (93)

This passage presents a scene of desire for the woman as represented by the accumulation of objects. In fact, the passage plays out a scenario of woman looking into the mirror and seeing the cultural image of woman surrounded by accoutrements. In the passage, the "women, pale with desire bent over as if to look at themselves." And what do they see; they see a series of signifiers, as evidenced in the various descriptions of the silk. The passage then describes what I have been arguing so far—the objects surrounding women stem from a desire to create a fantasy image of wholeness. The objects take on the role of language; language evokes a thing by means of a substitute, which the thing is not. Thus, we are always substituting for the original object. But as we have seen, the objects in their profusion prevent a crystallized image; rather desire moves onto increasingly more and more elaborate objects.

This desire for woman is the desire for embodiment. For to capture the image of woman would mean in effect to revert to the idealized image of the mother's face or the ultimate object of desire. The desire for the woman is the desire to render whole the viewer.[13] This, of course, is an impossibility, but the woman and her accoutrements offer the possibility of a fantasy of completeness. Her image promises the possibility of all objects coalescing into what the masculine subject desires, namely a readable text. In this connection, the inscription above the store, "The Ladies' Paradise," held up by "Two allegorical figures, representing two laughing, bare-breasted women" (6) reveals that the store and woman in the text cannot be read as simple allegory. Rather the text functions as pure desire, which cannot be represented fully.

The sublime excess with which Zola describes women and the items in the department store parallels the layout of the store itself. That is, the store is figured as a labyrinth or maze meant to entrap and seduce women into making purchases. This map of the department store resembles the function of language itself in its attempts to capture woman through a series of words used to describe her. The text, then, is one long labyrinth that initially tries to render woman canny in its elaborate and repeated use of description. But this canniness erupts into uncanniness as the repetitions evince that burying woman under a cloak of language results in the collapse of the buried text. Embedding woman in descriptions produces various layers of stories that resurrect her into a text that cannot be defined.

Baudelaire's "The Painter of Modern Life" offers a productive framework with which to read woman as image of desire in Zola's text. Baudelaire writes: "All the things that adorn woman, all the things that go to enhance her beauty, are part of herself; and the artists who have made a special study of this enigmatic being are just as enchanted by the whole *mundus muliebris* as by woman herself" (423–424).

For Baudelaire, and I would argue for the history of woman's representation, a woman cannot be separated from the series of objects that guarantee her fascination. This fascination is part of the desire for woman to be the guarantor of subjectivity. The word "enchant" derives from the Latin: to chant or to sing. For Baudelaire, woman possesses the power to charm and to cast a spell precisely because of her adornment. This adornment is the very function of desire, for the apparel composes the woman: "all the things . . . are part of herself" (423–424). She presents to the masculine subject an enigma, which is displaced onto the object. The object then comes to represent woman which marks her as composed of a series of signifiers.

Writing of an artist's representation of woman, Baudelaire posits: "When he describes the pleasure caused by the sight of a beautiful woman, what poet would dare to distinguish between her and her apparel? Show me the man who, in the street, at the theatre, or in the Bois, has not enjoyed, in a wholly detached way, the sight of a beautifully composed attire" (424). Woman then is a function of her attire suggesting that she as object of desire retains plasticity. To envision woman as the sum total of "beautifully composed attire" is not to render her into an object but rather to deconstruct the notion of what makes up identity. Paradoxically, capitalism advances identity as a series of signifiers whose meanings are fixed by the dominant culture, but it also signifies an identity capable of being changed. To see woman as a function of her attire is to read her as a text whose outer covering masks her identity. Clothing, then, becomes akin to language which is a function of history and culture. Composed of clothing, woman stands as the social signifier of her day. And fashion impresses onto her body a way to render her but not to fully define her, for her attire bears the weight and burden of signification.

In arguing that "beauty [is] enhanced by every kind of artifice" (428), Baudelaire posits the constructed nature of woman. The department store therefore in its presentation of fashion promotes the fascination with the ideal as against the natural or the real. In so doing, fashion presents to woman the many guises she wears. In wearing a guise, woman figures identity as performance, as against the rigidity of the phallic signifier. Baudelaire goes on to postulate: "Fashion must therefore be thought of as a symptom of the taste for the ideal that floats on the surface in the human brain, above all the coarse, earthy and disgusting things that life according to nature accumulates, as a sublime distortion of nature, or rather as a permanent and constantly renewed effort to reform nature" (426). Baudelaire suggests that woman cultivate artifice to distort nature. The object here is, of course, desire for the love object, which always already exists as artifice, as representation, outside what Baudelaire terms as "earthy and disgusting that life according to nature accumulates."

Implicit in Baudelaire's observations is the notion that to be womanly is indeed to take on the articles of how our culture registers a woman. This desire for artifice then is a desire to be the fantasy image of a woman or an ideal figure. This desire also registers for woman a textual identity that is based on the desire for ever more elaborate disguises. Disguise then masks that woman's image is always already a fantasy built on the bedrock of a supposed stationary subject that can be read definitively.[14]

The rise of the department store contributes to the making of woman's identity into a commodity for the stores' owners to manipulate, but paradoxically this seeming victimization and exchange of women's bodies results in a novel way to read woman's identity. The department store figures woman's identity as embodying performance and display. The objects surrounding women such as her clothing are built around a desire for a fabricated image. That is to say, underneath the societal image of woman is an empty figure as evidenced in the figure of the dummy in the text. The objects in the store then serve as a means of shoring up an image that may not be there to begin with.

The desire for woman's identity to represent a stable one masks a fear that she is always already outside that identity. Thus, desire in the text, in the form of the eroticization of objects that go into making the woman, moves along a continuum that never ends. The text records the impossibility of possessing the original object of desire, a fantasy image of woman; instead, desire moves on to substitutions, displacements, and replacements.

This desire to adorn woman in order that she may fascinate is closely aligned with the desire in the text to fashion a love story for the two main characters: Denise Baudu and Octave Mouret. This is no ordinary love story, for it functions as a spectacle for the workers to exchange gossip, opinions, and innuendo. The love plot for the store's workers becomes a fantasy escape where they can project their fears and desires. The department store, emblem of desire, is the setting for the workers to watch scenes of love. The erotic energy in the store plays itself out in the love plot. As Denise first enters the store, "there was mingled with her desire to enter it a vague sense of danger which rendered the seduction complete" (17). Everything in the store is primed to seduce her. She hears a succession of stories about the founding of The Ladies' Paradise, most notably the story of Madame Hédouin, who, as we have seen, meets her death "amidst the foundations" (28). Thus, storytelling about the store functions as desire. The women shoppers circulate stories about the acquisition of goods. Madame Marty displays her purchases at a gathering of friends:

> The bag became inexhaustible, she blushed with pleasure, a modesty like that of a woman undressing herself made her appear more charming and embarrassed at each fresh article she took out. There was a Spanish blonde-lace cravat, thirty francs: she didn't want it, but the shopman had sworn it was the last, and that in the future the price would be raised. Next came a Chantilly veil: rather dear, fifty francs; if she didn't wear it she could make it do for her daughter. (74)

In the passage, Zola presents an erotic scene of Madame Marty showing off her purchases. The desire for the object thus becomes a sensual display of the woman's body, and the desire for objects translates into a desire for the love plot to move forward.

This sensual display is a prelude to, and the impetus for, the love plot. The department store becomes the shrine of love. Zola remarks: "A fine dust rose from the floor, laden with the odour of woman, the odour of her linen and her bust, of her skirts and her hair, an invading, penetrating odour, which seemed to be the incense of this temple raised for the worship of her body" (225–226). Commercialism is linked with the desire for a love story and also with a wish to fabricate a love story of one's own. Commercialism—in its making possible the democratization of objects or at least the fantasy of possession—also brings about the desire to tell a love story.

The love plot is the spectacle for the consumption of the department store workers: Denise and Mouret become then the biggest display in the novel. Regarding Denise and the gossip of her coworkers, Zola writes: "But Mouret's sufferings were destined to increase, for he became jealous. One morning, in the office, before the board-meeting commenced, Bourdoncle ventured to hint that the little girl [Denise] in the ready-made department was playing with him."

> "How?" asked he, very pale.
> "Yes! she has lovers in this very building."
> Mouret found strength to smile. "I don't think any more about her, my dear fellow. You can speak freely. Who are her lovers?" "Hutin, they say, and then a salesman in the lace department—Deloche, that tall awkward fellow. I can't speak with certainty, never having seen them together. But it appears that it's notorious." (300)

The stories about Denise and her supposed lovers fuel a need for the workers to monitor Denise's and woman's sexual behavior. But the stories in a more complicated way turn on a fascination with the desire to be in the place of Denise or to identify with her. The circulation then of the love plot works to diffuse the desire to be in the position of a woman. Work on fantasy stresses the mobility of the subject, as Parveen Adams has observed: "Fantasy is laid out—in scenarios and the subject can take up now one position, now another in the scenario" (4).[15]

This means of identification is aligned with the desire to be the Other. The desire for objects and for woman cannot be separated from the desire to create a story of love as the following passage makes clear: "Amidst the crowded sea of customers, this sea of bodies, swelling with life, beating with desire, all decorated with bunches of violets, as though for the bridals of some sovereign" (378). Here desire for the store is aligned with the desire for the marriage or the love plot to succeed. Thus, the love plot indeed leads to the ultimate desire, marriage, or the acquisition of the place of the Ladies' Paradise.

But, as the text reveals, the novel needs the love plot to stimulate desire for the final acquisition of the woman or the language of conquest in the text. Clearly, whoever has the story in the text possesses the power to fascinate, to stimulate desire. The story then becomes a valuable commodity to be passed on and embellished with the accoutrements of desire.

The figure of woman is the figure in the story, and all of it is fabricated or embellished for the amusement of the workers in the store.

> All the counters were talking of nothing else but the governor's love affairs, amidst the press of business. The adventure, which had for months been occupying the employees, delighted at Denise's long resistance, had all at once come to a crisis; it had become known that the young girl intended to leave The Ladies' Paradise, not withstanding all Mouret's entreaties, under the pretext of requiring rest. And the opinions were divided. Would she leave? Would she stay? Bets of five francs circulated from department to department that she would leave the following Sunday. (355)

This inset piece on the love plot serves to figure woman as a series of stories being exchanged. Zola makes the story of the desire for woman conform to an already existing plot or story about her. The text, however, simultaneously reveals a different story about the image of woman: to traffic in the image of woman opens up the possibility for resistance and the denial of closure. The return of repressed woman's desire can be read in the traces of the remains of what is left over after the store's much-vaunted sales. The threat in the text of woman's revenge looms over the success of the store: Baron Hartmann tells Mouret: "I fancy they're [women] taking their revenge . . . They're getting tired of belonging to you" (279). Woman's desire cannot be suppressed or contained. The department store in its mazes and twists loses sight of one story to tell about woman. Instead multiple stories, including Denise's, inform the telling of the love plot.

The love plot functions as a kind of commodity in the text; it reflects the readers' and the employees' desire to see love conquering all. But Zola's plot reveals that even though Mouret wins Denise at the end through her withholding her sexuality—her "goods"—his emphasis is on the mechanics of plot itself and the artificiality of that construction. In other words, the love plot begins to resemble the text's point about the construction of women. Constructing woman as a multivalent sign, Zola points to the possibility of woman's desire escaping commodification. Similarly, the love plot in the mechanical gestures of the happy ending allows for the possibility of other plots and gestures. Using the love plot that contains the idea that virtue (sexual purity) will gain Denise her man, Zola emphasizes the love plot as a commodity to satisfy readers' desires for a "happy" ending. But the artificiality of this plot subverts the idea of a happy ending. At the same time that Zola's text contains a happy ending, he demolishes it with a critique of the monological desire for happy endings that bind loose ends and loose identities. The text's insistence on a succession of images and substitutions to describe woman tells a story of desire that cannot be contained. The desire to narrate woman cannot be foreclosed by the "happy" ending.

CHAPTER 5

SHE'S NOT THERE: *VERTIGO* AND THE GHOSTLY FEMININE

I have been leading up so far to what I would now like to term gothic identity; that is, one that resists the discrete categories of Victorian stable identity. This gothic identity is most clearly observable in forms of discourse, most identifiably in narrative returns from the dead. As we have seen throughout this study, narratives proliferate and return from the dead in an altered form. In *Our Mutual Friend*, first person narration is buried deep in the interstices of the multiplot novel but returns in the middle of the narrative and presents identity as an effect of doubling and death. In *The Ladies' Paradise*, the spectacle produces an identity that is a function of the parade; that is to say, identity becomes a succession of images: a cinema of the imagination.

The move to Hitchcock and *Vertigo* situates gothic identity as that which logically arises from fictional narratives to filmic narratives. That is to say, filmic narrative renders identity visible through the frame's display of phantoms of gender. Film visually erects the props of gender identity inasmuch as it is a ghost-producing technology that manufactures a replica of identity. For what is photography but a technological mode for narrative representations of returns from the dead? In demonstrating film as a spectral parade of gender, *Vertigo* links woman and her identity to the supernatural. Identity becomes an effect of the supernatural, and desire for the image is always a desire for the fake or the counterfeit to replicate a fantastical image of the original object that can never be duplicated. *Vertigo* thus presents identity as an effect of cultural stories of gender. This predicament is located in the way in which the film treats vision. Vision turns into vertigo resulting in the film's critique of the instability of the eye. This instability deconstructs the "real" and substitutes glimpses and flickerings of identity, calling into question stable notions of identity and narrative. Identity does not stay in its proper place because it is a production of shadows and specters.

Vertigo in presenting its love story is confronted by ghosts. Not only are the characters haunted by ghostly figures from the past—Madeleine is haunted by Carlotta, and Scottie is haunted by Madeleine— but the film narrative itself exhibits a ghostly effect. Hitchcock shot many scenes employing a fog filter. It is almost as if in this elegiac film Hitchcock is in love with the image but coextensively must reveal the image for what it is—a fake and a counterfeit. So in one of the most haunting of love stories, we find Hitchcock mounting a metacommentary on the status of film itself. Hitchcock is in love with the image, but the image is in a sense always the wrong image. Thus, what is so terrifying in the film is that the image comes back to haunt in a different form. Identity cannot be located in one person or in one film frame. Madeleine returns as Judy, and Scottie's identity is linked with Madeleine's. This haunting is an after effect stemming from master narratives about identity and gender in Western culture.

The layering of stories in *Vertigo*—the proliferation of stories—is truly gothic and produces a vertiginous effect. The film itself operates on the level of multiple live burials and returns from the dead: Scottie buries his story and it returns in Madeleine's story, and Madeleine/Judy's story is buried in the interstices of both Scottie and Elster's stories. Thus, *Vertigo* presents the difficulty of telling Madeleine/Judy's story. What would that story look like? I am claiming that her story leaks into everybody else's story producing its own ghostly effect. That is to say, when Madeleine/Judy speaks, who is speaking? The layering of these stories reveals that the supposed "real" will always return as the gothic other.

Vertigo positions identity as an effect of visual projection. Scottie, in watching Madeleine, can inhabit her through projection. He enters into the picture and becomes an image, safely through the filter of the screen. Rather than a discrete identity, film visually sets into play the dynamics of doubling and projection. *Vertigo* situates identity as a series of images. We find Madeleine at the art gallery observing a portrait of Carlotta after whom she has modeled herself. The camera focuses on the coil in Carlotta's hair and then cuts to Madeleine's hair which is an exact replication. All the while, Scottie is looking in on this scene of gazing into the mirror and seeing an image of desire. He longs for the image of the painting: the image that would guarantee perfection. But this desire for the dead woman—this live burial of the woman into an image—returns in the "real" woman, Judy, who is a layering of Madeleine, Carlotta, and all of the images she plays. One of the terrors of *Vertigo* is that the image of Madeleine/Judy does not stay fixed. The original is never the original but rather a gothic series of replications and fabrications.

Here *Vertigo* takes up the issue of origins. Origins can never be located definitively in one identity or person. Images and stories proliferate out of control suggesting that what one has put to rest returns in an altered form. Hitchcock combines the suspense mode with the gothic to formulate questions inherent in the narrative about gender and identity. The effect is one of ghostly returns upon the present, recalling a maze rather than any definitive conclusion about gendered identity.

Roland Barthes's hermeneutic code creates a model of suspense based on the formulation of an answer to a question inherent in the narrative. Thus, as he phrases it, "the hermeneutic terms structure the enigma according to the expectation and desire for its solution" (119). In the course of a narrative, we are presented with many false conclusions in the form of "the snare, the equivocation, the partial answer, the suspended answer, and jamming" (119); these are functions of narrative's delaying tactics. But how do we explain a narrative that in its very formulation blocks the questions proposed? That is to say, Barthes's model presupposes first that the question can be answered and second and, perhaps more important for my argument, that everyone can agree on the questions proposed. If we apprehend *Vertigo* through Scottie's point of view, then his questions participate in Barthes's hermeneutic code. Thus, for example, the central question at the beginning of the film rests on finding the key to Madeleine.

But in strikingly complex ways, the film articulates a different model of narrative. Instead of presenting the narrative as a sentence, as Barthes puts it, "to narrate (in the classic fashion) is to raise the question as if it were a subject which one delays predicating"[1] (120), *Vertigo* poses a dizzy array of mutually contradictory questions. The hermeneutic code would seem to operate as if there is one question, one answer, and one voice articulating that question throughout the narrative, even though several questions may arise during its course. As soon as we think we apprehend Scottie through point of view focalization, another possible story intervenes to qualify his point of view. This multiplication of stories calls forth the uncanny where one can meet up with one's double; so too the uncanny entails the horror experienced when one cannot resolve meaning, where meaning is comparable to a spiral rather than a particular destination. The function of stories within stories presages live burial, and, consequently, the unspeakable vertigo occasioned by repression. This vertigo is transferred onto the body of woman making her an uncanny figure who narrates stories that double Scottie's story.

Therefore, what is so disturbing about *Vertigo* is its insistence on multiple stories most effectively announced by Hitchcock's employment of numerous fades to black to mark the closure of a scene, and perhaps more significantly in Madeleine/Judy's story, which is a displacement of and thus a rewriting of Scottie's story. This displacement surfaces in the multiple voices in the text. M. M. Bakhtin in *The Dialogic Imagination* elaborates a theory of novelistic narrative discourse thus:

> Authorial speech, the speeches of narrators, inserted genres, the speech of characters are merely those fundamental compositional unities with whose help heteroglossia can enter the novel; each of them permits a multiplicity of social voices and a wide variety of their links and interrelationships (always more or less dialogized). These distinctive links and interrelationships between utterances and languages, this movement of the theme through different languages and speech types, its dispersion into the rivulets and droplets of social heteroglossia, its dialogization—this is the basic distinguishing feature of the stylistics of the novel. (263)

Even though Bakhtin writes here of the novel's stylistics, film too is a narrative that speaks in many voices: the director, the characters, the music, the scriptwriter, and so on.[2] The film itself presents identity as the effect of a series of ghosts or others, rather than a discrete identity. Scottie's speech or his point of view is informed by the dynamics of love, identity, and gender in western society. But *Vertigo* is heavily dialogized in its insistence on critiquing the monologic voice that structures these dynamics.

The detective story fueling the narrative most closely resembles Barthes's hermeneutic code, but overlapping that story is one detailing the dynamics of love and masculine and feminine identity. Scottie's predicament in the story—one involving the collapse of his masculine identity—is written onto the body of Madeleine/Judy. This displacement transfers his symptoms onto woman. So that the text we think we are watching is always informed by the subtext of what Scottie does not see. How can we detect Scottie, and what does his detection serve as a cover for? Perhaps *Vertigo* is a long sustained elegy to the dynamics of feminine representation—the image of woman at the service of her male producer/director (Scottie, Elster, Hitchcock). But in exposing the dynamics of representation, the film sounds a death knell for the operations of the hermeneutic code predicated on discovery and disclosure, given that Scottie asks the wrong questions. Thus, the film uses the gothic mode of live burials and returns from the dead to articulate a story about forms of oppression—film being one of them. In this way, it calls for new questions and new answers lying outside the structure of the sentence which is the unified western model of order, closure, and fixity (both for narrative and for identity).

If narrative is based on arrival, reflecting a male model of development,[3] then the film suggests that the suspense model, the hermeneutic code, is not an adequate model to address femininity. Perhaps the hermeneutic code in Hitchcock's later films, most notably, *Rear Window, Vertigo, Psycho, The Birds*, and *Marnie* rests on a false premise, a snare, so to speak. Hitchcock dismantles the structure of the sentence and woman's place in that sentence, which as Barthes has shown is the basic grammar of narrative. In doing so, Hitchcock alters the sentence, thereby querying the dynamic of gender relations in the sentence or narrative of time.

Vertigo details the *mise-en-abyme* of representation; one of the whirlpools of terror that the film conjures is the terror of falling, of not being able to control and close a narrative, of falling into a vortex of endless space and time. This falling is very much associated in the film with the figure of woman. To fall is to be in the feminine position, to be powerless. We have to understand the dichotomy, however, between Scottie's positioning of femininity and the film's positioning of it. Scottie's reading of femininity is full of terror because in part it suggests to him open-endedness, but the film offers an alternative reading—a positive one involving non-closure, and thus situated outside the order of the sentence.

Scottie, like the hysteric, suffers from reminiscences (Freud, *Beyond the Pleasure Principle 7*). The narrative is one long fixation leading back to Scottie's original trauma—his fear of falling. Scottie's compulsion to repeat is a narrative function of wishing to see his story displaced onto another character. Scottie, in effect, accomplishes a live burial of his story. Written onto his body is a form of paralysis—of what cannot come into existence as narrative. He thus occupies the role of the hysteric who transfers his symptoms onto Madeleine/Judy's body. In this scenario, he can watch safely, much like the film viewer, who through displacement avoids displeasure. Thus, we can say that *Vertigo* acts as one long dream of Scottie's in which the different segments replay his original trauma. What we see on the surface and what Scottie sees is the manifest content or the operations of the hermeneutic code. But the latent content is much more interesting; the film becomes Scottie's symptom in its disclosure of distortion. Freud elaborates this process of distortion in *The Interpretation of Dreams*: "Everyone has wishes that he would prefer not to disclose to other people, and wishes that he will not admit even to himself. On the other hand, we are justified in linking the unpleasurable character of all these dreams with the fact of dream distortion" (193).

The film works from the beginning to maintain the identification of Scottie with woman.[4] The title sequence begins with a woman's mouth; over this mouth the James Stewart credits appear. Right from the beginning, the film proposes woman's identification with a man's name. The title sequence conveys trauma around the face of the woman, and that terror is reflected in her eyes. Her eyes become the site of terror, the place from which Scottie will see. Therefore, the film announces that to be frightened is to be placed in the position of woman. She is the location of the vertigo: through her eyes, the spiral of falling appears.

Seeing in this film is very much gendered: in order to surmount a crisis in seeing, the narrative must work to locate the act of seeing through the eyes of the detective figure. In fact, the film uses superimposition to identify Scottie with Madeleine/Judy. In the original trailer to the film, there is a shot of Scottie looking into a store window display of flowers. Then, images of Madeleine/Judy are superimposed on his face. This superimposition uncannily links Scottie with the image of woman. One of the terrors the film evokes is this uncanny meeting with someone who is alike and different, calling forth this ghostly reminder of identification. Superimposition structures identity as a series of layers rather than oppositions. Superimposition thus technically represents the ghost as it reflects doubling, a non-closure of the image.

Further, the woman's face and her gaze in the opening credits announce the central question of the narrative—what would a woman's question and answer look like?[5] Scottie at the beginning of the narrative is very much in a passive position; to compensate for this masochistic position, he begins to occupy the sadistic position of the viewer who gains control through looking. Similarly, Norman Bates in *Psycho* is very much discomposed by the thought of "cruel eyes studying you." Scottie, to deflect the gaze from himself, from his story, displaces his story onto Madeleine's. He, in order not to be the story, makes Madeleine into the story. He buries his story, and in doing so, becomes haunted by the ghostly figure of woman who replays his predicament.[6] But the central paradox of the film is that Madeleine/Judy is never fully there—in the position that Scottie places her. She is always somewhere other. Thus, multiple ghosts structure the film.

The opening chase scene places Scottie in the position of woman: his fear is a fall into being the woman, of not being able to see coherently. In the subsequent scene with Midge, we see Scottie carrying a cane and speaking of wearing a "corset that binds." Clearly, his desire to take control of a narrative rests on a crisis of seeing. The idea of being robbed of one's eyes or the power to look and to control and define is very much aligned with the fear of symbolic castration, with the dread of not having control over one's story. The transference from Scottie's story to Madeleine's then involves Scottie's attempts to initiate a narrative and closure of his own choosing, something that was denied him by the contingency of the policeman falling to his death.

This crisis of seeing is most pointedly played out through the formal aesthetics of the "vertigo shot." This shot involves a simultaneous zooming forward and tracking backward of the camera, conveying the sensation of vertigo. The narrative structure of the film proceeds precisely in this fashion. On the surface level and according to Barthes's model of the hermeneutic code, the story works to make us think we are proceeding forward, such as in the movement of a sentence, but the more forward we go, the more we are taken back to the trauma experienced by Scottie in the opening scene of the film. We may then say that the film operates on a snare: we think we are solving the question of Madeleine, but the buried question of masculinity is covered over and hidden to protect the power of the phallus. The repression recurs in the story of Madeleine, but Scottie remains blind to this identification. He, as detective figure, must figure the key to the story, but like Oedipus, Scottie himself is implicated in the dynamics of the story he tries to solve. The detective figure is the one then who has a guilty secret, and, as I have been arguing, that secret involves Scottie's identification with Madeleine. As he puts it concerning Madeleine's mysterious behavior, "If I could just find the key . . . and put it together."

While on the surface, the detective plot moves us forward, Scottie's compulsion to repeat the trauma from his own past displaced onto the story of Madeleine takes us back to his original trauma. In this way, Scottie wanders away from his own story, which would place him too much in the position of woman, and instead enters the plot of the detective story. Elster asks Scottie: "Do you believe that someone out of the past, someone dead, can enter and take possession of a living being?" Scottie is, in a sense, possessed by the figure of woman; he is haunted by being placed in the position of woman in his original trauma. Just as Elster says of Madeleine, in attempting to explain her behavior, "She'll be talking to me about something; suddenly . . . she is somewhere else," Scottie, through Madeleine's narrative, places himself "somewhere else." In this way, he becomes a ghost, by not being there. The overlay of stories in the film substitutes for Scottie's story. This overlay of stories is formally announced by the film's use of fog filters, as if to suggest a ghostly remainder of what we are actually seeing on the screen. In employing shots that are not fully exposed, Hitchcock announces Scottie's being haunted by something lying outside of his consciousness. Also, the film gets darker as it proceeds on its narrative course. This technique of chiaroscuro suggests flickerings from a mode outside of consciousness.

That this original trauma gets reworked onto the body of woman is no accident. The film's opening scene involving Scottie's trauma is juxtaposed with the scene between Midge and him. This juxtaposition is crucial: for the latter scene encompasses the dynamics of the masculine projection of the fear of falling onto the figure of the woman. As observed earlier, Scottie carries a cane and wears a corset, and the scene replays his vertigo and ends with Midge cradling him in her arms, like a mother. The scene's comic dialogue on Midge's occupation—designing women's lingerie—clues us in to the dynamics of male/female relations in western society. The white brassiere, which hangs on Midge's desk, designed by an aircraft engineer and made to work on the principles of the Cantilever Bridge, can function as the prop, the stand-in for the masculine ego. That is to say, this article of clothing is an uplift, a decoy, thus figuring woman as a series of signifiers designed by the masculine subject. But the humor underscores the frail foundation of this agreement.

The seemingly forward movement of the love plot is a function of the death drive and Hitchcock's deconstruction of western love that is founded on the conjunction between love and death. To love Madeleine, Scottie must turn her/Judy into a *memento mori*, an object to be looked at from a distance, a figure in the painting, into Carlotta, whom Madeleine emulates in her supposed death. Edgar Allan Poe in "The Philosophy of Composition" has infamously claimed: "The death . . . of a beautiful woman is unquestionably the most poetical topic in the world" (982). What moves Scottie is not Madeleine's presence, but his recollection of her as it is played out in the second half of the film in Scottie's refashioning of Judy.[7] Thus, he memorializes Madeleine through his narrative by continually returning to scenes from the past. Scottie's fascination with observing Madeleine's obsession with the portrait of Carlotta recapitulates his own fixation with immobilization.

He becomes obsessed with Madeleine at the moment when he hears her story from her husband, Galvin Elster. This story seduces Scottie: for in many ways it is his own story. Hitchcock shoots this scene employing narrative as a means of gaining power. That is to say, Galvin towers over Scottie feeding him the story of Madeleine; Scottie is seated in a chair and shot from high angle, making him seem vulnerable and weak. To narrate for Scottie is to turn woman into a dead object, to avoid that which unnerves him throughout the film, the fear of being the dead object, or the fear of being in her place. It is no accident that when Scottie first begins to follow Madeleine, Hitchcock sets the scenes at the graveyard and the art museum—all sites of memorialization. The concatenation of the film image, the art gallery, and the grave all suggest the attempt to bury the image and its subsequent return from the dead. The gravestone and the painting act as means of preservation, but simultaneously they call forth the fixation on death.[8]

Woman is aligned with this fixation on death, and here the doubling between Scottie and Madeleine is most evident. At one point in the film when Scottie performs his detective work, he follows Madeleine from her house in his car for quite some time, and she leads him back to his own house. This scene is a return home for Scottie and symbolically suggests what he cannot see—that Madeleine's obsession with her past is a displacement of Scottie's compulsion to repeat as a means to avoid displeasure. The scene recalls the vertigo shot: Scottie thinks in his narrative that he is moving forward to uncover the secrets in Madeleine's life, but all the while, he is being propelled backward by the forces of repression of his own story.

Scottie here is linked with Madeleine, and it produces an uncanny effect. In a sense, he desires to formulate his own story about Madeleine, but from this point on in the narrative his story is buried alive in hers. Home is never the place he thought it was because it always leads back to her. In this way, her narrative takes control over him, and he is inhabited by the ghosts it evokes. Freud locates the uncanny as an unresolvable contradiction: that which is familiar and strange coextensively. Scottie's journey home is a circuitous one; he travels in circles. Perhaps what turns out to be so uncanny is Scottie's identification with Madeline, with his inability to fix the difference. As Scottie tries to move forward in the narrative, he is continually taken back to the figure of the woman, which he tries to repress in himself. Thus, gender in its staging of ambivalence haunts the film.

The film narrative returns Scottie to his home which is the place occupied by Madeleine. To move away from his trauma, he must view her as uncanny, as that which leads him back to something that he already knows and simultaneously does not know, thus invoking in him feelings of dread and horror. Condemned to repeat the fear of falling, of his own death, of in fact mirroring the woman, Scottie moves on to a succession of stories all involving the inability to escape from the past and his trauma.

The uncanny is nowhere more evident than in Scottie's obsession with the past which gets reworked in Madeleine's fixation on Carlotta Valdes. It is actually Scottie who suffers from a crisis in identity manifested in his obsession with his eyes. This obsession is aligned with his being able to narrate a story to himself, which the film portrays by privileging Scottie through the use of focalization. For if Madeleine is supposedly inhabited by the specter of Carlotta, then it would seem as if Scottie too is haunted by the specter of being in the position of woman—of the feelings of helplessness manifested in his vertigo. This feeling of the uncanny, which is crystallized through Scottie's unfolding of the story of Madeleine, accounts for Scottie's simultaneous love for and wish for Madeleine to be dead. For her to be dead would perhaps put an end to what she represents for him unconsciously, which as I have been arguing is his identification with her. An apt tripling in the text would seem to be that between Madeleine/Carlotta/Scottie. Madeleine is purportedly inhabited by Carlotta, but Scottie is haunted by Madeleine and Carlotta's past, which involves loss and suicide. Perhaps here *Vertigo* makes its most important critique on gender relations: if woman serves as the figure of the repressed to prop up the masculine ego, then she will return with a vengeance to confound all attempts to realize identity at her expense.

Several critics interpret the film as a straightforward portrayal of gender relations with Madeleine/Judy playing the role of the masochist and Scottie occupying the place of the sadist.[9] But Scottie's identification with Madeleine/Judy is a function of his sadomasochism. In punishing Judy through his obsession with making her into Madeleine, he actually punishes himself by his simultaneous identification with her and his disavowal of her. To disclaim this identification, he makes her into a fetish object. But this supposed visual difference actually begins to unravel through the alternation in the film between love and death. Love it would seem involves a movement forward, a movement that does not have a script already formulated in the mind. But Scottie's love is tied to death in the sense that he repeats a script of his own making, already mapped out. This script is one of destruction, sadomasochism, and hatred—all present within him but transferred onto the body of Madeleine/Judy.[10] This dynamic again recalls the vertigo shot: love involves a movement forward, representing life; and repression entails a movement backward, signaling death. In this way, the core of the film demonstrates an ambivalence about gender, and the ghostly returns from the dead involve a psychological dynamic of repression.

The horribly painful scene in the clothing store where Scottie tries to remake Judy into Madeleine reverts to the scene that opens the film—the shot of Scottie dangling from the roof gutter. In this shot, Scottie is the image, and he is the image precisely because of his inability to control the situation. In a very great sense, he is overpowered by his experience. To compensate for his feelings of powerlessness, he makes Judy relive his experience of vulnerability by making her into an image. He thus revenges himself on a substitute figure. But still the identification with her is very much a part of this dynamic. In part, he sees himself in her. It is almost as if he occupies the position of Narcissus looking in the pool of water and seeing Judy/Madeleine. He is simultaneously in love with himself and in love with death. Scottie's neurosis then involves being compelled to repeat the past in the present, thus leading him literally to a narrative dead end and to his obsession with death.

In the scene in the clothing store, Judy laments, "You want me to be dressed like her." And immediately following in Scottie's apartment Judy asks, "If I let you change me . . . will you love me?" Love then becomes a function of being what one is not, and this encapsulates a wish to refabricate one's image into something else. This scenario replays Scottie's own insecurities about his identity. Scottie's ideal formulation of himself would ensure that he is in control of the narrative to mask his trauma of feeling powerless. His need to make Madeleine into an ideal image corresponds to his desire to see himself as the all-powerful detective figure. If he can be someone else through Judy's being someone else, then he can disavow his original trauma. Judy's transformation into Madeleine is full of images of rebirth. Hitchcock uses a fog filter to make it appear as if Madeleine is rising from the dead. But these images are also tinged with death: it is no accident that Madeleine gets reincarnated wearing the suit in which she supposedly fell to her death.

Scottie is, in a sense, inhabited by the woman, in his fixation on Madeleine's clothing. He is simultaneously haunted by the lost female, Madeleine, and the feminine in himself that he tries to disavow. The obsession with Madeleine/Judy's clothing reflects paradoxically his wish to ensure difference but also his desire to be in her place. By identifying too closely with her previously in his dream sequence, his only recourse is to go mad. He has disturbed the separation between the sexes that the fall into gender assures with one's entry into the symbolic order or the law of the father. His sadistic treatment of Judy is therefore in part punishment for his identifying too closely with Madeleine. Judy then becomes the scapegoat figure on whom he can safely project his simultaneous hatred and love for woman.

Paradoxically, Scottie occupies the position that he feared all along—that of a woman. This feeling of powerlessness the film locates in Scottie's inability to control the narrative. He works very hard to be the detective, to find the key to Madeleine's illness, but, as we know, Elster situates Scottie in the position in which Scottie places Madeleine/Judy. So Scottie plays the masochist to Elster, the sadist. It is Scottie whom Elster makes into his "apt pupil," just as he has made Madeleine into an "apt pupil." Thus, the identificatory relationship between Scottie and Judy/Madeleine becomes even more complex. In the ending sequence of the film, Scottie says to Judy/Madeleine, "I was the made-to-order witness." Here he speaks of his witnessing Madeleine's death from the window in the tower. As witness, Scottie again does not control the narrative; he watches events that happen outside his purview. But paradoxically, being a witness also gives Scottie the illusion of scopic control. In other words, being able to say, "this is what happened." But that illusion rests on a falsity. Scottie thinks he possesses the key to Madeleine, but she is not in the identity or narrative place where she is supposed to be. Here Hitchcock calls into question the illusion of masculine power and control. *Vertigo* through its complex working of gender illuminates the idea that power rests fundamentally on a sham, on an illusion that one works very hard to maintain, creating potential for dismantling and disruption.

Perhaps this notion of disruption appears most forcefully in the dream sequence after the inquest where Scottie is forced to listen to the coroner's narrative. This narrative again places Scottie in the feminine position. The official refers to "Mr. Ferguson's weakness," "his fear of heights," and "his lack of initiative—he did nothing" to prevent Madeleine's death. Immediately following this scene, we see Scottie sleeping in his bed. Flashes of light appear, suggesting a breakdown or crisis in vision. Madeleine and Carlotta's flowers break up into shapes suggesting a deconstruction of the vision about Madeleine and himself that he has tried so hard to maintain up to this point. Scottie's identification with Madeleine is crystallized in the dream, for he essentially dreams Madeleine's dream in which she stands "by the gravestone looking down into it"; this is her "grave." Scottie too walks toward an open grave, and then the next image shows his head falling; the subsequent image portrays him falling onto the red tiles of the mission roof where Madeleine supposedly fell to her death. The dream portrays a dissolution of the self—it is as if he is being taken over by the ghost of Madeleine.

If dreams are wish fulfillments, then Scottie indeed wishes to die—to occupy the place of Madeleine. But the dream presents a conundrum— he falls in love with a woman because she is obsessed with death. Falling in love then corresponds to falling into the grave where one is not in a position of control. Falling in love is much like the vertigo that Scottie experiences in the opening scene, for falling in love leads to some sort of original trauma about gender relations and power. That is to say, falling in love entails giving oneself up to the contingency of another's existence. Preserving the dead object though the dynamics of the death drive would enable the person to freeze the love object in an image of desire, and the image of that desire is always a dead woman.

Immediately following the dream sequence, Hitchcock cuts to the mental hospital, and we see an image of Scottie, catatonic, sitting in a chair. He has become the figure of woman fixed in a portrait, much like Carlotta's portrait. Scottie has awakened from his dream and found it true, resulting in complete paralysis. He takes on the persona of Madeleine, for the dream presents to Scottie a mirror image of him- self that he cannot interpret. The dread and horror caused by the dream and its overlappings of identity is the final link that causes Scottie's breakdown. The dream brings to the surface something that Scottie has been trying to repress: his desire to die, to be situated in the grave and the coextensive wish to preserve Madeleine in a fixed ideal image of desire.

The film overlaps its stories in an endless array of displacements and transferences, thus producing a vertigo feeling in its deployment of identity and stories about identity. Identity and stories cannot stay in their proper places; they move around indiscriminately. Thus, *Vertigo* seems to be inhabited by phantoms of gender identities that float from one story to the next. Scottie comes to occupy the position of Carlotta/Madeleine. We remember Carlotta's story: Her lover kept their child and then Carlotta "became the sad Carlotta . . . and the mad Carlotta." Finally, she died "by her own hand." And then Madeleine is inhabited by Carlotta; Madeleine looks down into Carlotta's grave. Finally, to complete this triangle, Scottie, completely broken down, is inhabited by the ghosts of Madeleine/Carlotta. Their obsession with death mirrors Scottie's, and Carlotta and Madeleine's "madness" reflects Scottie's fear of going mad. As Madeleine puts it in her dream, she fears walking "into the darkness," for then she will "die." Scottie too struggles against this darkness throughout the narrative. Scottie writes onto his body in the form of catatonia, his fixation on death, his fixation on his trauma. He is back to where he started out, frozen by fear. He has no story to tell; as Tzvetan Todorov puts it, "absence of narrative" equals "death" (74).

Narration is transferred onto the body of the woman whom he can train and rehearse to speak his words that are ventriloquized by his desires. This guarantees his desire to ward off his death. When Madeleine dies, his story short-circuits, and he is mute temporarily. The narrative is resuscitated when he begins to find a substitution in Judy. For Scottie, narrative is inextricably tied to memorialization, like the portrait and the gravestone. Telling a story then means killing the object, rendering her lifeless as opposed to his articulation. But *Vertigo* exposes that telling a story through another leads to ghostly apparitions and ultimately to a dead-end.

The drive to the mission is a drive toward death. Laura Mulvey has spoken of Marion's drive to the Bates Motel in *Psycho* as being her drive toward death (related by Professor William Simon, lecture on Hitchcock at New York University, May, 2001). This death drive is inextricably linked with the desire to repeat and leads back to the opening of the film, which announces Scottie's trauma. The film then is structured in the form of a spiral always coiling back to an original moment that is never mastered or resolved. The film basically wanders from plot to plot (Scottie's plot, to Madeleine's plot, to Judy's plot), but is always—through the dynamics of displacement—repeating in some form or another Scottie's trauma. So while on the surface, Scottie says that he has "to go back into the past once more," that past is Madeleine's past and not Scottie's. Thus, Scottie always avoids his own past.

Perhaps the ending is so disturbing because for the first time in the film (at least consciously) Scottie is brought face to face with what he has been eliding all along—the specter of death. This specter appears in various guises. What surfaces in the cruel scene in the mission when Scottie forces Judy to reclimb the tower steps is that Scottie's actions are informed by the meaninglessness of the story he had fabricated about Madeleine. One of the deaths that Scottie confronts at the mission is the death of narrative. In other words, his life is meaningless, without a story, but particularly the story he had told himself about Madeleine. Scottie's actions are thus fueled by a narrative death. Without Madeleine's story, he, in effect, does not exist. His anger rests on his fury that actually Galvin Elster was in control of the narrative all the time. The story was not supposed to turn out this way; it was supposed to follow Scottie's desires and wishes. His vertigo is very much involved with the fear of losing his identity and the coextensive fear of nothingness, of falling into a void. This fear of nothingness is related to being in time, and thus in narrative, which, of course, involves contingency. This idea is played out in the sequoia sequence that focuses on the passage of time. While there, Madeleine thinks of "all the people who've been born and have died while the trees went on living." We are shown a cross-section of a tree where important historical dates are marked off, such as the Magna Carta's signing in 1215. And then Madeleine places herself in the historical time line of the tree and says, "Somewhere in here I was born, and there I died." This scene startlingly recalls Scottie's preoccupation with being in time, with being haunted by time, with wandering to avoid death, but as the ending sequence reveals, he is haunted by the death drive.

As Scottie forces Judy up the steps of the tower, he says, "We're going up and look at the scene of the crime." Scottie thinks that the scene of the crime involves the staged death of Madeleine. But the scene of the crime reverts to the opening sequence of the film: the original scene of the crime where Scottie unintentionally caused the death of another. He is doomed to repeat his past by causing the death of Madeleine/Judy. In the most terrifying scene of the film when Scottie and Madeleine are kissing and we are led to think that perhaps the couple may be reconciled, we are shown an eyeline match from Madeleine's point of view. We view a shadowy figure, and Madeleine screams and falls to her death. We then see the figure of a nun who says, "I heard voices."

What are we to make of the gothic introduction of the nun figure at the ending of the film? We know that nuns play an important role in the gothic novel. The nun is usually a figure from the past who mysteriously returns from the dead and haunts the present as in *The Monk* or *Villette*. I want to claim here that the nun is the symbolic marker of the ghost—the uncanny remainder of what has not been dealt with. That is to say, the nun represents the ghostly articulation of what cannot be spoken in the narrative: the nun as ghostly apparition mirrors the positioning of Madeleine/Judy in the film. Significantly, the nun and the female heroine of the gothic novel are doubled: Raymond in *The Monk* thinks he is eloping with his beloved Agnes, but the figure turns out to be an animated corpse. In *Vertigo*, the nun erupts into the frame, but her story is framed. She thought she "heard voices," but those heard voices cannot begin to narrate her story. Her appearance is truly uncanny because it is so unexpected and unexplainable. Here is an image without definitive meaning, and the story collapses into nothingness. The nun represents the conjunction of love and terror and what cannot be articulated about it in the film narrative.

But the nun's veil also suggests her potential for disruption. The nun in gothic stories is a transgressive figure who usually was buried alive for some transgression. The veil recalls the habit; the nun is inhabited and hidden—she represents what cannot be known or represented directly. The scene between Scottie and Madeleine/Judy is broken up by the figure of another, by the figure of the nun, who fractures the self/other dichotomy announced by masculine and feminine polarized positions. Thus, in the ending, as in almost every other relationship in the film, we are presented with the dynamic of the triangle that upsets binary oppositions. The third party will always throw into confusion neat distinctions. What does Madeleine/Judy's gaze signify? Perhaps her look lies outside representation. What she sees cannot be explained, but it does involve terror and death. But this terror and death is not simply negative. It also points to the death knell of representation and woman's place in it.

We could also read this scene as a representation of Madeleine/Judy looking into the mirror. She sees the ghostly figure of a nun.[11] A nun, a no one, which is the place she occupies in Scottie's system of gender relations. The nun too wears a habit—a costume—which announces her being inhabited by another. This is what haunts Madeleine throughout the film: the specter of her place in western society as played out by the dynamics of western love. As Scottie tries to transform her through changing the color of her hair, he opportunes, "Judy, please it can't matter to you." In this film love and terror prove inextricable. *Vertigo* then announces that, given this system of gender oppression that exists under the guise of love, the only thing Madeleine/Judy can do is to die. The film image always already turns woman into an animated corpse. In the production notes to the film Kim Novak speaks of her identification with the Judy character in that upon her arrival in Hollywood everyone wanted to change her.

But paradoxically, the figure of the nun at the ending also suggests the death of representation—the death of the sentence or the plot in which Madeleine/Judy has been placed. The nun implies that there will always be another story, another contingency that one had not accounted for. She represents the uncanny return of what has not been dealt with—the repression of woman's desire. She figures the supreme moment of anxiety that has been elided all along. Hitchcock clearly was influenced by Michael Powell's and Emeric Pressburger's *Black Narcissus* (1947), which focuses on the repression of feminine desire and its damaging effects in a story about nuns who attempt to bring civilization to an isolated community in the Himalayas. Almost every character in *Black Narcissus* is haunted by memories of love and

death. The caretaker of the palace "lives with ghosts of by-gone days."
And when Sister Clodagh leaves the palace after Sister Ruth has tried
to kill her and instead has fallen to her death, she says, "I shall have my
ghosts to remind me" of the events that occurred at the palace. The
hauntings in *Vertigo* and in *Black Narcissus* involve returns of the
repressed. And each film posits what happens when feminine identity
is obscured: it will return to haunt Scottie's narrative of detection.

The nun would seem to be the uncanny figure that stands in for the
return of the past upon a present. Just as Scottie thinks that he has the
key—that he has returned to his past and uncovered the deception
practiced upon him—the nun surfaces to disturb his sense of the
familiar. As nun, she is the uncanny force beyond his control; she is
the shadow haunting his realm of knowledge. Therefore, she is the
unknowable—she represents the figure of woman in the film. The nun
is the internal eruption of the idea of what we cannot know or represent directly; she embodies the terror of what lies outside language.

Scottie's narrative and the narrative of western love predicated on
controlling the image cannot prevail. There will always be another to
rewrite the narrative, to insert herself in the figure, a nun—a no one
who speaks the last lines in the film: "I thought I heard voices."
Perhaps these are the voices of the other who will be heard despite the
narrative sentence in which Scottie places Madeleine/Judy and ultimately himself. Earlier in the film when Madeleine tells Scottie about
her dream and he tries to puzzle it out, he explains to her, "You see
there's an answer for everything." The film works against finding the
answer to woman.

The last image is one of Scottie with his arms spread out in a passive
position. The film uses the gothic archway to position Scottie as if he
is in a coffin. This image recalls Madeleine's positioning of her arms just
before she jumps into the San Francisco bay. Scottie, himself, has
turned into the animated corpse. In life as in death Scottie becomes
Madeleine and occupies his place *D'Entre les Morts*. From the beginning of the film, Scottie is framed by images of death from which he
cannot escape. In a sense he is both alive and dead; he is haunted by
this in-between position, in effect, of being a ghost. The film exposes
cultural practices that place woman in a secondary position. This
involves a long slow death; in many ways the film is both an expose of
and an elegy to the practice of love in western society. If narratives are
structured in this way, then how does one move outside this narrative?
At the threshold of narrative, *Vertigo* indeed presents a dizzy array of
voices.

CHAPTER 6

GRAVE NARRATIONS: DICKENS'S
LATER WRITINGS

GREAT EXPECTATIONS AND THE ART OF GRAVETELLING

This chapter returns to Dickens to make the claim that in *Great Expectations* he pioneered a new narrative mode based on live burials, doubling, and layering. This new form of narration is gothic and makes its appearance in full force in *Great Expectations*. We have come to view the Victorian novel as representative of high realism; however, I argue that the Victorian novel is obsessed with buried secrets, returns from the dead, and ghosts. Narration itself at the supposed apogee of high realism becomes inhabited by ghostly presences, announcing the limitations of realism. Two forms of narration represent what I term gothic narration—the multiplot and first person narration. The multiplot novel which became the standard form for the Victorian novel layers stories; in a sense, then, this form rehearses the live burial of a story so that another story can continue. This layering of stories mimics doubling and shadows as one story impinges upon another story. The multiplot novel as Bakhtin has shown speaks in many voices.[1]

I posit that the voices of the Victorian novel are engaged in a dialectic of deanimation and reanimation; that is to say, these voices speak as if from the grave and are resurrected in the course of the narrative. However, these voices ultimately occupy a space of narration that is in-between. The buried story is supplanted by the current story but still exerts an influence on the current story. The form of the Victorian novel suggests flickerings from other worlds. In fact, its mode is superimposition where each story is linked to the shadows and layers of the other story. The multiplot novel thus in its very form continually brings to life the dead and buried. Nothing in these plots is ever dead or closed.

The other form of narration that recalls the gothic is first person. *Great Expectations* tells a story entailing narrating from the grave.[2] We begin the novel at the site of the grave where Pip contemplates the gravestones of his family. This gravesite informs the telling of the story—we begin the story at the ending of life, and the novel functions as a kind of ruin after this traumatic opening. Dickens had already explored first person narration in *David Copperfield* and *Bleak House*. The difference between those novels and this later one is that in *Great Expectations* it is as if Dickens shows retrospective narration to be a return from the dead. One could claim that all retrospective narration reanimates the corpse of the former self, but in this novel the return from the dead is not all together successful. That is to say, Pip is stuck in the nether world of the dead/alive. First person narration in this novel involves an emptying out rather than a fulfillment. The voice is characterized by exhaustion, almost as if it were narrating from the grave.

Whereas in *David Copperfield* the narrative voice is marked by an elegiac tribute to childhood, in *Great Expectations* the return to childhood seems to be characterized by a dead-end. The expectations for first person narration cannot be fulfilled given the narrator's attempts to wrestle with a language that is now informed by returns, doublings, and ghosts. Thus, Dickens situates *Great Expectations* at the limits of realism and the novel: the subject narrates a new kind of story—one that is inhabited by the ghosts of others and the ghostly alterity of language itself. In *Great Expectations*, identity cannot be separated from the gothic; realism is not an adequate means to depict the mind's terrors.

Retrospection in *Great Expectations* involves looking backward at a lost object. The contemplation of that lost object produces a ghostly effect. Pip's attempts to render his story entail confronting a specter that is aligned with the dead. The horror is how to reconcile the dead with the living. Therefore, the narrative seems particularly haunted because of this simultaneous looking forward and backward. To look into the mirror for Pip is to confront ghosts, and, in effect, he becomes his own ghost in the sense that his thoughts become ghost-like, filled with forebodings, shadows, and flickerings from outside consciousness.

As he is continually troubled by ghosts, Pip cannot find the connection between his past self and his first person narrative voice. In this way, retrospection is linked to the disjunction between words and objects. Pip's first lesson on the marshes is an apprehension that words can only ever approximate meaning—metaphor is the gothic nightmare troubling the autobiographer. Dickens adds to the gothic novel by foregrounding the ruination of character the moment Pip posits it.

That the novel begins at the grave is telling. Whereas Pip names himself at the very beginning: "I called myself Pip, and came to be called Pip" (3), this name making is immediately supplanted by the tombstone inscriptions. The novel is marked by others potentially inhabiting Pip's body. Not only is Pip haunted by the bodies of others, but this haunting crosses over into his mind which becomes the site for haunting in the novel. The narrative home of Pip's retrospective narration is haunted by the project of telling a life. The very foundation of narration begins from the ruin of the graveyard where the gravestones serve as a reminder of decay and ruin. Pip learns language at the graveyard, but he also apprehends that language is its own graveyard, when he relates:

> My first most vivid and broad impression of the identity of things, seems to me to have been gained on a memorable raw afternoon towards evening. At such a time I found out for certain, that this bleak place overgrown with nettles was the churchyard; and that Philip Pirrip, late of this parish, and also Georgiana wife of the above, were dead and buried; and that Alexander, Bartholomew, Abraham, Tobias, and Roger, infant children of the aforesaid, were also dead and buried; and that the dark flat wilderness beyond the churchyard, intersected with dykes and mounds and gates, with scattered cattle feeding on it, was the marshes; and that the low leaden line beyond, was the river; and that the distant savage lair from which the wind was rushing, was the sea; and that the small bundle of shivers growing afraid of it all and beginning to cry, was Pip. (3–4)

Pip is never at home in his own house because it is informed by the apprehension that language involves what is outside the self, and thus can never fully be incorporated in the self. Pip learns that the self can only be explained in metaphor as evidenced by "the small bundle of shivers growing afraid of it all and beginning to cry, was Pip." Pip thus is continually displaced by the ghosts and residues of language. His mind is haunted, and the phantasmagoria that begins the novel is peopled with the terrors linked to the self and its recognition that language is inhabited by doubles.[3]

Pip also learns another very important lesson at the site of the grave. Not only does language represent the potential terror of what lies beyond it—what cannot be explained—but he also discovers that in telling his story he enters the realm of the dead where one is subject to specters and inhabitations by others. In meeting up with his double, Magwitch, Pip encounters his first displacement from the self. Layers inform the telling of the self—the self can only ever be told through telling another story. It is as if this haunted self transforms into replicas that produce the self as a replicant, a zombie.

The meeting with Magwitch interrupts Pip's musings on language and the self. It is almost as if Magwitch embodies the attendant horrors of creating someone in one's own image. Commentators have focused on Magwitch's creation of Pip, Miss Havisham's creation of Estella, and Miss Havisham's creation of Pip.[4] But the supreme creation in the novel is the displacement of the creation of Pip onto a substitute figure, Magwitch. Magwitch then represents the horror of creating someone in one's own image. The convict announces the horror of Pip's creation of himself. Thus, at the moment of retrospection, there is always a fragment, a leftover that invokes the lines "What was it?" —lines that Pip later speaks about Estella when he subconsciously recognizes the connection between her and her mother. Pip relates about Magwitch: "As I saw him go, picking his way among the nettles, and among the brambles that bound the green mounds, he looked in my young eyes as if he were eluding the hands of the dead people, stretching up cautiously out of their graves, to get a twist upon his ankle and pull him in" (6–7). Magwitch, the chained convict, links Pip's project of narration to the dead.

That is to say, the convict forges the link between criminality and the telling of one's story, as several critics have demonstrated.[5] But the convict also represents the figure from the other world who appears as an apparition—"a man started up from among the graves," telling Pip to "Hold your noise" (4). The convict serves as the figure *par excellence* for being dead/alive. That is to say, socially he does not exist, but simultaneously he engenders all kinds of imaginative fancies in Pip's mind. He comes from the dead, but he also animates something in Pip's mind about narration and life and death—narration entails meeting up with ghosts and entering the terrifying realm of the dead/alive.[6] As Magwitch leaves Pip on the marshes, Pip imagines that "The man was limping on towards this latter [gibbet], as if he were the pirate come to life, and come down, and going back to hook himself up again" (7).

Magwitch is depicted in scenes where he exchanges places with the dead. To narrate is to associate with ghosts—to confront ghostly doubles that take one to another world. This other world is coextensively terrifying and exhilarating because it invokes the uncanny place of being both dead and alive. Magwitch also calls to mind the machine-like uncanny figure of the automaton and the resultant fear of being carted off to the realm of the dead. Magwitch's click in his throat ("Something clicked in his throat, as if he had works in him like a clock, and was going to strike") (19) links him to a machine and recalls the nether world between life and death.

Ironically, as Pip begins his life story it can only ever be about death. The moment he begins to narrate, he is confronted with the gothic displacements and eruptions that signal live burial. That is to say, we begin the text expecting an unfolding of plot and character; instead, plot and characters double back on themselves and occupy an in-between place of dying and coming back to life. The narrative itself proceeds in fits and starts, much like the click in Magwitch's throat which recalls the effect of simultaneously being inanimate and being recalled to life or to narration. Narration in *Great Expectations* exists in this space of being dead/alive, thus producing a haunting effect.

It is as if the novel's impulse to narrate a life must begin at the end. This beginning at the ending is fraught with the tensions of coextensively being recalled to life and the sense of a life that is dead. Here, lies the grave irony of *Great Expectations*: how to tell a life when that life is in a sense exhausted or dead. This gives the narrative a particularly gothic feel, for where one expects fullness one gets the fragment or ruin. Dickens's great achievement in *Great Expectations* is to form a narrative whose subject matter is its own ghostly formation: to tell a life retrospectively is to be confronted by ghostly figures that lead one to the realm of the dead.

Therefore, the novel seems more like an inscription on a gravestone than a journey forward that one comes to expect from the bildüngsroman. Autobiography in this novel never strays far from the opening associations of subjectivity with death. What Dickens then adds to the gothic novel is the association of storytelling with the grave. We find in many gothic novels the obsession with death and corpses; in *Great Expectations*, narration seems to be aligned most closely with death. Thus, the narrative is informed by its own inscription on the gravestone. The tone of the novel is one of mourning—it is as if Pip cannot tell the story of the self because replications keep taking over his telling of the story. As soon as Pip begins to speak, another story obtrudes into his consciousness. The narrative then is characterized by displacement and transference. In other words, Pip's story is never fully available to himself as his: as soon as he begins to speak, doubles appear such as Magwitch, Orlick, or Wopsle. As he tells his story, readers are tempted to prompt him: What was it?

One of the reasons that Pip is so enthralled by Miss Havisham and her ruined life is that it mirrors his in the sense that the relation of his autobiography stands on the ruins of language and the mourning of that exigency. The ruined house in the novel parallels the ruin of autobiography. As Pip writes the ruin of Miss Havisham's house, he displaces his own ruin.

> It was spacious, and I dare say had once been handsome, but every discernible thing in it was covered with dust and mould, and dropping to pieces. The most prominent object was a long table with a tablecloth spread on it, as if a feast had been in preparation when the house and the clocks all stopped together. An epergne or centre-piece of some kind was in the middle of this cloth; it was so heavily overhung with cobwebs that its form was quite indistinguishable; and, as I looked along the yellow expanse out of which I remember its seeming to grow, like a black fungus, I saw speckled-legged spiders with blotchy bodies running home to it, and running out of it, as if some circumstance of the greatest public importance had just transpired in the spider community. (84)

The scenes of ruin showcase houses and objects, while Pip's ruin entails his coming home to the self. The home in *Great Expectations* is associated with a gothic ruin.

The description runs riot as if all of the energy in the novel is directed toward the piling up of words, but underneath that piling is a ruin that mirrors Pip's state of enervation. Pip is continually in danger of entering the spectacle of the descriptive world to evade the spectacle of his own identity. That is to say, he focuses on description as a means to avoid confronting the contemplation of himself. He can only ever be a construction based on another story as is driven home when he realizes:

> As I looked round at them, and at the pale gloom they made, and at the stopped clock, and at the withered articles of bridal dress upon the table and the ground, and at her own awful figure with its ghostly reflection thrown large by the fire upon the ceiling and the wall, I saw in everything the construction that my mind had come to, repeated and thrown back to me. My thoughts passed into the great room across the landing where the table was spread, and I saw it written, as it were, in the falls of the cobwebs from the centre-piece, in the crawlings of the spiders on the cloth, in the tracks of the mice as they betook their little quickened hearts behind the panels, and in the gropings and pausings of the beetles on the floor. (303)

As the passage demonstrates, Pip views a panorama of his own ruined consciousness. He sees his life as if he is watching a moving parade of his diseased mind. It is as if he has become a metaphor without a self. His is a story already written by the forces of the gothic tale of Miss Havisham's life. The descriptions in the novel at times seem more animated than the people in them, showing all the more forcefully the difficulties Pip has in trying to reanimate himself.

In this connection, it is no accident that the novel, unique among Dickens's novels, has no illustrations. It is almost as if the visage of Pip cannot be established definitely; it can only be glimpsed through the shadowy words that Pip uses to describe himself. For us to see an image of Pip would in fact disturb the notion of himself as a ghostly presence, for what properly would a ghost look like? Much like the horror film that stages the most horrific action offscreen, the novel must hide Pip pictorially. For at the core of his identity is the blank, the absence. To make himself present through the image would be to define the terror at the heart of his representation. To show an image would be to posit a concrete identity when the novel is at pains to disperse his identity among other characters and scenes.

Great Expectations seems to be not only Pip's epitaph but also Dickens's epitaph on the act of autobiography. The novel, supposedly about the origins of Pip, turns into a story about multiple and conflicting origins. As Pip the narrator goes back in time to his origins, he meets up with a self and a narrative home that is haunted by many presences. The narrative home is haunted by multiple origins. The mourning entails this: one has great expectations that one's self is available to one, but the text demonstrates over and over that one cannot own the self. In a world without origins, Pip wanders and is lost. This state is reflected in the form of the multiplot novel.

Many commentators have explored the influence Darwin's ideas exerted on *Great Expectations*.[7] I want to combine Darwinian ideas about multiple origins and the uncanny to suggest that when Pip returns home, he expects to find himself; instead he is confronted by ghosts that refuse to stay in their proper places. Darwin writes enthusiastically about the fecundity of the "great Tree of Life, which fills with its dead and broken branches the crust of the earth, and covers the surface with its ever branching and beautiful ramifications" (130). What seems so wondrous and life affirming to Darwin is a source of anxiety to Pip because he finds that origins are impossible to establish and what is dead is never dead; instead, it lives on. His narrative is one long lament about the indeterminacy of origins. While the creature in

Frankenstein continually asks the question "Who was I," Pip in a sense knows all too well that the self is a product of not one but many.

This inspires terror about the telling of the self. The novel over and over inscribes scenes of terror such as when Pip first visits Miss Havisham's house, he relates as he is leaving:

> It was in this place, and at this moment, that a strange thing happened to my fancy. I thought it a strange thing then, and I thought it a stranger thing long afterwards. I turned my eyes—a little dimmed by looking up at the frosty light—towards a great wooden beam in a low nook of the building near me on my right hand, and I saw a figure hanging there by the neck. A figure all in yellow white, with but one shoe to the feet; and it hung so, that I could see that the faded trimmings of the dress were like earthy paper, and that the face was Miss Havisham's, with a movement going over the whole countenance as if she were trying to call to me. In the terror of seeing the figure, and in the terror of being certain that it had not been there a moment before, I at first ran from it, and then ran towards it. And my terror was greatest of all, when I found no figure there. (64)

The scenes of terror all seem related to the phantasmagorical depiction of identity. That is to say, identity in this text moves onto other beings—at the site of identity, there is always another. This moving spectacle of identity shifting is associated with many scenes in the novel that involve a kind of spectral parading of identity. As we have seen, the opening of the novel shifts from Pip's identity to Magwitch's.

As Pip is telling his story, he impersonates himself; coextensively, the multiplot involves other impersonations that impinge upon Pip's identity. It is as if the novel stages identity as a series of images that shift backward and forward into one another, much like superimposition. In this way, the novel represents identity much like the cinematic device of a series of moving images, but in the novel, they literally move into one another. The novel stages identity as a scene within a scene, as we have gleaned from Pip's apprehension of his identity at the graveyard. The rest of the novel deploys a layering of identities through the multiplot rather than a depiction of an autonomous identity. What this means is that identity is always presented through many different veils and screens.

As we have seen, the novel replaces identity with another image, as in the first chapter with Pip and Magwitch. The novel also stages identity through the dynamics of the multiplot. That is to say, identity is displaced onto another story by the function of the multiplot. It is as if we get to one stage of Pip's expectations and then we crisscross onto another stage, involving another story. This depiction of identity arises out of terror, as I have suggested, because to go home is to consort with the terrifying idea that one can never go home and one is never at home with the self; rather, one is confronted by multiples presences or ghosts that disturb the notion of a unitary self.

Not only is Pip never at home in his narration, but the home is the site for terror in the novel, as evidenced in Mrs. Joe's home and Satis House. Even Pip's residence in London, Barnard's Inn, is fraught with images of the grave and live burial, as Pip describes:

> We entered this haven through a wicket-gate, and were disgorged by an introductory passage into a melancholy little square that looked to me like a flat burying-ground. I thought it had the most dismal trees in it, and the most dismal sparrows, and the most dismal cats, and the most dismal houses . . . that I had ever seen. I thought the windows of the sets of chambers into which these houses were divided, were in every stage of dilapidated blind and curtain, crippled flower-pot, cracked glass, dusty decay, and miserable makeshift; while To Let To Let To Let, glared at me from empty rooms, as if no new wretches ever came there, and the vengeance of the soul of Barnard were being slowly appeased by the gradual suicide of the present occupants and their unholy interment under the gravel. A frowzy mourning of soot and smoke attired this forlorn creation of Barnard, and it had strewn ashes on its head, and was undergoing penance and humiliation as a mere dust-hole. (173)

The images of the burying-ground, decay, and death mirror Pip's death in life. But in a curious way, they also point to a narrative energy that is directed away from character and onto words. It is as if Pip uses words and particularly metaphor as a cover to mask the terror and lack at the center of his self. Houses then become particularly ghostly because they act as a substitute for what Pip cannot reveal about himself.

As already mentioned, the novel's focus on the multiplot moves away from the revelation of character. The novel then is characterized by textual drift that continually asks the question, what was it? This idea surfaces in its most horrific form when Pip receives the letter from Wemmick telling him not to go home. Pip relates his nightmare involving the contemplation of don't go home.

> When at last I dozed, in sheer exhaustion of mind and body, it became a vast shadowy verb which I had to conjugate. Imperative mood, present

tense: Do not thou go home, let him not go home, let us not go home, do not ye or you go home, let them not go home. Then potentially: I may not and I cannot go home; and I might not, could not, would not, and should not go home; until I felt that I was going distracted, and rolled over on the pillow, and looked at the staring rounds upon the wall again. (367–368)

What is it about the home that inspires this nightmare vision of a "shadowy verb"?

I want to advance the argument here and claim that going home is precisely what Pip tries to avoid in the novel. In the Victorian novel, going home involves a confrontation with a place that Victorians revered and marked as the site of the feminine, as evidenced in Ruskin's famous "Of Queen's Garden's," where he relates: "And wherever a true wife comes, this home is always round her. The stars only may be over her head, the glow-worm in the night-cold grass may be the only fire at her foot; but home is yet wherever she is; and for a noble woman it stretches far round her, better than ceiled with cedar, or painted with vermilion, shedding its quiet light far, for those who else were homeless" (122–123). In the Victorian novel, going home is the return to a feminine space that is not the benign and peaceful place that Ruskin describes; rather, it evokes a place that recalls an ambiguity about language and origins.

To go home is to go home to the shadows of language, an act that entails a confrontation with ambiguity. To conjugate essentially means to join together, and the dream above evokes terror because the joining entails the masculine and feminine. Going home in the Victorian novel is a going home to the entangled bank that in essence knows no gender. As Darwin describes at the very ending of *The Origin of Species*: ". . . whilst this planet has gone cycling on according to the fixed law of gravity, from so simple a beginning endless forms most beautiful and most wonderful have been, and are being, evolved" (490).

Going home involves having a home to go home to, but Pip is homeless. Dickens restructures the gothic novel by announcing the ruination of paternity. That is to say, the novel erects a gravestone to the marker of paternity. Pip might think he is going home to himself to claim himself, to own himself, to father himself, but the novel shows repeatedly that this quest cannot obtain. Instead, the novel is characterized by the mutability of gender, by a gender that cannot stay in its proper place.

Joe is the figure who most represents this gender instability, for while masculine in many regards, he is the maternal figure *par excellence* in the novel. One of the most affecting scenes is when he nurses Pip back to health after his illness. To be a gentleman in this novel is to be Joe—a combination of masculine and feminine. Several characters occupy multiple subject positions, in-between genders, so to speak, such as Miss Havisham. The novel simultaneously mourns the loss of a passing world where everything has a fixed place, but it also celebrates the potentiality of this new world where categories are not determined by gender.

Nowhere is this more evident than in the shifting meaning of the word "gentleman" in the novel. Pip wants to be a gentleman, but he comes to learn that "no man who was not a true gentleman at heart, ever was, since the world began, a true gentleman in manner" (181). Over and over the novel interrogates the "true" meanings of words and substitutes in their place a redefinition that is multiple and shifting and not based on definitive meaning. Dickens replaces discrete categories of gender with phantoms of gender. Not only does Pip not have a home, but also words in the novel do not have a definitive home. The novel then privileges a plurality of meaning that for Pip as we have seen can be terror producing. Words after Darwin are divorced from origins; they float free in a drift of meaning. Like a verb to be conjugated, they cannot stop multiplying into new forms and meanings.

At first glance, one might be tempted to argue that the overall tone of the novel is pessimistic, that its tone is one of mourning, as I have already stated. But this is not the entire case. The novel seems to present a much more ambivalent view of decay, dying, and ruination. Out of the decay and ruin of Pip's expectations, and as I have been arguing narrative expectations, arises a new kind of narration—one that is characterized by gothic layerings, the fragment, and the ruin. This may seem negative, but actually the great achievement of *Great Expectations* is to supplant the fairy tale of the bildüngsroman, where the hero is rewarded for his maturation, with the contingency of experience. In other words, *Great Expectations* moves away from the fairy tale where everything is mapped out and there is a definitive ending to the ambiguity of the real. Pip relates:

> She had adopted Estella, she had as good as adopted me, and it could not fail to be her intention to bring us together. She reserved it for me to restore the desolate house, admit the sunshine into the dark rooms, set the clocks a going and the cold hearths a blazing, tear down the cobwebs, destroy the vermin—in short, do all the shining deeds of the young Knight of romance, and marry the Princess. (231)

One of the terrors that Pip has to face is that there is no benevolent parent figure controlling the outcome of his life; there is only the self. This idea stems from Darwin and the death of the idea of God as the creator of life. Instead, evolution posits a random and chaotic origin.

Pip comes to learn that in the place of parents and benevolent figures, he must substitute the self, which is a terrifying thought for him. Instead of a guiding figure, Pip is faced with the silence of the universe. Pip desires a dialogue with a creator; he fabricates in his head intricate stories about his creator, as evidenced in the passage above. In the place of intentionality and order in the universe, we have the silence of Pip's language with no response. In effect, the world before Darwin imagined a dialogue with someone in the universe; post-Darwin, one is haunted by the silence of space. However, this silence Pip fills with his words. In a sense, Pip has no progenitor, no one to model himself after. The hauntings in the novel stem from a cacophony of dead voices all trying to impinge upon his story.

As we have seen from our discussion of *Our Mutual Friend* where Dickens writes a postscript in lieu of preface recounting his near death by railway accident, Dickens has a need to narrate compulsively to ward off death. He cannot quite say goodbye to his readers and prolongs the farewell by creating another venue to narrate—a postscript where he relates: "I can never be much nearer parting company with my readers for ever, than I was then [railway accident], until there shall be written against my life, the two words with which I have this day closed this book:—THE END" (894). In writing the postscript, Dickens resuscitates himself as he creates a narrative that supposedly ends the novel but also prolongs it. We see this obsession with narration as a means to ward off death also enacted in his public readings which, stressful as they were, were thought to have led to his premature death. The multiplot, a mode of narration that Dickens perfected, replays this obsession with layers of stories as a way to avoid the Victorian unease with the disappearance of God.

The multiplot novel consequently replaces the scriptural word. *Great Expectations* becomes the repository for a character's confrontation with his own demons and ghosts as he negotiates a world without God and without attendant meaning. Dickens turns narration into a kind of salvation. The hero of the Dickens story in this retrospective account is a hero only because of his ability to narrate his story. Much like Sisyphus who must endlessly toil every day to roll the rock up the hill only to have it fall back again, Pip compulsively records because that is his only recourse.

As we have seen, ghosts in this novel proliferate. Several commentators have argued that the Victorian preoccupation with ghosts compensated for the loss of God and the consequent need for the supernatural to replace God.[8] Dickens uses narrative as a means to deal with ghosts and what they represent. Pip is haunted throughout the novel, as we have seen, and he compulsively repeats actions because he cannot read the text of himself. He thus is continually haunted by a presence outside his consciousness. As he pushes Miss Havisham around her room he ponders: "It was like pushing the chair itself back into the past, when we began the old slow circuit round about the ashes of the bridal feast" (239). It is my contention that the narrative rehearses this repetition/compulsion through the dynamics of the double ending. Much like the ghosts in the novel proper, the double ending engenders a published ending and a buried ending that surfaces as the ghosts in the novel do. The ghost appears in the form of a narrative that cannot be put to rest because of multiple sightings and multiple readings.

The doubleness of the ending creates a multiplication of the story, a proliferation of a narrative that cannot end properly. The multiple ending takes the novel back to the grave ending that opened the novel. We have a novel that begins at the end, at the site of the grave or death; and at the same time, we have a novel that ends with life, with the endless recalling of the multiple ending. In other words, the grave narration that I have argued for previously competes with being recalled to life by narration. The search for origins as we have seen leads to multiple and contradictory origins. The attempt to reach conclusions then erupts into a fecundity of possibility. Just as there can be no definitive origins, there can be no conclusions, only endless branchings off into a kind of ghostly residue of meaning. Instead of a novel that ends, we have a novel that returns to the possibility of another contingency.

The potential terror lying outside language that characterizes Pip's unease for most of the novel Dickens transforms through the double ending into multiplicity of meaning and a celebration of ambivalence. In many ways, *Great Expectations* takes up where *Frankenstein* had left off in that the former suggests a Victorian horror about identity. Whereas Pip views himself and sees a kind of hydra, reflected in the multiplication of doubles in the story, such as Orlick and Wopsle, the double ending may be said to superimpose this state with hybridity. Pip looks at himself and sees a ghost, a residue that continually frightens him. He posits his identity only to see it dispersed and multiplied. The immobilization and paralysis that follow Pip Dickens counteracts with the fructification of the double ending. What this means is that Pip has no parent in the novel—as we have seen, the narrative mourns the death of a parent and the child's sense of being alone in the world. In a sense, Pip has no one with whom he can engage in a dialogue. To surmount this obstacle, Dickens replaces the monologue of Pip's retrospective narration with a dialogue with his readers—in doing so, he substitutes the lack that Pip experiences in the novel with the multiple voicing of narration.

Instead of the terror occasioned by the voice, by the fear of don't go home, we have the voice at the ending not going home and reveling in the idea that one indeed is homeless—that to be homeless is to recognize that the voices from the grave refuse to stop talking. The double ending takes the ruination that is at the heart of *Great Expectations* and erects another competing structure. While Pip stands at the ruins of Satis House he relates: "There was no house now, no brewery, no building whatever left, but the wall of the old garden. The cleared space had been enclosed with a rough fence, and, looking over it, I saw that some of the old ivy had struck root anew, and was growing green on the low quiet mounds of ruin" (482). This competing structure is a hybrid that celebrates variety and diversity. Thus, the textual drift that accounts for much of the narrative's sadness is replaced with a wandering that is life affirming. In this way, the double ending evokes ghostly returns that form such an important motif in the novel. The ghost comes back because there is unfinished business, and that unfinished business must be related through the form of another story.

If Pip represents the hysteric in the novel, that is to say, his narrative seems particularly marked by a kind of paralysis reflected in his first person narrative which embeds stories within stories, never fully coming to terms with his own story; then, the double ending suggests the embracement of the multiplication of story, of story that cannot be blocked off or stopped because of the effects of repression.[9] The double narration then erupts into a resurrection of narrative, without an end-stop.[10] In fact, the double ending replays the novel's obsession with each story being contaminated by another story. It is as if the novel stages through the multiplot a kind of writing that bleeds into other stories. In the same way, the double ending encodes the effects of an after writing that recalls the ghost who will not be silent.

The double ending demolishes the frame of the novel. The novel may begin with Pip at the gravesite, but it quickly transforms into multiple and competing stories that are terror producing for Pip. Conversely, the ending remains poised on the brink of dialogue. Through the double ending, Dickens erects an epitaph with two outcomes that put him at the center of a dialogue with his readers. Instead of the voice that does not respond, we have voices that engage in a dialogue about the ending of the text. The double ending marks Dickens's attempt to deal with the contingency of Pip's experiences in the novel.

Great Expectations also refers to Pip's narrative never quite measuring up to its original intentions; we have seen that the novel demolishes unique and discrete origins. Dickens uses narrative as a way to compensate for the sense of unease that Pip feels through much of the novel. Thus, the separation that the novel engenders through the voice of Pip is replaced with relation—the act of Dickens telling the story of Pip. As we have seen, Dickens used his public readings to keep his works alive—to recreate his texts anew and to engage his audiences in his work.[11] Dickens capitalized on his voice to establish a connection with his audiences. The crowds adored him and were greatly affected by the dramatics of the readings. Dickens, the storyteller, is laid to rest at the ending of *Great Expectations*, but his voice keeps returning through the dynamics of the double ending. Just as nothing can ever be said to rightly begin, nothing can ever be put to rest— endless links keep forming and joining together to create recombinations of meanings.

NARRATION AS RESURRECTION: *A TALE OF TWO CITIES*

While *Great Expectations* imagines a life as told from the grave, *A Tale of Two Cities* creates a world where one is dead but is continually resurrected by narrative. A disembodied voice narrates in *A Tale*. The novel is obsessed with buried writing and its subsequent resurrection. Dickens wrote *A Tale of Two Cities* in 1859, a particularly tumultuous time in his own life when he separated from his wife and began a series of public readings that were to continue until his death in 1870. Why during this particular time in his life did Dickens turn to the historical novel, and particularly a novel concerning the French Revolution, and why did he break up the narrative into a tale of two cities: London and Paris? Further, what is the connection among history, revolution, and the family? And why does Dickens write an historical melodrama? I want to explore the doubleness in the text between Dickens the novelist and Dickens the melodramatist.

It is my contention that *A Tale* inaugurates an innovation in Dickens's narrative style, that is to say, the embedded narratives reflect an obsession with narrative itself. Encrypted in the narrative are spectral presences and haunting obsessions that are brought to life through the process of narration. *A Tale* takes as its subject matter revolution, being buried alive, and resurrection—the first concerns the French Revolution, the second Dr. Manette and his imprisonment in the Bastille, and the third Dr. Manette's rebirth. Of course, there are many other forms of revolution, live burials, and resurrections in the novel. The linkage of the three that seems to have been overlooked in critical commentaries however is to narrative itself. I want to claim that the true revolution in the text are the narrative innovations and narrative's ability to transcend the historical moment. Dickens creates in *A Tale* his own buried story of being recalled to life, and that recall is tied to narration.

Peter Ackroyd relates that around the time of the publication of *A Tale* Dickens took to carrying a card that read "Charles Dickens, Resurrectionist, In Search of a Subject" (169). In the place of history, Dickens replaces the words of someone who can resurrect materials from the dead fragments of history and make them immemorial. Narrative then for Dickens at this time takes on monumental meaning as it comes to embody a replacement for the scriptural word, as I have argued earlier in the section on *Great Expectations*. As resurrectionist, Dickens assumes the role of the creator. Whereas Frankenstein creates a creature in his own image, Dickens takes as his subject matter the act of creation itself in a world after Darwin, after God. He relates in the preface to *A Tale*: "When I was acting, with my children and friends, in Mr. Wilkie Collins's drama of *The Frozen Deep*, I first conceived the main idea of this [*A Tale's*] story. A strong desire was upon me then, to embody it in my own person; and I traced out in my fancy, the state of mind of which it would necessitate the presentation to an observant spectator, with particular care and interest." I want to explore the question what does it mean "to embody" the story in Dickens's "own person?" Right from the beginning, we see Dickens's obsession with embodiment. Embodiment entails the creator (Dickens) giving life to what is dead. The buried alive story of *A Tale* is Dickens's bringing to life the grave of history.

Whereas time for Darwin is imagined as a glorious evolution, as indicated in his closing remarks in *On the Origin of Species*: ". . . whilst this planet has gone cycling on according to the fixed law of gravity, from so simple a beginning endless forms most beautiful and most wonderful have been, and are being, evolved" (490), time in *A Tale* is a historical nightmare where one is alienated from the self. The narrative is marked by a dread of time, by a being in time that one cannot make sense of. The narrator tells us of the effect of time: "The water of the fountain ran, the swift river ran, the day ran into evening, so much life in the city ran into death according to rule, time and tide waited for no man, the rats were sleeping close together in their dark holes again, and the fancy Ball was lighted up at supper, all things ran their course" (133). The description of the passage of time involves a haunting sense of death lurking in the background, and Lucy seems to be haunted by the "echoes of all the footsteps that are coming by-and-by into our lives" (121). The narrative is marked by the ghosts of time; history is the ghost that comes back to haunt the characters.[12]

The only recompense would seem to be an ordering in time through the act of narration. Dickens replaces being in time with melodrama, a structural device that ultimately rings hollow. While Christina Crosby posits that "the 'melodramatic imagination' is an extreme instance of the Victorian historical imagination, a conceptualizing of history as home, as the recoverable origin of man, something lost which can be found, which will in the finding reveal man to himself" (75), I maintain that melodrama is simply a stylistic device that marks the ability of the creator to arrest time in the form of a story, but one is always aware of the story-like quality to this formulation. What seems particularly strange about the narrative of A Tale is the formal orchestration of the scenes, in particular the mob scenes in Paris.

Dickens combines the aesthetic with the dramatic to capture the staged scenes of horror in the text:

> The grindstone had a double handle, and, turning at it madly were two men, whose faces, as their long hair flapped back when the whirlings of the grindstone brought their faces up, were more horrible and cruel than the visages of the wildest savages in their most barbarous disguise. False eyebrows and false moustaches were stuck upon them, and their hideous countenances were all bloody and sweaty, and all awry with howling, and all staring and glaring with the beastly excitement and want of sleep. As these ruffians turned and turned, their matted locks now flung forward over their eyes, now flung backward over their necks, some women held wine to their mouths that they might drink; and what with dropping blood, and what with dropping wine, and what with the stream of sparks struck out of the stone, all their wicked atmosphere seemed gore and fire. The eye could not detect one creature in the group free from the smear of blood. (321)

The emphasis on the gory spectacle in the above passage calls attention to the formal aesthetics of artifice. One is continually reminded of the spectacular spectacle Dickens describes; it is as if in describing the bloody terrors of the murderings, Dickens description runs riot. Character here does not matter; what matters is the petrification of character into type.

Much has been made of Dickens's resorting to melodrama in his novels, and words such as sentimentality and excessiveness hover over his work. But Dickens used melodrama as a narrative device that seemingly would resolve contradictions but ultimately announce the limitations of a fairy-tale conception of character as either good or bad. Melodrama while on the surface upholds Victorian values simultaneously calls them into question. Dickens in *A Tale* desires a double story: one that celebrates melodrama and one that offers a severe indictment of a culture that perpetuates the fantasy that melodrama offers. Melodrama is a temporary fix to the problems that being in time creates, but essentially melodrama is continually superceded in the text by forces that come back to haunt, that come back to remind that the ghosts of time cannot be put to rest by melodrama. Essentially, for Dickens melodrama offers the culture a collective fantasy that history is knowable.

The forces of the melodrama are always superimposed onto the gothic presentation of character that Dickens employs in *A Tale*. So being in time is linked to the unfolding of character in time, and *A Tale* is in many ways innovative in this regard. Instead of characters unfolding in time, we get a gothic presentation of character that involves secrets and mysteries at the heart of the self. Dickens presents character in the form of doubles that cannot be reconciled. Characters become separated from themselves by the act of decapitation; that is to say, the names that Madame Defarge knits in her register become divorced from the self through the removal of the face, the site of identity. The novel is obsessed with the face not being able to guarantee whom the person is, such as with the confusion between Sydney Carton and Charles Darnay. The spectacle of the guillotine and decapitation suggests that the self is interchangeable. The terror of revolution is linked to the terror of the self. Not only is the self alienated from itself, but also people are alienated from one another. At the beginning of the text, which is told for the most part in the third person, we have an irruption into the first person.

A wonderful fact to reflect upon, that every human creature is constituted to be that profound secret and mystery to every other. A solemn consideration, when I enter a great city by night, that every one of those darkly clustered houses encloses its own secret; that every room in every one of them encloses its own secret; that every beating heart in

the hundreds of thousands of breasts there, is, in some of its imaginings,
a secret to the heart nearest it! . . . .In any of the burial-places of this
city through which I pass, is there a sleeper more inscrutable than its
busy inhabitants are, in their innermost personality, to me, or than I am
to them? (12–13)

It is almost as if Dickens uses the forces of the backdrop of a melodramatic history to cloak the mysteries of character. In a sense, then,
Dickens employs history as a means to evade character.
One must ask the question what is the relation between history and
the self? In historical time, history is conceived in this novel as a spectacle, of spectacular moments in time, as when the crowd invades the
Bastille and wreaks horror and bloodshed. The self, in the novel, however, is characterized by evasion, by a refusal to look inwards at the
self. Instead, the self looks outwards and is characterized by a sense of
puzzlement reflected in Carton's dialogue with himself in the mirror:

"Do you particularly like the man?" he muttered, at his own image;
"why should you particularly like a man who resembles you? There is
nothing in you to like; you know that. Ah, confound you! What a
change you have made in yourself! A good reason for talking to a man,
that he shows you what you have fallen away from, and what you might
have been! Change places with him, and would you have been looked
at by those blue eyes as he was, and commiserated by that agitated face
as he was? Come on, and have it out in plain words! You hate the
fellow." (99)

Carton erects a pantomime in front of the mirror with himself as the
actants; in doing so, he embodies the idea that the drama and melodrama can articulate the voice, but they cannot embody it. Rather,
history, along with the self, is a nightmare lurking outside consciousness to be viewed in the form of the grand spectacle of melodrama. It
is as if the self watches the self in a melodrama and then acts; interiority is something that someone performs. Dickens uses history as a narrative that all the more encodes secrets through the transformation
into melodrama. Melodrama transforms being in time into a legible
narrative, but A Tale is at pains to reveal that the legible narrative is a
cover up, and underneath the melodrama is the buried secret of the
impossibility of revealing character and history.
History is that which follows us like a ghost; it is a return upon a
present that must be dug up, but Dickens reveals history to be a narrative that fails in trying to show progress and rationality. Instead, we
are left with a narrative informed by returns, ghosts, and doubles.

That character, history, and melodrama are related in this text is no accident, and the ruling principle that links them is terror—terror in the face of trying to read the narrative of ourselves in history. Hayden White elucidates the problem historical narrative tries to grapple with: "Historiography is an especially good ground on which to consider the nature of narration and narrativity because it is here that our desire for the imaginary, the possible, must contest with the imperatives of the real, the actual" (4). Dickens creates in *A Tale* the impossibility of recovering history given that the real—life in the city of London— mirrors the double of Paris. Thus, history is always in conflict with the actual.

Live burials inform the structure of *A Tale*; that is to say, embedded stories form the content of the novel. The multiple stories— Dr. Manette's buried manuscript relating his life story and Carton's disembodied story at the ending of the text—would seem to suggest a return from the dead, but the return from the dead is not successful. Rather, the novel positions live burials as remaining on the brink of encryption and revelation. The true horror of the novel is linked to the blocked voice—to voices that we never hear, such as Lucy's, Madame Defarge's, and her sister's voice. Their voices are encrypted in the historical narrative. It is almost as if the text is blocked by the forces of history; the forces of history mandate a closing off of what is most secretive and mysterious about one. History, in its privileging of the law and legitimacy, sustains the silencing of the voice, for it always describes a conflict between desire and the law. History mandates a melodramatic self, one that is legible; however, the effects of history— rupture, disjunction, and fragmentation—mark Dickens's text.

Dickens needed history as a cover for a way to articulate family life; thus, the tale of two cities—London concerned with the familial, and Paris, concerned with the historical—mirrors one another and continually doubles back on one another. In this way, Dickens writes a precursor to the sensation novel under the guise of the historical novel. Henry James wrote in *The Nation* in 1865 about Wilkie Collins, "[He] introduced into fiction those most mysterious of mysteries, the mysteries which are at our own door" (quoted in Botting 131).[13] In writing a historical novel, Dickens returns to the home; this makes the novel particularly uncanny because it is as if each narrative's ghostly voice haunts the other. As Freud tells us in his essay on "The Uncanny," it involves that which has been repressed and returns: "On the one hand it [the uncanny] means what is familiar and agreeable, and on the other, what is concealed and kept out of sight" (224–225).

One of the buried stories in the text is the story of the home, which cannot be articulated in the text of London; it can only surface in the revolution text. In other words, what the revolution speaks, the domestic cannot. In *A Tale*, we have a novel with a secret. Another doubling in the text is the uncanny dialogue each plot has with one another. Dickens tries to separate the texts from one another—to decapitate them, so to speak, but they continually come together in peculiar ways. The more the novel moves away from the home to the historical story—the more it is brought back.

So much of *A Tale* involves live burials; in reading the text one is continually aware of something being left out and subsequently revealed or not revealed. Just as characters are alienated from one another and appear as gothic reflections rather than counterparts, so too the reader is estranged in this text. Part of this estrangement is connected to the elision of the home. The narrative itself is filled with spectral presences whose voices are silenced; they are on the brink of being recalled to life as is Carton's disembodied voice at the ending. The spectacular spectacle of the mob scenes allows the reader to enter into the moving parade of images, but the stilted melodrama of the family does not encourage identification.

Why in writing a story about history does the home obtrude into the tale, not as a separate entity, but inextricably linked to the terrors of revolution? Lucy relates that while sitting in her home, "I have sometimes sat alone here of an evening, listening, until I have made the echoes out to be the echoes of all the footsteps that are coming by-and-by into our lives" (121). This passage resembles Frankenstein's horror after creating the creature, when he relates an excerpt from Coleridge's "The Ancient Mariner."

> Like one, on a lonesome road who,
> > Doth walk in fear and dread,
> And, having once turned round, walks on,
> > And turns no more his head;
> Because he knows a frightful fiend
> > Doth close behind him tread. (60)

In the passage from *A Tale*, Lucy previews the forces of history impinging on her familial life, while, in the *Frankenstein* passage, Frankenstein is haunted by that which he has created. He cannot get away from what he tries to repress. Similarly, in *A Tale*, the tale itself cannot escape the forms of oppression that history constructs and the family then adopts. The London family in the text—Charles Darnay and Lucy Manette—is haunted by the revolution in the Paris text, which actually originates in the familial home of Madame Defarge, whose sister was captured and held captive by Darnay's uncle and his brother. History may be about the spectacle of bloodshed, but it originates in the home, which in the text is the originary site for terror.

The terror of the revolution and the sublime descriptions of the bloodshed that Dickens orchestrates seep into the familial world of order and restraint. Using the revolution as a counterpoint to a story of love, Dickens links the terrors of the revolution to the terrors occasioned by the family. The family secrets—Lucy does not know that Charles Darnay is an assumed name and the rape of Madame Defarge's sister—are the locus for the sense of unease that the text generates about forms of oppression. Underneath the domestic bliss of the romantic love of Lucy and Charles is dread and secrecy. "Among the echoes then, there would arise the sound of footsteps at her own early grave; and thoughts of the husband who would be left so desolate, and who would mourn for her so much, swelled to her eyes, and broke like waves" (256). The footsteps and echoes haunt the domestic bliss. They provide a counter-voice to the narrative of tranquility, and thus love cannot be divorced from terror.

What get left out of history are the family secrets that point to the real terror in the text. While the disorder of the revolution may seem far removed from the Victorian home emblematized by the Manette household, that household is also another form of a prison where Lucy is locked in and listens to the echoes of the footsteps in which she will be swept up. Contrary to a one-dimensional reading of the family as the source of love and order, the text offers a critique of the family that is blind to its inclusion in the social circumstances that make history. The monster that is history is located in the home that preserves secrets so as to legitimate power.

The strange passage about how each person is a mystery to each other: "every human creature is constituted to be that profound secret and mystery to every other" (12) illustrates the impossibility of fully knowing another human being. At the heart of relationships are secrets, and the night shadows passage makes clear that secrets are housed within the family. "A solemn consideration, when I enter a great city by night, that every one of those darkly clustered houses encloses its own secret" (12). The home is the originary site for secrets and their burial.

The text cannot articulate the critique of the family directly, but like Dr. Manette who obsessively works on his shoes as a way to repress the traumatic memory of his imprisonment in the Bastille, the text must obsessively replay the melodramatic plot of love and goodness at the heart of the London family story to block the problems originating from family secrets. The text, in presenting the terrors of the streets of Paris, gestures toward what cannot be articulated in the family of Charles and Lucy and Dr. Manette. The unarticulated voices of the dialogue that fail in the London passages (and here I mean to point to the absence of dialogue among the family members) are heard in the interstices of the mob scenes. The buried alive story in the text is the unarticulated story of the family. In place of dialogue, Dickens substitutes melodrama. In a novel about a love relationship, there is little dialogue among the participants. Much of the force of the novel is directed toward the spectacular scenes of carnage in Paris.

The most embedded story suffers from the most oppression, and the most embedded stories involve being encased in a house or prison. The former involves the sister of Madame Defarge and the latter Manette being encased in the Bastille prison. Both situations involve crimes against a family; it is Manette who has been the witness to the brutal treatment of the underclass by the aristocratic family of Evrémonde. Crimes, therefore, originate in the family, and they are the source for the historical revolution. However, this revelation is withheld from the reader until two-thirds into the narrative. As the narrative moves forward in time, it uncovers its internal secrets. It too performs the work of resurrection and digging to recover the past. However, there are some secrets that remain buried in the text.

Competing with secrets in the text is a wish to reveal—to insert into history the voices of the oppressed. The narrative seems to be particularly obsessed with narrating stories and revealing secrets. In "The Eighteenth Brumaire of Louis Bonaparte," Marx has written: "They cannot represent themselves, they must be represented" (200), referring to the power dynamic between masters and workers. Certain characters in the text are given the authority of voicing stories: Dr. Manette is the prime example. He buries his story in the Bastille prison in a written narrative which, uncovered, is later used against him to convict Charles Darnay. Encased in Dr. Manette's story is the story of Madame Defarge's family. The narrator remarks about the young brother of the raped woman: "Nothing human could have held life in the boy but his determination to tell all his wrong. He forced back the gathering shadows of death, as he forced his clenched right hand to remain clenched, and to cover his wound" (402). Even at the moment of death, narrative here is linked with life, with "his determination to tell all his wrong." All of the layerings of stories suggest, however, that it is almost impossible to find the originating story. All the stories in the text compete with one another for a hearing; some get heard, but others remain buried, on the brink of discovery.

The fragmentation of story suggests that there will always be the possibility of another resurrection. The fragmentation also presages an eternal return, an eternal circle that gets repeated because of the forces of repression. Thus, narrative in the text is resurrection in that it performs the work of uncovering the past that is history.

In the introduction to *A Tale*, Andrew Sanders relates: "The writing of letters by those condemned to the guillotine was by no means uncommon during the first French Revolution. Boxes of such letters survive in the Archives Nationales in Paris, . . . None reached its intended destination . . ." (vii). The impulse of the prophetic narrative at the ending resurrects the voices of the dead through the voice of Sydney Carton as articulated by the narrator. In the place of language not reaching its destination, which the text demarcates as a doubling without correspondence, the ending merges the voices together and for the first time voices are in true dialogue with one another.

Dickens as author has a choice about how to present the voice of Carton at the ending. He creates a narrative voice that is possessed by the ghost of Carton. In doing so, he embraces mutuality, rather than the separation that all the doubles in the text suggest. While the voices of the murdered in the annals of history did not have a hearing, the voice here is preserved through the act of narration. Communication is possible without the confines of history and time.

The ending of the text with Carton's death and resurrection through narrative orchestrates Dickens's solution to death—which is the continual rebirth of story through narration. It is through narration that death can undergo a rebirth. That is to say, as we have seen the text is obsessed with the march of time that inevitably leads to death. The only thing that can suspend death is narration. To supplant the vicissitudes of everyday life, Dickens substitutes the melodramatic imagination coming back as ghost and speaking its story over and over. And as a prelude to this sublime positioning of narration, Dickens resorts to another text concerning death and resurrection: "I am the Resurrection and the Life, saith the Lord: he that believeth in me, though he were dead, yet shall he live: and whosoever liveth and believeth in me shall never die" (464). Dickens takes the scriptural word and substitutes in its place the word of the ghost whose voice will never die. This voice lives on precisely because it has a story to tell—Carton's face in death is described as "sublime and prophetic" (464).

The ending then gives great importance to the act of commemoration: one of the women to be murdered asks for paper to write down her thoughts, and the narrator imagines what Carton's would have been. The narrative at the ending wants to figure a beginning, wants Carton's voice to plot the course of events. "I see a beautiful city and a brilliant people rising from this abyss, and, in their struggles to be truly free, in their triumphs and defeats, through long long years to come, I see the evil of this time and of the previous time of which this is the natural birth, gradually making expiation for itself and wearing out" (465). In essence, the sublime ending positions narrative as a replacement for scripture, and the narrator embodying the voice of Carton takes over the role of a creator.

The narrator embodying the voice of Carton at the ending, in essence embodying Carton, leads one to ask who is speaking. To have a dead person prophesize the future through the medium of the narrator is to create a suspended time, where finally embodiment occurs between two persons. In the rest of the text, we get a doubling of characters that suggests alienation; however, in the ending, through death and resurrection of the voice a true connection occurs. Dickens and Carton, through the prophetic voice, are in dialogue with one another, and their dialogue is about crossing the line between death and resurrection.

To be buried alive is, as Freud contends in "The Uncanny," probably one of the uncanniest feelings, for it recalls a return to the womb. The gothic foregrounds the trope of live burial, which produces dread and horror. In Dickens's strange imagination, however, live burial becomes a source of fecundity—it is only through death or being beyond time—that one can be fully alive. That is to say, the place of narration is a liminal space between life and death where one is fully alive to the march of death or of plotting. The prison motif pervasive in Dickens also inspires a breaking out, and it is this space that I am claiming for narration.

In *A Tale*, plot represents an inevitable drive toward the end—to the heroic sacrifice of Sydney Carton. Thus, the novel is predicated on the forward drive of an inescapable history. Here I want to link history to ghostly repetition. The drive forward in the text is interrupted by numerous returns to a traumatic event that has not been mastered. Along with characters who are traumatized by their pasts and who live as if suspended in a time that doubles back on itself, the narrator, in his attempt to embody his buried-alive characters, speaks from the grave. Part of the strangeness of this narrative voice entails our never being sure where the voice originates.

Not only are the characters haunted by their pasts, but the narrator also falls prey to his story. That is, in writing a story about death and resurrection, the narrator speaks from an in-between space, a space that is not quite locatable. To embody a story in one's own person, as Dickens stated he wanted to do in the Preface, necessarily entails a disembodiment, an occupying of a body that is both dead and alive. Part of this disembodiment is a linguistic one, that is, the novel is full of marks and traces and buried writing that repeat the linguistic predicament of the narrator as he tries to resuscitate his characters imaginatively. Of course, here I adopt a Derridean stance where once one begins to speak, one speaks from the other—language can only ever approximate meaning. But to stop here would not capture the complexity of Dickens's project. In an uncanny way, Dickens's texts coextensively disembody and embody language. For it is in the dead-alive space where narration fully achieves continual echoes of an imaginative force that literally cannot end. Narrative continually recalls Dickens to life.

We see this avoidance of closure in many of Dickens's endings. In *Great Expectations*, we have the double ending; in *Our Mutual Friend*, The Postscript in lieu of Preface; and in *A Tale of Two Cities*, Sydney Carton's suppositional narrative juxtaposed with his sacrificial act. The narrator writes: "One of the most remarkable sufferers by the same axe—a woman—had asked at the foot of the same scaffold, not long before, to be allowed to write down the thoughts that were inspiring her. If he had given any utterance to his, and they were prophetic, they would have been these" (464). The narrator, embodying the voice of the disembodied Carton, proceeds to recount a montage of scenes that he (Carton) sees. This forward-driving account from the voice of the dead is all about seeing, but it is not enough to see, one must recount what one sees. Thus, the narrator gives Sydney his power to forecast—this is the true resurrection and the life. Perhaps at the ending Dickens faces Carton and gives him the final words of an "I" that must be heard.

The final words of the text may be read in another way. Just as in *The Frozen Deep* where Wardour's death represents Dickens's imagining a world without him, the words of sacrifice in *A Tale* are about Dickens's death in the text. "It is a far, far better thing that I do, than I have ever done; it is a far, far better rest that I go to than I have ever known" (466). In embodying Carton, Dickens is disembodied, and it is this ghost-like place that is the proper ending to a tale that will not and cannot end. One cannot imagine a proper rest for Carton. For he too is continually recalled to life in the numerous retellings of his story. The entire narrative then may be said to be suspended between death and resurrection.

Through the narrator giving voice to Carton's voice, the text ends with a superimposed voice, with a layered voice that is unlocatable in time and space, producing a ghostly effect. While the text begins located squarely in time: "It was the best of times, it was the worst of times" (1), it ends poised on the brink of a suppositional time. In using the suppositional, the novel refuses to close, pointing to the possibility of other voices. In the place of a historical truth, Dickens imagines an evolutionary truth that contains the possibility of dynamism. Thus, we have the resolution of the story through the forecasting of the future, which leads back to the lessons of history that the novel puts forth.

In ending the story with multiple voices—the voice of the narrator and Carton's prophetic voice—Dickens resuscitates all the dead voices that have been encrypted in the text through multiple layerings. One imagines an army of disembodied voices—voices without heads speaking from the land of the dead. At the ending of a text about history, Dickens imagines what life would look like from the land of the dead. He presents us with a voice without a home—the ghost of Carton walks. The novel embraces the uncanny place of being poised between life and death. In choosing to prophesize, Dickens simultaneously presents us with the melodramatic moral drama of death, sacrifice, and redemption, but he also leaves open the possibility for other voices to speak in the space of Carton and the narrator's voice. We remember that the ghost returns because all has not been articulated. Thus, the novel ends in an in-between space. There is no frame to close the novel. The beginning sets into motion time, but the ending presents dream-like suppositional moments in time that move into one another rather than end-stop. In the face of history, the imagination must conjure ghosts; only then can it present its alternative—the possible supernatural. For Dickens, memory and commemoration in the form of narrative are the solution to the forces of history. The prophetic words suggest the melodramatic script, but the in-between spaces document the complex, unresolvable nature of the conflicts that Dickens orchestrates.

WANDERING AND PLOTTING: DICKENS'S JOURNALISTIC WRITING

I have maintained that in Dickens's later writing, beginning with *A Tale of Two Cities*, there is an increased emphasis on death and narrative as a compensatory form of resurrection. We see this obsession with death and narrative played out in Dickens's journalistic writing, most notably, *The Uncommercial Traveller* and *The Lazy Tour of Two Idle Apprentices*. During this time period of the 1850s, Dickens also began his series of public readings during which he acted out scenes from his novels. These public readings garnered him much acclaim and gave Dickens the opportunity to form a bond with his audience. This bond is a different kind from the one Dickens had established with his readers. Through the public readings Dickens could establish a form of dialogue with his readers. Instead of reading in private, people could see a performance of the written text with Dickens as the actor. These public performances brought to life the dead words on the page, and through them, Dickens continually resurrected his much-loved works. The public readings then kept alive the force of the words on the page through the actual voice of Dickens the actor. One of Dickens's favorite works of literature was *The Arabian Nights*. In that tale, we remember that Scheherazade, to avoid her own death, keeps herself alive by narrating a different tale to the Sultan each night. In the same way, in this later period of his life, Dickens obsessed with death—articulated in the form of the gothic— continually employs narrative as a means of rebirth.

Resurrection in the novels and in the journalistic writing is linked to Dickens as a writer, and it is my contention that the public readings and the obsession with the gothic in these works connect Dickens the writer to the ghost who continually returns and haunts. Thus, Dickens's narratives are never properly done; they always come back in some form or other, whether in the form of the public readings, the multiplot, or double endings. In a sense, the gothic in Dickens involves the story that brims over, not the lack of a story. Dickens's wandering imagination is also aligned with the ghost, for it can never find a resting place; it is continually on the move. The model for wandering in these texts is walking, and Dickens's creative imagination is put into play as he walks the streets of the vast city of London. It is as if London becomes the labyrinth to house his inexhaustible imagination.

Walking the streets of London, Dickens becomes the ghost who does not have a home. Dickens is continually recalled to life walking the streets of London, and that recall is linked to plotting. In a letter written in 1846, in the midst of writing *Dombey and Son* in Switzerland, he laments about

> the absence of streets and numbers of figures. I can't express how much
> I want these. It seems as if they supplied something to my brain, which

it cannot bear, when busy, to lose. For a week or a fortnight I can write prodigiously in a retired place . . . and a day in London sets me up again and starts me. But the toil and labour of writing day after day, without that magic lantern, is IMMENSE!! (*Letters of Dickens Vol. 4*, August 30, 1846, 612)

While many commentators have argued that Dickens celebrated the domestic in his novels, the gothic side of Dickens renounces the home in favor of a homelessness reflected in a shifting panoramic landscape.[14] Dickens leaves the home to experience the unfamiliar—in essence, to be haunted.

In the journalistic writing, Dickens destabilizes the home resulting in a radical identity—one that is homeless. Dickens in the journalistic writing goes outside the home to truly feel at home through an imaginative traveling. I am claiming that Dickens created a new form of narrative, one that is based on the multiplot, to reflect his wandering gothic imagination. This gothic imagination locates itself in the moving parade of images of the city that float in and out of Dickens's mind. Walking allowed him to search "for some pictures I wanted to build upon" (Ackroyd 563).[15] In the first issue of *The Uncommerical Traveller*, Dickens states his purpose in writing the series of essays:

I am both a town traveler and a country traveler, and am always on the road. Figuratively speaking, I travel for the great house of Human Interest Brothers, and have rather a large connection in the fancy goods way. Literally speaking, I am always wandering here and there from my rooms in Covent-Garden, London—now about the city streets: now about the country bye-roads—seeing many little things, and some great things, which, because they interest me, I think may interest others. These are my brief credentials as an Uncommercial Traveller. Business is business, and I start. (28)

Through walking and through the transmutation of walking into narrative, Dickens window-shops for his readers. That this walking is linked to the ever changing face of the city brings us back to Darwin and the absence of origins; rather, there are multiple origins and multiple branchings off leading to evolution as a dynamic and ever-changing force in the world. Similarly, the city and walking for Dickens give him a model for shifting images that float into one another. They are not static but are linked through an imaginative accretion.

Dickens creates a wandering narrative style that mirrors the wandering spectacle of the metropolis. Adopting the role of the *flaneur*,[16] who walks the city streets and observes as a journalist would the very by-ways of the impressions created by the spectacle, Dickens creates in *The Uncommercial Traveller* documentary impressions of the city. In doing so, he engenders an imaginative panorama that is labyrinthine and all encompassing. He, in fact, becomes what Baudelaire has termed "a kaleidoscope endowed with consciousness" (400).[17] He can continually see the city in a different way as it is forever changing its dimensions. He resembles the roving eye that moves and records the modern metropolis from different angles. Plots and stories merge in and out of one another, much like the device of the moving picture.[18]

Furthermore, walking allows him to continually postpone the ending, for walking propels new plots. Dickens links walking to living; he wrote to Forster in 1854, "if I couldn't walk fast and far, I should just explode and perish" (xviii). The style of writing that Dickens perfected in his journalistic writing and in the novels represents his unease with remaining still; for him, being still presages a slow death of the imagination that must be kept in continuous motion. This style of writing is aligned with the vagabond. Dickens writes: "My walking is of two kinds; one, straight on and to a definite goal at a round pace; one, objectless, loitering, and purely vagabond. In the latter state, no gypsy on earth is a greater vagabond than myself; it is so natural to me and strong with me, that I think I must be the descendant, at no great distance, of some irreclaimable tramp" ("Shy Neighborhoods," *The Uncommercial Traveller* 119).

Peter Ackroyd tells us that *The Uncommercial Traveller*, which Dickens wrote in between *A Tale of Two Cities* and *Great Expectations*, documents "the wanderings of a man haunted by his past and images of death" (873). While I agree with Ackroyd that Dickens in the latter part of his life is haunted by his past and death; coextensively, walking and plotting allow him to be reborn. What I want to claim, then, is that the ghost that forms the basis for horror for the gothic imagination turns out to be life affirming in Dickens in the sense that the ghost leads to narration. Instead of the ghost forecasting live burial, as in Poe's *The Fall of the House of Usher*, the ghost presages continual resurrections.

"Night Walks," written in 1860, encapsulates the beauty of the gothic in Victorian narration. Rather than representing the terrors of the imagination, Dickens uses the occasion to champion the beauty of the imagination arising out of death and decay. In "Night Walks," Dickens creates a paean to the return of the dead when he writes:

> It was a solemn consideration what enormous hosts of dead belong to one old great city and how, if they were raised while the living slept,

there would not be the space of a pin's point in all the streets and ways for the living to come out into. Not only that, but the vast armies of dead would overflow the hills and valleys beyond the city, and would stretch away all round it, God knows how far: seemingly to the confines of the earth. (154)

This phantasmagoria of the dead returning allows Dickens to imagine a London peopled by a vast army of the dead.[19] Rather than terror, the emphasis is on the mind expanding to imagine the scene. In using the words "overflow," and "stretch," Dickens points to the vitality of the dead people populating the city. Dickens uses the gothic to recall the sublime resurrection of the dead. In so doing, he resuscitates his own imaginative powers and starts to see connections between the dead and the living. It is as if the gothic enables Dickens to come to important philosophical realizations about life and death in the story. Also, the conjuring of the dead people gives him the impetus to imagine the vast city of London populated by the dead. In a sense, the dead during the night are a vital part of the living. Throughout the story, Dickens attempts to abolish demarcations between the living and the dead. The writing in "Night Walks" pivots on ambivalence—Dickens creates an imaginative space where opposites are reconciled.

Furthermore, the passage conveys the idea that what is dead is never dead; but rather gets reconstituted—the dead return to life. As Dickens walks, he sees a series of images that never die through his imaginative resuscitation. The night walks transform the city into a source of great fecundity; the city itself resembles the entangled bank that Darwin describes at the ending of *On the Origin of Species*: "Whilst this planet has gone cycling on according to the fixed law of gravity, from so simple a beginning endless forms most beautiful and most wonderful have been, and are being, evolved" (490). The city becomes the site for the recycling of the dead, and the living evolve and create because of the recognition of the effect of the past upon the present. The ghost text that follows the Victorian author is Darwin's, for the ghost announces the correspondence of descent in that nothing is ever dead but is linked through the concept of evolution. One is tempted to ask who is speaking in the text: is it the voice of Dickens or is his voice being channeled by ghosts? This multiple voicing creates a London with many voices funneled through the voice of the narrator. In this way, Dickens creates a poetics of the city that combines elegy and lyric celebration.

As Dickens walks his mind becomes ghost-like, filled with images of death, but these images provide the impetus for a creative outpouring.

Dickens needs the trappings of the gothic to explore the passageways of his mind. The gothic becomes the site then for the mind's confrontations with terror and beauty. Instead of being overwhelmed, the mind portrays the plenitude of life. Through the dead coming to life, Dickens explores the ever-changing dynamism and exuberance of the city, and it is only through the gothic that Dickens can present narrative as encyclopedic.

Walking serves as the means to get lost; it does not prescribe arrival, but rather a creative and dissonant disorientation as it leads to several different byways. As we have seen, Freud's essay on "The Uncanny" relates his own experience with the strange and familiar as he walks the streets of Paris and keeps ending up in the red-light district. This sense of repetition produces anxiety for him. For Dickens, in the journalistic writing, however, getting lost is the prelude to an imaginative transport. Dickens looks into the face of terror and sees narrative ambivalence in the form of a vast imaginative space that is without a home and without a proper destination.

Furthermore, walking allows Dickens to use the city as a lens with which to portray the psychology of mind. Many commentators continue to fault Dickens for eliding psychology; however, psychology for Dickens is not obvious but hidden through mystery, doubles, and structural burials of repressed desires that return. To put it another way, Dickens explores psychology through the ghostly trappings of the gothic reflected in the exterior. He needs the gothic apparatus to shadow character rather than represent it directly. Character psychology for him wanders and refuses to stay in one place; this as we have seen he accomplishes through the dynamics of the multiplot. Psychology for him is akin to a dream where one is not fully aware of all of the connections in it.[20] In "Night Walks," in the middle of his night wanderings, he asks an astonishing series of questions that align creativity, dreaming, and plotting with the mental travellings of the mad person.[21]

> Are not the sane and insane equal at night as the sane lie a dreaming? Are not all of us outside this hospital, who dream, more or less in the condition of those inside it, every night of our lives? Are we not nightly persuaded, as they daily are that we associate preposterously with kings and queens, emperors and empresses, and notabilities of all sorts? Do we not nightly jumble events and personages, and times and places, as these do daily? Are we not sometimes troubled by our own sleeping inconsistencies, and do we not vexedly try to account for them or excuse them, just as these do sometimes in respect of their waking delusions? Said an afflicted man to me, when I was last in a hospital like this, "Sir I can frequently fly." I was half ashamed to reflect that so could I—by night. (153)

Character involves a series of poised questions, not arrival and answers. It also entails a wandering sense of identity: that is, bodies wander and are not confined necessarily to one body. Like a moving image, identities are not static but instead merge with one another. The multiplot, like the dream text, jumbles events and personages by moving on from one story to the next. This night walk state is a source of fecundity because it cannot be confined in space or time. As the mad person can fly, so too the imagination can fly.

The meditation on the power of the imagination and its connection with madness builds to the startling conclusion of the story when Dickens confronts his double, the tramp without an identity who vanishes into the night, and we are left with the image of clothes without a body.

> Suddenly, a thing that in a moment more I should have trodden upon without seeing, rose up at my feet with a cry of loneliness and houselessness, struck out of it by the bell, the like of which I never heard. We then stood face to face looking at one another, frightened by one another. The creature was like a beetle-browed hare-lipped youth of twenty, and it had a loose bundle of rags on, which it held together with one of its hands. It shivered from head to foot, and its teeth chattered, and as it stared at me—persecutor, devil, ghost, whatever it thought me—it made with its whining mouth as if it were snapping at me, like a worried dog. Intending to give this ugly object, money, I put out my hand to stay it—for it recoiled as it whined and snapped—and laid my hand upon its shoulder. Instantly, it twisted out of its garment, like the young man in the New Testament, and left me standing alone with its rags in my hand. (154–155)

Walking in the text leads to startling revelations about identity and the self. As we have seen, the first recognition is one of similarity between the sane and the insane. This final confrontation is a more personal realization. Dickens ends the story conjuring a replicant of himself, who is not only inexhaustible, but uncontainable. He produces a ghostly figure, who at the ending, vanishes. The story involves looking into the mirror and seeing an image of horror, the tramp, who is more inhuman than human. But the story does not end with an image of terror. Instead, it evokes a more acute realization about identity. Dickens in looking into the mirror imagines a double who runs off, presaging that the self is not locatable; it remains homeless.

In essence, all encounters with the self lead to a missed connection. In other words, Dickens through the text peoples the city—embodies the city—with disembodied ghosts, first with the dead people coming to life, and second, with the tramp vanishing without his clothes. We are led to ask the question, do not night walks lead to disembodiment? As one wanders the streets, not only is he or she without a home, but without a proper body. Dickens looks into the mirror of himself and sees a figure without clothing; instead of terror, we are left with a deeper understanding of Dickens's imagination as being truly spectral. That is, its force stems from recognizing that he needs terror to produce beauty. It is only through the strange that he can express his inexhaustible imagination. By dissolving his own self, he is overtaken by the dead. This does not evoke terror; rather, it inspires a true ambivalence, a home without a home, an authorial self without a covering, forced to wander.

Dickens's special affinity for the dead leads him to imagine a self that in effect never ends. To conspire with the dead is to open up new avenues for the representation of the self in fiction. His correspondence with the dead allows him to continually be reborn through projection and doubling. Through correspondence with the dead, he can try on new faces. Even though the faces terrify him, they also provide him with a plot that continually resurfaces in a different form. In "Travelling Abroad," Number 10 of *The Uncommercial Traveller*, published in 1860, Dickens relates: "Whenever I am at Paris, I am dragged by an invisible force into the Morgue. I never want to go there, but am always pulled there. One Christmas Day, when I would rather have been anywhere else, I was attracted in, to see an old grey man lying all alone on his cold bed, with a tap of water turned on over his grey hair, and running drip, drip, drip, down his wretched face until it got to the corner of his mouth, where it took a turn and made him look sly" (88). Dickens goes to the morgue on special days: Christmas and New Year's. Both days we associate with new beginnings: Dickens needs the gothic trappings of the morgue to rejuvenate himself.[22] These holidays are also associated with conviviality among friends. Dickens is drawn like a magnet to the morgue scenes, allowing him to represent the exuberance of death. The dead inspire an exhilarating sense of the vitality of telling the story. It is only the dead who can bring Dickens through narrative to life.

And Dickens is haunted by the figure of the dead man who follows him around Paris like a ghost. Everywhere Dickens goes, he pictures this man. "That very day, at dinner, some morsel on my plate looked like a piece of him" (90). Even the smell of Dickens's apartment at the hotel "never failed to reproduce him" (90). The picture of the dead man is akin to the transformations effected by plot. Dickens views the dead man in everything he encounters. He sees the dead man's image superimposed upon other images and other senses even. The dead man is the necessary obsession for narration to proceed. As Dickens walks around Paris, the dead man's image proliferates.

While the confrontation with one's double usually leads to death in gothic tales, such as in *Frankenstein* and *Dr. Jekyll and Mr. Hyde*, Dickens uses the double not for fragmentation, but for multiplication, primarily multiplication of the story. Freud in "The Uncanny" relates regarding the double: "From having been an assurance of immortality, it becomes the uncanny harbinger of death" (235). He further explains that the double resurrects the primitive fear of the dead. "Most likely our fear still implies the old belief that the dead man becomes the enemy of his survivor and seeks to carry him off to share his new life with him" (242). The encounter with the double produces fear but coextensively pleasurable moments of recognition. In a very strange way, Dickens visits the morgue to be embodied with other bodily forms. These bodily forms allow Dickens to try on new personae and to experience a sense of connection and correspondence. That the people are dead rehearses Dickens's obsession with his own death and resurrection through the depiction of other bodies that die and return. Images of death spark the desire to forestall the ending through a series of intricate imaginings.

Dickens's encounter with the many strange people in his travels creates not only a kaleidoscopic eye where he moves from scene to scene and records and reaches profound conclusions, but his travels also engender a kaleidoscopic "I." Through his "kaleidoscope eye," Dickens can lose himself in others. The city allows for this transformation in identity.[23] The poetics of the city inspires a multitude of recognitions. In the journalistic essays, Dickens presents two cities in one: he transforms the gothic city into the poetic city. In doing so, he resembles Keats's poetical character: Keats writes that the poetical character "is not itself—it has no self—it is every thing and nothing—It has no character" (Letter to Richard Woodhouse, October 27, 1818, 279). In exploring the streets of London, Dickens merges with his surroundings. It is as if the city provides him with different identities that allow him to occupy a space between embodiment and disembodiment.

Curiously, Charles Baudelaire in *The Painter of Modern Life* establishes a link between the artist and the convalescent who in a sense returns from the dead. He writes about Poe's *The Man of the Crowd*:

> Sitting in a café, and looking through the shop window, the convalescent is enjoying the sight of the passing crowd, and identifying himself in thought with all the thoughts that are moving around him. He has only recently come back from the shades of death and breathes in with

delight all the spores and odours of life; as he has been on the point of forgetting everything, he remembers and passionately wants to remember everything. (397)

Creativity arises out of the space between the living and the dead; as Dickens walks the streets he is brought back to life by the vitality of what his mind associates with the cityscape.

Dickens's imagination needs to restage death to resurrect narration. In *The Lazy Tour of Two Idle Apprentices*, written in 1857, he writes a gothic tale, a piece of diablerie. This diablerie represents a link between narration and the diabolic. In the midst of the mundane wanderings of the two idle apprentices, the undead appears. In fairy tales, the narration is impelled by a command, by someone saying something such as: "Don't go into the forest." Of course, children go into the forest, and this represents a function of the narrative moving forward. In "The Bridal Chamber" (a story in *The Lazy Tour*), there are two commands: die, which the old man repeats to his young wife; and live, which the ghost of the young wife says in her haunting of him. The resulting story hangs in between the words die and live. But these words are not oppositional, for the dead old man lives a haunted life. Where does the living reside in this text?

To be idle for Goodchild, the stand-in for Dickens, represents a kind of death. The fourth chapter begins with Goodchild's attempt to be lazy and idle. However, he cannot manage to be either. Idle says to him: "To me you are an absolutely terrible fellow. You do nothing like another man. Where another fellow would fall into a footbath of action or emotion, you fall into a mine. Where any other fellow would be a painted butterfly, you are a fiery dragon. Where another man would stake a sixpence, you stake your existence. If you were to go up in a balloon, you would make for Heaven; and if you were to dive into the depths of the earth, nothing short of the other place would content you." Idle further says, "A man who can do nothing by halves appears to me to be a fearful man" (448). Idle's sublime description of Goodchild portrays Idle's dread and awe at Goodchild's demonic energy. This energy precludes idleness and is the source for Dickens's strange imaginings in this story.

Energy in "The Bridal Chamber" is most realized in the obsessive interplay among the characters and narrators. We begin with a third person narrator relating the camaraderie between Goodchild and Idle, we move to an account of Goodchild's visit to the lunatic asylum, then to the old man's story of the bride, and finally to Goodchild's carrying Idle down the stairs. The profusion of stories points to how narratives are layered over one another—buried atop one another, so to speak. These buried narratives slowly come to life, but only when Goodchild is reduced to a death-like state. As I have stated earlier, to be idle is in a sense to die, but now I want to complicate the argument by claiming that idleness is the state where channeling can occur—the story of the dead man can enter Goodchild.

In this regard, Goodchild stands in for the bride, imprisoned in the chamber of listening. "Mr. Goodchild believed that he saw two threads of fire stretch from the old man's eyes to his own, and there attach themselves. (Mr. Goodchild writes the present account of his experience, and, with the utmost solemnity, protests that he had the strongest sensation upon him of being forced to look at the old man along those two fiery films, from that moment)" (452). The chamber represents the inner sanctum where Goodchild dies to gain access to the dead man's story. Literally, to be idle is to be a ready vessel for the transmission of the story, but being idle also might lead to death by horror. If the narrator remains under the power of the dead man for too long, he risks death. "The two fiery lines extending from the old man's eyes to his own, kept him down, and he could not utter a sound" (460–461).

Coming face to face with his readers keeps Dickens alive. In this way, we can read the story as an allegory for Dickens the storyteller and his imaginative work of resurrecting matter from his imagination. Why does Dickens need the mode of the gothic to tell this story? The sublimity of his imagination mimics the lunatic's. As a prelude to the story proper of the bride, Dickens visits the lunatic asylum. The inclusion of the lunatic asylum story links the narrator to the lunatic in the sense that like Dickens the lunatic obsessively repeats an action. Through narration, Dickens can obsessively bury secrets and bring them to life. The narrator recounts that the lunatic is "stooping low over the matting on the floor, and picking out with his thumb and fore-finger the course of its fibres." Then the narrator realizes: "I thought how all of us, God help us! in our different ways are poring over our bits of matting, blindly enough, and what confusions and mysteries we make in the pattern. I had a sadder fellow-feeling with the little dark-chinned, meager man, by that time, and I came away" (449). Being in time entails plotting the course of the matting. The work of the lunatic is aligned with Dickens's narrative work: the profusion of narratives and the obsessive need to narrate suggest a compulsive repetitive action.

The story stages multiple returns from the dead. It is as if narrative cannot contain the self in one frame and in one time or space. The ghost of the man in the story is compelled to narrate: "I must tell it to you" (452), and he too is haunted by the ghost of the wife whom he murdered. She takes over his narration by repeating to him the word "Live" (461). Thus, the dead man lives through narrating, and Dickens dies to be the conveyor of this tale about life and rebirth. In fact, each character in the story vies to be in the position of the narrator; each in an uncanny way is infected by the compulsion to narrate, and Dickens as the Goodchild figure is first forced to listen and then compelled to narrate the story. The multiplication of narrators forecasts the many layers of meanings that the story unfolds.

Subjectivity in this little tale never stays put; it moves from one person to the next as each wrestles with the other for control of the narration. The ghost of the old man recounts: "*We* were there. She and I were there. I, in the chair upon the hearth; she, a white wreck again, trailing itself towards me on the floor. But, I was the speaker no more. She was the sole speaker now, and the one word that she said to me from midnight until dawn was, 'Live!' " (461). The demonic energy of the story comes from the characters' struggle with death; the only way they can surmount death is by coming back as ghosts who tell their stories. In this story, everyone comes back to life to narrate; consumed by the desire to narrate, each character cannot properly be put to rest. And Dickens through telling the story occupies the innermost heart of the chamber—the bridal chamber. In this tale of male camararadie, with Mr. Idle (Wilkie Collins) and Mr. Goodchild as the characters, Dickens marries narrative.

The Lazy Tour stages its own return from the dead by foregrounding the return to the home in the midst of a walking tour. Even though Dickens goes outside the home, he is compelled to return home for the real story of the bride to begin. The site of the home, where one should feel most secure, is full of ghosts, murders, and violence. The home thus represents an uncanny place where "everything that ought to have remained . . . secret and hidden . . . has come to light" (224). We read the story then as a meditation on the uncanny: during the course of the tale many secrets are uncovered through the act of narration. The story continually stages resurrections, but there still remain many layers of live burials. Just as the ghost of the dead man keeps multiplying, one gets the sense that this tale may spin out of control through the revelation of secrets that are buried deep within the home. Narration, taking on the character of the haunted house, runs the risk of being short-circuited by the final revelation that would be the most horrific one. Instead, it must be deeply buried and transposed to the mad man.

To be buried alive as most certainly the lunatic is in the asylum is a terrible fate, but it is also from this space that the narrative moves to a live burial that is suspended between life and death. This space of being buried alive is the space of suspension. The narrative repeats a story or stories of death. In the retellings, traces may be heard. The buried-alive story is a space of ambivalence—dead/alive, neither here nor there. From the zombie-like state emerges a new subjectivity— one that is conflicted and multiple. The numerous returns and reworkings of stories open up a space that is not closed or fixed. The gothic in this tale enables Dickens to bury secrets and then to bring them to light, but the final revelation is always concealed because of the forces of repression. The chamber is haunted precisely because of the many networks of narrative passageways that have not fully been explored.

We know that Dickens was obsessed with the possibility of his own death. As Peter Ackroyd relates in the introduction to *The Mystery of Edwin Drood*:

> He broke the habit of a lifetime by agreeing to a series of public readings even while he was engaged on a piece of fiction. In previous years he had kept the activities apart, for the sake of his energy as well as his health. But now, even while deep in the composition of *The Mystery of Edwin Drood*, he agreed to give a series of "farewell readings" to his adoring public. He finished them at great cost to his strength. (xi)

Walking, writing, and reading for his public in a sense forestalled the ending. As Tzevtan Todorov has put it: "Narrative equals life; absence of narrative, death" (74). In the Postscript in Lieu of preface to his last completed novel, *Our Mutual Friend*, Dickens relates his near death by railway accident, during which he observed many mangled bodies. He, in fact, went back into the derailed carriage to save his current number of *Our Mutual Friend*. At the ending of the Postscript, he writes: "I can never be much nearer parting company with my readers for ever, than I was then, until there should be written against my life, the two words with which I have this day closed this book:—The End" (894). In the midst of death and carnage, he retrieves the man-uscript of one of the numbers of *Our Mutual Friend*. In going back into the railway carriage, he resuscitates his work. The only thing that can stop him is his literal death, until there should be written against his life: The End.

What would a world without Dickens as storyteller look like? What would his literal end presage for his body of work? *The Mystery of*

Edwin Drood is full of images of the graveyard: Durdles is a stonecutter who makes inscriptions on tombstones. "Durdles stumbl[es] among the litter of his stony yard as if he were going to turn head-foremost into one of the unfinished tombs" (48). The novel itself stands as an unfinished tomb, a paradox which explains nicely the incomplete novel. *The Mystery of Edwin Drood* ends poised on the brink of knowledge. Dickens's death while writing *The Mystery of Edwin Drood* leaves us with a profound understanding of narrative, death, and rebirth in his works.[24] The fact that he did not complete the novel, that he died during its writing, replays in an uncanny way the central preoccupation in his writings during his later period: death, rebirth, and narrative. In fact, Dickens could not have staged it better himself if he had written his own death.

What remains is a story that cannot end, that will not end, that remains a mystery forever at its core. The unfinished novel continually engages in a dialogue with readers. Dickens the author has disappeared through his death, but the words on the page keep coming back to undo the death of the author. The unfinished story leaves open the potential for more plotting and more mystery. The novel is ghost-like in that its work is never finished. In this last work, Dickens is truly homeless; the present tense of the text continually unfolds. Cut off from an ending, the fragmented text continually calls for new possibilities, thus continually staging its own return from the dead.

The unfinished tale evokes the ghost of the author, continually wandering the unfinished tomb of his work. One cannot imagine a quiet death for Dickens, as he continually comes back to haunt though the process of resurrecting the words on the page. Without a proper ending, the text exhibits multiple possibilities and endless ramifications for plot.

CONCLUSION

Throughout this study, I have been arguing for a double reading of Victorian fiction. On the one hand, the Victorians thought of the home as a sacred space; on the other, that home became the site for undoing ideas about gender and identity. The home indeed turned out to be a haunted one, unable to carry the weight of stable ideas about identity. I have argued that the texts in *Gothic Returns* represent stories that are buried and return as an effect of haunting. It is my contention that the Victorian novel is haunted by its own ghosts— namely, the ghost of the feminine that returns figuratively through narrative. As we have seen, the Victorians were obsessed with origins, with a return home. This return home is the structural beginning point for most Victorian novels. I have argued that the figure of woman haunts Victorian ideas about identity and home and conse-quently narrative homes. The Victorian novel thus is a haunted house. It is simultaneously about returning home and not being there in the place where one is supposed to be. This effect is uncanny, and is asso-ciated with the figure of woman. The home and therefore identity turns into something that is both familiar and strange.

While many novels focus on the development of the individual and his or her leaving home to mark this development, the novels I discuss cannot get away from the home. That home, however, is transformed by the ghost in that the ghost always suggests a problem with coex-tensively being there and not being there. The ghost wanders and circulates freely undercutting that the home may be a limiting force. The home is no longer the ideal home in that the ghost turns the home into a haunted house. And in Dickens's journalistic pieces, he emphasizes the delights of wandering and being estranged from home. He confronts the fears associated with home by creating scenarios in which homelessness inspires an embracing of ambiguity, thus allowing for an imaginative freedom.

The ghost is the remainder of what has not been dealt with, and narrative serves as the means with which to articulate what has been buried. Narrative represents resuscitation. Freud in *Five Lectures on*

Psychoanalysis writes: "*[O]ur hysterical patients suffer from reminiscences.* Their symptoms are residues and mnemic symbols of particular (traumatic) experiences" (16). The novels I discuss are in a sense all versions of hysterical symptoms, and the ghost or the remainder of the story represents the attempt to articulate what has been buried. Reminiscences call forth the ghost of memory; each story is layered with multiple meanings—that is to say, stories overlap one another in a continuous proliferation of meaning.

One could very well argue that all narrative is informed by doubling, by ghostly presences lying underneath the surface, but it is my contention that Victorian authors created narratives that structurally and thematically focused on ghostly returns, double narratives, and the multiplot. This doubling is tied to a crisis in origins, for Darwin's ideas about the origins of species recall the ghost—that is, the ghost is the figure for no definitive origin. It is an entity without a home. In fact, the ghost represents the nonclosure of the body. Darwin's ideas point to a crisis in ownership, that is to say, the ghost suggests that which cannot be legally bound. Too, in the continuum of inheritance, there is an entangled legacy that disturbs origins and endings.

The psychological dynamic of the gothic produced uncanny narratives where stories become haunted by something other, something lying just outside consciousness. This residue of the other suggests the return of the past upon the present. The buried voice is never dead but lurks waiting to be reborn. Therefore, stories never end but proliferate into startling eruptions of ghostly effects, such as the double, the spectacle, or superimposed identities.

The novels, journalistic essays, and film I have focused on present narrative and therefore identity as excessive in that something is always left over. This view of identity is what I would like to term gothic identity. Gothic identity stages identity as an effect of doubling and multiple voicing, producing a superimposed identity, rather than a discrete one. As the century progressed, this gothic identity became consolidated in the photograph and in film where the image is predicated on the shadow or the specter. Technology through the apparatus shows the disjunction between the self and its representation. This is an important point, because it demonstrates the ambivalence surrounding masculine and feminine gender positions that the Victorians worked so hard to keep separate. The self is never coextensive with its representation because representation is an effect of the social.

Gothic identity begins with *Frankenstein* where identity is not one but many, stitched onto the body of the creature. Identity is not fixed or closed but takes as its image the labyrinth in gothic fiction. Identity is an effect of entanglement forecasting the social as an effect of the past returning to haunt the present. Thus, identity is one of the returns from the dead. This identity in its multiplicity calls into question one way to read identity. A reproduced identity or a tampered with identity suggests that the original can be manipulated. The spectral demonstrates that identity can never be fixed—there is always a residue.

The gothic in Victorian fiction is concerned with identity, and this excessive identity that is buried and returns sees itself mirrored in the multiplot novel that reproduces the contagion of identity in the contagion of story. Narratives proliferate out of control. The tortuous story lines in the Victorian novel suggest multiple retellings. For what is the multiplot novel other than the reproduced residue of story? The ghost returns because it is in love with narration and life. In this way, we can posit a salutatory effect of the ghost speaking in these novels. The ghost speaks in another voice; it refuses to stop narrating. In effect, it suggests that stories are never done; there will always be someone or something to come back and begin narrating again.

NOTES

INTRODUCTION

1. See Frederic Jameson for an explanation of the connection between time and subjectivity in the postmodern world. He maintains: "[P]ersonal identity is itself the effect of a certain temporal unification of past and future with the present before me; . . . such active temporal unification is itself a function of language, or better still of the sentence, as it moves along its hermeneutic circle through time. If we are unable to unify the past, present and future of the sentence, then we are similarly unable to unify the past, present and future of our own biographical experience or psychic life" (72).

2. See, for example, Kenneth W. Graham, Ed. *Gothic Fictions: Prohibition/Transgression*; George E. Haggerty, *Gothic Fiction/Gothic Form*; Clive Bloom, Ed. *Gothic Horror: A Reader's Guide From Poe to King and Beyond*; Jerome Cohen, *Monster Theory: Reading Culture*; David Punter and Glennis Byron, *The Gothic*; Ruth Robbins and Julian Wolfreys, Eds. *Victorian Gothic: Literary and Cultural Manifestations in the Nineteenth Century*; Julian Wolfreys, *Victorian Hauntings: Spectrality, Gothic, the Uncanny, and Literature*; Terry Castle, *The Female Thermometer: Eighteenth Century Culture and the Invention of the Uncanny*; Vijay Mishra, *The Gothic Sublime*; Andrew Smith, *Gothic Radicalism: Literature, Philosophy and Psychoanalysis in the Nineteenth Century*; and Elizabeth R. Napier, *The Failure of Gothic: Problems of Disjunction in Eighteenth Century Literary Form*.

1 SURVIVAL OF THE UNFITTEST: COLLINS'S *THE HAUNTED HOTEL* AND *THE WOMAN IN WHITE*

1. Eve Kosofsky Sedgwick makes this point: "Of all the Gothic conventions dealing with the sudden, mysterious, seemingly arbitrary but massive inaccessibility of those things that should normally be most accessible, the difficulty the story has in getting itself told is of the most obvious structural significance" (13).

2. Tamar Heller argues: "Through the recurrent image of buried writing Collins represents social and textual marginality, as well as a subversiveness lurking beneath the surface of convention" (1). Heller does not discuss *The Haunted Hotel* in reference to her argument.

3. Lyn Pykett reports: "In a recent (1992) brief review of critical work on Collins in the last twenty years, Peter Thorns suggested that much of it 'locates Collins's merit as a novelist' not in 'the very conspicuous and thrilling surfaces of his stories,' but 'in his subtexts' " (2).

4. See D. A. Miller who posits: "Characters who rely on utterly unlegal standards of evidence like intuition, coincidence, and literary connotation get closer to what will eventually be revealed as truth" ("Cage" 114).

5. Ann Cvetkovich explains Hartright's secrets in terms of his class accession. She argues: "We might suspect that Walter Hartright, the writer of the Preamble, is hiding more than just his narrative's sensational qualities" (110). She goes on to suggest that his secret involves "his accession to patriarchal power and property, making it possible for him to marry her [Laura] despite their class difference" (111). My argument differs from hers in that I am claiming the secrets in the text revolve around woman's identity that Hartright fails to detect.

6. Jenny Bourne Taylor views Laura as "a proper 'self-made' woman who has really been made by others in the theatre of a simulated family" (130).

7. A. D. Hutter maintains: "Detectives are . . . inevitably concerned with the problem of knowledge, a problem only intensified by the urban upheaval of the world in which they move, by the disorder, the multiplicity of detail, the constant impinging presence of other people, other accounts, other viewpoints" (178).

8. Tzvetan Todorov makes this point in *The Poetics of Prose* (73–76).

9. Patrick Brantlinger posits: "If the content of the sensation novel represented a challenge to bourgeois morality, one way that challenge shows up structurally is in the undermining of the narrator's credibility" (43).

10. Mark M. Hennelly, Jr. argues that Hartright achieves self-discovery by linking ratiocination with his "heart-felt love" (94). He further claims: "Often the figure bent on detection assumes the role of an archetypal quester attempting to resolve the primordial conflict between order and chaos, to discover the golden key" (92). Finally, he asserts that "Hartright ultimately detects the sensations of real love under his discarded courtly love pose" (102). My argument centers on Hartright's lack of self-awareness and his resulting inability to read the identities of Laura and Anne.

11. Hennelly points to the incongruity of Hartright's claim. "This description of the novel as an objective and rational document seems oddly inaccurate, given that *The Woman in White* was one of the most famous sensation novels, noted for its capacity to create suspense and excitement" (110).

12. D. A. Miller argues that "the detective story is invariably the story of a power-play" ("Roman" 198).

13. For a differing view, see Winifred Hughes who argues that in Collins's novels "victory belongs to rationality, defeat to the failure of reason"(142).

14. For a differing reading of the detective and his or her ability to restore order to mystery, see Patrick Brantlinger who claims: "The mysteries in *Lady Audley's Secret, Uncle Silas, The Woman in White,* and *The Moonstone* . . . function like those in later mystery novels and do not connect with anything outside themselves. In each case, though much that is violent and terrifying happens along the way, the mystery turns out to be soluble, unlike the larger mysteries raised by *Bleak House* and *Our Mutual Friend.* The worst evils that can be perpetrated by individuals are unmasked, but the instant of their revelation is usually also the instant of their exorcism. The paradox is that sensation novels—and mystery novels after them—conclude in ways that liquidate mystery: they are not finally mysterious at all. The insoluble is reduced to the soluble" (47–48). Clearly, I disagree with Brantlinger, in that I claim that the mystery of woman's identity is never solved in *The Woman in White.*

15. Hutter explains the connection between detective fiction and dreams and play. "Detective fiction intensifies a quality present in dreaming, in literary experience, and indeed in all those activities our culture defines as 'play' by taking as both its form and its subject a conflict between mystery and unifying solution" (192).

16. Jonathan Loesberg claims that the "sensation novel sees the problem [of women's identity] in its legal and class aspects rather than in its psychological aspect" (117). I would argue that Collins's point here is to suggest that the legal and class aspect precludes a psychological rendering of woman by the male detective. A psychological reading, therefore, does exist, and we find it located in the gothic plot, as I argue.

17. Cvetkovich argues concerning Walter Hartright: "Physical sensations that threaten to overwhelm the perceiver must be transformed into mysteries to be explained" (119).

18. Brantlinger explains the connection between the detective and criminal. "The equivocations and silences of Collins's narrative personae suggest these transformations of metaphysical-religious knowledge into the solution of a crime puzzle and of the omniscient narrator into a collaborator with his disreputable character doubles, the criminal and the detective" (46).

19. In this connection, see W. H. Auden's "The Guilty Vicarage" where he maintains that the ritual nature of detective fiction entails the detective as priest who performs an exorcism.

20. The sensation novel as Collins saw it was as Walter M. Kendrick points out "potentially subversive of the belief that fiction is and must be mimetic" (73).

21. Brantlinger posits: "In the sensation novel, the Gothic is brought up to date and so mixed with the conventions of realism as to make its events seem possible if not exactly probable" (37).

22. See D. A. Miller who argues: "The novel's 'primal scene,' which it obsessively repeats and remembers . . . as though this were the trauma

it needed to work through, rehearses the 'origins' of male nervousness in female contagion—strictly, in the woman's touch" ("Cage" 110).

23. Jonathan Loesberg argues that in sensation fiction "the constant concern [is] with identity and its loss" (117).

24. See Elisabeth Bronfen's *Over Her Dead Body: Death, femininity and the aesthetic.*

25. Tamar Heller explains: "The colonization of Marian's voice is particularly villainous, but it is only a more obvious version of Hartright's own strategy for containing Marian's narrative energy" (134).

26. Hutter claims: "What saves Poe and Conan Doyle from sterility is not that, like Collins, they came first, but that the relentlessly logical process of ratiocination is thrown into question by a deeper irrationality" (176).

2   PHANTASMAGORICAL NARRATION IN *BLEAK HOUSE*

1. J. Hillis Miller writes: "The novel is a complex fabric of recurrences. Characters, scenes, themes and metaphors return in proliferating resemblances" (62).

2. Numerous commentators have debated the effect of the two narrative voices in *Bleak House*. Virginia Blain argues that the two narrative voices reproduce the "vexed question of the division between the sexes near the heart of the novel's meaning" (71), whereas Audrey Jaffe claims that "the idea of omniscience as all-knowing is . . . undermined by Esther's narrative, which, as supplement, to use Derrida's term, reveals a lack in what is supposed to be complete" (163–164). Katherine Cummings suggests: "Structurally speaking, *Bleak House* is a twin narrative. It faces in two directions (past and present); it incorporates two worlds (private and public); and it is told in two voices, one of which is serious, often pained, mimetic or realistic, the other parodic, playful, and deliberately artificial. Their mixture produces uncanny and undecidable effects" (183). Cynthia Northcutt Malone argues that the two narratives produce "the division that always operates within the 'I.' " (109). D. A. Miller maintains that the "two separate systems of narration . . . are unequal and unrelated" ("Discipline in Different Voices" 140). As my argument makes clear, I am not advocating for a division between the two narrators, but rather for a crossing over and a narrative facing of one another, which as I argue produces terror and horror.

3. Christine Van Boheemen-Saaf writes: "From the very beginning . . . Esther's 'self' is split into two halves, one 'buried' and unmentionable, one obsessively concerned with conformity to patriarchal views of feminine identity" (55).

4. Eve Kosofsky Sedgwick writes of " 'live burial' as a structural name for the Gothic salience of 'within' " (5).

5. Eve Kosofsky Sedgwick, in this vein, argues that "The immobilizing and costly struggle, in the hysteric, to express graphically through her bodily hieroglyphic what cannot come into existence as narrative, resembles in this labor of the paranoid subject to forestall being overtaken by the feared/desired other, by himself mimetically reproducing the perceived or projected desire/threat of the other in a temporally paralyzed form" (vi).

3 SHADOWING THE DEAD: FIRST PERSON NARRATION IN OUR MUTUAL FRIEND

1. All quotations are from the 1985 edition.

2. Patrick O'Donnell explains "Dickens' growing sense that identity is a linguistic effect or a figure of speech, a represented form of indeterminacy that reveals its foundation in the 'unrepresentable' " (248).

3. In the 1997 introduction to the novel, Adrian Poole writes: "Most of the life in Dickens's last completed novel tends to a state of suspended animation. Nothing seems certainly dead nor entirely alive" (ix).

4. O'Donnell argues that "Dickens is compelled to give up for good the 'private self'—that idealized and narcissistic embodiment of knowledge, control, and desire—for a version of the 'public self,' split up or spread amongst the novel's characters" (248).

5. Nicholas Royle writes: "This novel is about living on, not as the triumph of continuing to live but as a movement of return or haunting which comes back" (49).

6. See O'Donnell who argues that "In Dickens' last-completed novel identity has become (to use Bakhtin's terminology) 'pluralized' to the extent that Dickens' most successful ventriloquistic spectacle is a most public abandonment of the private, coherent 'self,' though the novel retains skeletal traces of the attempt to preserve an older, more masterful version of identity" (248). I argue, however, that the multiplot novel completely replaces the private, coherent self.

7. Nicholas Royle contends that "Our Mutual Friend stages the dispersal of fictional realism" (48).

8. Peter Garrett claims that one of the reasons why the multiplot novel became so important in the period from the late 1840s to the late 1870s was to embody inclusiveness. "To multiply plots is to divide the fictional world, to disrupt the continuity of each line in order to shift from one to another, to disperse the reader's attention" (1). He also writes of the multiplot novel's dialogism, of the "continuing play of perspectives that resists monological resolution" (94).

9. See Lacan who argues that "man cannot aim at being whole . . . while ever the play of displacement and condensation to which he is doomed in the exercise of his functions marks his relation as a subject to a signifier"

(*Écrits* 287). See also D. A. Miller who argues that "closure, though it implies resolution, never really resolves the dilemmas raised by the narratable" (*Narrative and its Discontents* 267).

10. We know that Dickens took long walks through the streets of London religiously and that he got many of his ideas from observing city life.

11. In a similar vein, see John Kucich who writes that Dickens's style is an "expression of textual euphoria, the verbal trace of an energy that cannot be named in terms of what it represents" (170).

12. For various readings of John Harmon's narration see Carol Hanbery MacKay who argues that "John Harmon's soliloquy takes on the dimensions of an epic quest, a Romantic quest for imaginative freedom modified by a Victorian's 'socializing vision' " (258). Albert Hutter focuses on dismemberment's ability to turn into "patterns of detecting, articulating, and resurrecting" (158) in Harmon's narration. My argument differs from theirs in that I postulate that imaginative freedom and articulation are made impossible by the disarticulation embodied in Harmon's story.

13. In this connection, see Lacan who postulates that "the ego of the subject" cannot be "identical with the presence that is speaking to you" (*Écrits* 90).

14. See, for example, Carol Hanbery MacKay who writes: "Readers and critics alike have found this exposition problematic, usually seeing its length and form as implausible and awkward" (255). Garrett Stewart refers to Harmon's interior monologue as "a long and improbable monologue" (192).

15. Albert Hutter in his generally excellent analysis of dismemberment and articulation in *Our Mutual Friend* writes of the Victorian "period's fascination with bringing the dead back to life" (149). As my argument makes clear I focus on representation's problem of rendering the animate inanimate through language.

16. Various critics argue that Harmon finds himself through narrative. See, for example, Robert Keily who posits a correlation between authorship and identity when he articulates: "He [Harmon] cannot find himself without assuming authorship of his own life and yet he fears that in trying, he may trace a design that reveals him as a mirror image of the dreaded 'venerable parent' " (275). Carol Hanbery MacKay postulates: "This unique form [Harmon's soliloquy] takes the romance quest through the life-and-death wasteland of self-isolation towards an identity revitalized, because it is community shared" (258). Finally, Albert Hutter argues that "like Venus, Harmon patiently and gradually pieces together the events of his own life and the lives of those around him until he can form a more satisfying whole" (157). I argue, however, that this wholeness is an impossibility. The piecing together that Hutter writes of is never realized in the guise of self-articulation.

4 SHOPPING FOR AN "I":
ZOLA'S *THE LADIES' PARADISE*
AND THE SPECTACLE OF IDENTITY

1. Peter Brooks argues that "Mouret's establishment figures a culture in which a woman, through the relay of the economy, commercial and erotic, established by man, is forced to accept herself as other; she is foreclosed from her own desire, never in full possession of her own body" (*Body Work* 154); while Rachel Bowlby proposes that Mouret's project of commercial seduction effects a "colonization of the mind designed to produce new areas of need and desire" (70).

2. For studies describing the potential destabilizing effects of the department store, see David Chaney who posits that "The real fear [of the department store] was that circumstances gave women an effective choice which ran counter to conventional contemporary expectations about female submissiveness" (29). Rita Felski similarly postulates that "if consumer culture simply reinforced women's objectified and powerless status, it becomes difficult to understand why the phenomenon was attacked so vehemently as a threat to men's traditional authority over women" (66).

3. See David Chaney who posits: "Panoramic perception organises a jumble of impressions through a synoptic perspective, the sensations may be blurred and discontinuous but they are held together by our admiration for the spectacle and by our gratification with the service rendered" (27).

4. Joseph Litvak in his work on the nineteenth century and theatricality argues: "[I]f the self is treated . . . as not just a text but a contingent cluster of theatrical roles, then it becomes possible to make a spectacle of the impervious, domestic, sexual, and aesthetic ideologies for which, and in which, it is bound (xii), thus in a sense turning the look back on the spectacle itself.

5. See Felski who writes that the "crowd scenes of Zola's novel, [are] where the seething mass of female shoppers assumes a sinister, even demonic, quality" (73).

6. Barbara Vinken maintains that "Zola's naturalism . . . shows itself unable to overcome its fetishistic predicament" (247).

7. Kaja Silverman postulates: "The image of a woman in front of the mirror playing to both the male gaze and her own, has become a familiar metaphor of sexual oppression" (183).

8. Stephen Heath writes that "Men and women may be differentiated on the basis of biological sex but that differentiation is always a position in representation . . . the individual is a sexed being in representation, always represented by his or her sexuality" (109).

9. Drucilla Cornell makes a similar point: "[W]e cannot know once and for all who or what she is, because the fictions in which we confront Her always carry within the possibility of multiple interpretations, and

there is no outside referent, such as nature or biology, in which the process of interpretation comes to an end" (88).

10. See Freud, "Three Essays on The Theory of Sexuality."

11. See Judith Butler who writes of the "ungrieved and ungrievable loss in the formation of what we might call the gendered character of the ego" (136). Diana Fuss in *Identification Papers* argues similarly that "All identification begins in an experience of traumatic loss and in the subject's tentative attempts to manage this loss" (38).

12. Diana Fuss in "Homospectatorial Fashion Photography" has argued that "The images by fashion photography operate both ways: as defenses (or screens) against the early interruption of the homosexual-maternal continuum, but also more importantly as defenses against the pain that this psychical rupture continues to inflict on the adult subject" (734).

13. See Mitchell and Rose, who argue that "the absolute Otherness of the woman . . . serves to secure for the man his own self-knowledge and truth" (50).

14. Lacan's assertion that woman does not exist as translated by Mitchell and Rose means "that phallic sexuality assigns her to a position of fantasy" (137).

15. In a similar vein, Cora Kaplan argues that fantasy is "a scenario in which the shifting place of the subject is a characteristic part of the activity" (151).

5   She's Not There: *Vertigo* and the Ghostly Feminine

1. See a concomitant view to Barthes in Noel Carroll who maintains: "Suspense arises when a well-structured question—with neatly opposed alternatives—emerges from the narrative and calls forth an answering scene" (100).

2. See Bellour who argues that "Hitchcock himself has been extremely conscious of this crisscrossing effect between his vision (the vision of the mise en scène) and that of the different characters, that he's chosen to appear within his films to mark ironically by a kind of initial a certain place which is precisely the place of the enunciator" (98).

3. See Bellour who argues: "Classical American cinema is founded on a systematicity which operates very precisely at the expense of the woman . . . by determining her image, her images, in relation to the desire of the masculine subject who thus defines himself through this determination" (97).

4. Tania Modleski maintains that "despite all his attempts to gain control over Madeleine, Scottie will feel himself repeatedly thrown back into an identification, a mirroring relationship, with her and her desires, will be unable to master the woman the way Galvin Elster and

Carlotta's paramour are able to do" (92). My argument differs from Modelski's in that I combine narrative displacement with gender identification.

5. Shoshana Felman posits that woman is that which cannot be seen given the tenets of realism when she writes: "realism is inherently unable to see [her]" (6).

6. Lawrence Shaffer writes: "*Vertigo* haunts us because, more poignantly than any other film, it shows how 'looks' haunt our lives—lives that are kaleidoscopes of superimposed slides, through which we fall, wander, lose ourselves" (385).

7. See Denis De Rougement's study of the Tristan myth in *Love and the Western World*, where he asserts that "Love and death, a fatal love, is aligned with the sweetest songs" (15).

8. Ann West argues: "As Todorov suggests, the love of someone in the form of a statue or painting, as for a place of historical meaning or a shrine, represents a kind of love of the dead or necrophilia, which is a common theme of the fantastic" (165).

9. See, for example, Mulvey who argues "Her [Judy's] exhibitionism, her masochism, make her an ideal passive counterpart to Scottie's active sadistic voyeurism" (37). Bellour in a similar vein states: "I think that a woman can love, accept and give a positive value to these films only from her own masochism" (97).

10. See Jean LaPlanche who states that: "In *Beyond the Pleasure Principle*, he [Freud] attributes, as a tendency towards death, a repetition compulsion whose major piece of supporting evidence is, however, the psychoanalytic phenomenon par excellence: transference" (122).

11. See Eve Kosofsky Sedgwick's important work on veils in *The Coherence of Gothic Conventions* where she argues that "the veil is the locus of the substitution of one person for another" (149).

6 GRAVE NARRATIONS: DICKENS'S LATER WRITINGS

1. See *The Dialogic Imagination* where Bakhtin writes: "This double-voicedness in prose is prefigured in language itself (in authentic metaphors, as well as in myth), in language as a social phenomenon that is becoming in history, socially stratified and weathered in the process of becoming" (326).

2. In this connection, see Peter Brooks's *Reading for the Plot* where he relates: "As Sartre argued, autobiographical narration must necessarily be 'obituary' " (114).

3. Deborah A. Thomas relates that "in his short fiction between *A Tale of Two Cities* and *Great Expectations*, Dickens seems to have been especially preoccupied with the idea of multiple images of the same person" (86–87).

4. See, for example, Jeremy Tambling who maintains: "*Great Expectations* certainly recognizes itself to be about the creation of identities, imposed from higher to lower, from oppressor to oppressed" (18).

5. See, for example, Philip Collins, *Dickens and Crime* and Jeremy Tambling, "Prison-Bound: Dickens and Foucault."

6. *Frankenstein* begins the inextricable association of life with death when Victor creates a creature from dead body parts. Also, his narrative marries his obsession with creation to his obsession with self-destruction.

7. See, for example, Gillian Beer, *Darwin's Plots: Evolutionary Narrative in Darwin, George Eliot and Nineteenth-Century Fiction.*

8. See Peter Brooks's *The Melodramatic Imagination* where he asserts that "Melodrama becomes the principal mode for uncovering, demonstrating, and making operative the essential moral universe in a post-sacred era" (15).

9. See Peter Brooks's *Reading for the Plot* where he argues that the narrative is characterized by repression. "The Expectations will in fact only mask further the problem of the repressed plots" (117).

10. Peter Brooks argues in *Reading for the Plot*: "It is with the image of a life bereft of plot, of movement and desire, that the novel most appropriately leaves us" (138). I argue, however, that the novel through the double ending keeps wishing to formulate new plots.

11. In a letter to Daniel Maclisse, Dickens wrote about his acting the role of Wardour in *The Frozen Deep*, "The interest of such a character [Wardour] to me is that it enables me, as it were, *to write a book in company* instead of my own solitary room, and to feel its effect coming freshly back upon me from the reader" (quoted in Brannan 84).

12. In this connection, see Hayden White, who argues that "narrative strains to produce the effect of having filled in all the gaps, to put an image of continuity, coherency, and meaning in place of the fantasies of emptiness, need, and frustrated desire that inhabit our nightmares about the disruptive power of time" (11).

13. At this time, Dickens separated from his wife. The novel's obsession with secrets and mysteries mirrors Dickens's own life and his own fraught relationship with his wife. We know that sensation fiction emerged in part through the relaxing of the divorce laws, most notably the Matrimonial Causes Act of 1857 that made divorce a bit easier to obtain. Thus, through the publication of the divorce proceedings, people had access to familial accounts of discord and rupture.

14. Homelessness is a recurring theme in almost all of Dickens's novels.

15. The imaginative wandering that Dickens employs in the journalistic writing is very much connected to the apprehension of life as a series of pictures, which traveling by railroad produced.

16. See Michael Hollington's "Dickens the Flâneur," where he writes: "The flâneur is a kind of hero of modern civilisation, going amongst the crowds to withstand the assaults of successive, disparate, infinite

visual stimuli, mediating and imaginatively transforming mundanities into 'secular illuminations' "(82).

17. Baudelaire writes of the *flaneur*: "Thus the lover of universal life moves into the crowd as though into an enormous reservoir of electricity. He, the lover of life, may also be compared to a mirror as vast as this crowd; to a kaleidoscope endowed with consciousness, which with every one of its movements presents a pattern of life, in all of its multiplicity, and the flowing grace of all the elements that go to compose life. It is an ego athirst for the non-ego, and reflecting it at every moment in energies, more vivid than life itself, always inconstant and fleeting" (400).

18. For connections between Dickens and the cinema, see D. W. Griffith who maintained: "I invented that idea (cross-cutting from one scene to another to heighten tension) . . . but it was not by any means my own. I discovered it in the work of Dickens" (*New York Globe*, May 2, 1922). Also Graham Petrie explains that "Eisenstein's famous essay 'Dickens, Griffith and the Film Today' showed in fascinating detail how Dickens had evolved a system of structuring his novels by means of editing and of presenting action through a series of rapidly shifting angles and viewpoints that the Russian director was to use as a basis for his own montage techniques" (187).

19. Michael Hollington tells us that "George Henry Lewes spoke of his [Dickens's] imagination as approaching to hallucination" (85).

20. Ned Lukacher maintains: "In the culture of psychoanalysis, Dickens has always been the figure of both its prehistory and its future" (336).

21. Fred Kaplan maintains regarding Dickens that the "dream state was his domain, permeating his fiction and non-fiction . . . [and became] a metaphor for his exploration of what he considered the most meaningful aspects of human consciousness and the human predicament" (212).

22. John Forster writes of Dickens's "profound attraction of repulsion" (Vol. 1, 14).

23. In writing of the *flaneur*, Baudelaire explains: "The crowd is his domain, just as the air is the bird's, and the water that of the fish. His passion and his profession is to merge with the crowd. For the perfect idler, for the passionate observer it becomes an immense source of enjoyment to establish his dwelling in the throng, in the ebb and flow, the bustle, the fleeting and the infinite" (399).

24. In his introduction to *The Mystery of Edwin Drood*, Peter Ackroyd relates: "It seems possible that Dickens knew that this book, so concerned with death and disappearance, would be his own final work. In some sense he identified the book with death itself, and may have been loath to complete it" (xiii).

WORKS CITED

Ackroyd, Peter. *Dickens*. London: Sinclair Stevenson, 1990.

Adams, Parveen. "Per Osc[cillation]." *Male Trouble*. Eds. Constance Penley and Sharon Willis. Minneapolis: University of Minnesota Press, 1993. 3–25.

The Arabian Nights: Tales from a Thousand and One Nights. Trans. Richard Burton. New York: Modern Library, 2001.

Auden, W. H. "The Guilty Vicarage." *The Dyer's Hand and Other Essays*. New York: Random House, 1962. 146–158.

Bakhtin, M. M. *The Dialogic Imagination*. Trans. Caryl Emerson and Michael Holquist. Austin: University of Texas Press, 1981.

Barthes, Roland. "Delay and the Hermeneutic Sentence." *The Poetics of Murder*. Eds. Glenn W. Most and William W. Stowe. New York: Harcourt Brace Jovanovich, 1983. 118–121.

Baudelaire, Charles. "The Painter of Modern Life." *Selected Writings on Art and Literature*. Trans. P. E. Charvet. New York: Penguin, 1972. 390–435.

Beer, Gillian. *Darwin's Plots: Evolutionary Narrative in Darwin, George Eliot and Nineteenth-Century Fiction*. Cambridge: Cambridge University Press, 2000.

Bergstrom, Janet. "Alternation, Segmentation, Hypnosis: Interview with Raymond Bellour." *Camera Obscura* 3–4 (Summer 1979): 71–103.

The Birds. Dir. Alfred Hitchcock, Universal, 1963.

Black Narcissus. Dir. Michael Powell and Emeric Pressburger, Universal, 1947.

Blain, Virginia. "Double Vision and the Double Standard in *Bleak House*: A Feminist Perspective." *Bleak House: Charles Dickens*. Ed. Jeremy Tambling. New York: St. Martin's Press, 1998. 65–86.

Bloom, Clive, Ed. *Gothic Horror: A Reader's Guide From Poe to King and Beyond*. New York: St. Martin's Press, 1998.

Botting, Fred. *Gothic*. New York and London: Routledge, 1996.

Bowlby, Rachel. *Just Looking: Consumer Culture in Dreiser, Gissing and Zola*. New York: Methuen, 1985.

Brannan, R. L., Ed. *Under the Management of Mr. Charles Dickens: His Production of the Frozen Deep*. Ithaca: Cornell University Press, 1988.

Brantlinger, Patrick. "What is 'Sensational' about the 'Sensation Novel' "? *Wilkie Collins: Contemporary Critical Essays*. Ed. Lyn Pykett. London: Macmillan, 1998. 30–57.

Bronfen, Elisabeth. *Over Her Dead Body: Death, femininity and the aesthetic*. New York: Routledge, 1992.

Brontë, Charlotte. *Villette*. Oxford: Oxford University Press, 1998.

Brooks, Peter. *Reading for the Plot: Design and Intention in Narrative*. Cambridge: Harvard University Press, 1984.

Brooks, Peter. *Body Work: Objects of Desire in Modern Narrative*. Cambridge: Harvard University Press, 1993.

Brooks, Peter. *The Melodramatic Imagination: Balzac, Henry James, Melodrama, and the Mode of Excess*. New Haven: Yale University Press, 1976 and 1995.

Butler, Judith. *The Psychic Life of Power: Theories in Subjection*: Stanford: Stanford University Press, 1997.

Carroll, Noel. *Theorizing the Moving Image*. Cambridge: Cambridge University Press, 1996.

Castle, Terry. *The Female Thermometer: Eighteenth Century Culture and the Invention of the Uncanny*. Oxford: Oxford University Press, 1985.

Castle, Terry. "Phantasmagoria and the Metaphorics of Modern Reverie." *The Horror Reader*. Ed. Ken Gelder. Routledge: London, 2000. 29–46.

Chaney, David. "The Department Store as a Cultural Form." *Theory, Culture and Society* 1–3 (1983): 22–31.

Cohen, Jeffrey Jerome. *Monster Theory: Reading Culture*. Minneapolis: University of Minnesota Press, 1996.

Coleridge, Samuel Taylor. "The Rime of the Ancient Mariner." *The Portable Coleridge*. Penguin: New York, 1983.

Collins, Philip. *Dickens and Crime*. Bloomington: Indiana University Press, 1968.

Collins, Wilkie. *The Haunted Hotel*. Oxford: Oxford University Press, 1999.

Collins, Wilkie. *The Law and the Lady*. Oxford: Oxford University Press, 1999.

Collins, Wilkie. *The Woman in White*. London: Penguin, 1999.

Cornell, Drucilla. *Transformations*. New York: Routledge, 1993.

Crosby, Christina. *The Ends of History: Victorians and 'the woman question.'* London: Routledge, 1991.

Cummings, Katherine. "Re-reading *Bleak House*: The Chronicle of a 'Little Body' and its Perverse Defense." *Bleak House: Charles Dickens*. Ed. Jeremy Tambling. New York: St. Martin's Press, 1998. 183–204.

Cvetkovich, Ann. "Ghostlier Determinations: The Economy of Sensation and *The Woman in White*." *Wilkie Collins: Contemporary Critical Essays*. Ed. Lyn Pykett. London: Macmillan, 1998. 109–135.

Dacre, Charlotte. *Zofloya*. Peterborough: Broadview, 1997.

Darwin, Charles. *On the Origin of Species*. Cambridge: Harvard University Press, 1964.

De Man, Paul. "Autobiography as De-facement." *The Rhetoric of Romanticism*. New York: Columbia University Press, 1984.

De Rougemont, Denis. *Love in the Western World*. Trans. Montgomery Belgion. New York: Pantheon, 1956.

Dickens, Charles. *Dombey and Son*. London: Penguin, 1970.

Dickens, Charles. *The Letters of Charles Dickens, Volume 4, 1844–1846*. Ed. Kathleen Tillotson. Oxford: Clarendon Press, 1977.

Dickens, Charles. *Our Mutual Friend*. London: Penguin, 1985.

Dickens, Charles. *Bleak House*. London: Mandarin, 1991.

Dickens, Charles. *David Copperfield*. London: Penguin, 1996.

Dickens, Charles. *Great Expectations*. London: Penguin, 1996.

Dickens, Charles. *Our Mutual Friend*. Introduction, Adrian Poole. London: Penguin, 1997.

Dickens, Charles. "The Lazy Tour of Two Idle Apprentices." *The Dent Uniform Edition of Dickens' Journalism, Volume 3: "Gone Astray" and other Papers from Household Words*. Ed. Michael Slater. London: Dent, 1998.

Dickens, Charles. *A Tale of Two Cities*. New York: Oxford University Press, 1998.

Dickens, Charles. *Oliver Twist*. Oxford: Oxford University Press, 1999.

Dickens, Charles. "The Uncommerical Traveller." *The Dent Uniform Edition of Dickens' Journalism, Volume 4: The Uncommerical Traveller and Other Papers 1859–70*. Ed. John Drew and Michael Slater. London: Dent, 2000.

Dickens, Charles. *The Mystery of Edwin Drood*. New York: Alfred A. Knopf, 2004.

Doane, Mary Ann. "Woman's Stake: Filming the Female Body." *Feminism and Film Theory*. Ed. Constance Penley. New York: Routledge, 1988. 216–228.

Felman, Shoshana. "Women and Madness: The Critical Phallacy." *Diacritics* 5 (Winter 1975): 2–10.

Felski, Rita. *The Gender of Modernity*. Cambridge: Harvard University Press, 1995.

Forster, John. *The Life of Charles Dickens*. London: Chapman and Hall, 1872–1874.

Foucault, Michel. *Madness and Civilization*. New York: Vintage, 1988.

Freud, Sigmund. "Three Essays on the Theory of Sexuality." *The Standard Edition of the Complete Psychological Works, Vol. 7*. Trans. James Strachey. London: The Hogarth Press, 1953. 123–243.

Freud, Sigmund. "Five Lectures on Psycho-analysis." *The Standard Edition of the Complete Psychological Works, Vol. 11*. Trans. James Strachey. London: The Hogarth Press, 1953. 9–55.

Freud, Sigmund. "The Moses of Michaelangelo." *The Standard Edition of the Complete Psychological Works, Vol. 13*. Trans. James Strachey. London: The Hogarth Press, 1953. 211–236.

Freud, Sigmund. "The Uncanny." *The Standard Edition of the Complete Psychological Works, Vol. 17*. Trans. James Strachey. London: The Hogarth Press, 1953. 219–252.

Freud, Sigmund. *Beyond the Pleasure Principle*. Trans. James Strachey. New York: W. W. Norton, 1961.

Freud, Sigmund. *The Interpretation of Dreams*. Trans. James Strachey. New York: Avon, 1965.

Fuss, Diana. "Homospectatorial Fashion Photography." *Critical Inquiry* 18.4 (Summer 1992): 713–737.

Fuss, Diana. *Identification Papers*. New York: Routledge, 1995.

Garrett, Peter. *The Victorian Multiplot Novel: Studies in Dialogical Form.* New Haven: Yale University Press, 1979.

Graham, Kenneth W., Ed. *Gothic Fictions: Prohibition/Transgression.* New York: AMS Press, 1989.

Griffith, D. W. *New York Globe*, May 2, 1922.

Grosz, Elizabeth. *Jacques Lacan: A Feminist Introduction.* London: Routledge, 1990.

Haggerty, George E. *Gothic Fiction/Gothic Form.* University Park: Penn State University Press, 1989.

Heath, Stephen. "Difference." *Screen* 19.3 (1978): 51–112.

Heller, Tamar. *Dead Secrets: Wilkie Collins and the Female Gothic.* New Haven: Yale University Press, 1992.

Hennelly, Mark M., Jr. "Reading Detection in *The Woman in White.*" *Wilkie Collins: Contemporary Critical Essays.* Ed. Lyn Pykett. London: Macmillan, 1998. 88–108.

Hoffmann, E. T. A. "The Sandman." *Tales of Hoffmann.* Trans. R. J. Hollingdale. London: Penguin, 1982. 85–125.

Hollander, Anne. *Seeing Through Clothes.* New York: The Viking Press, 1978.

Hollington, Michael. "Dickens the Flâneur." *The Dickensian* 77 (1977): 71–87.

Hughes, Winifred. *The Maniac in the Cellar: Sensation Novels of the 1860s.* Princeton: Princeton University Press, 1980.

Hutter, Albert. "Dismemberment and Articulation in *Our Mutual Friend.*" *Dickens Studies Annual: Essays on Victorian Fiction* 11 (1983): 135–175.

Hutter, A. D. "Dreams, Transformations and Literature: The Implications of Detective Fiction." *Wilkie Collins: Contemporary Critical Essays.* Ed. Lyn Pykett. London: Macmillan, 1998. 175–196.

Jaffe, Audrey. "*David Copperfield* and *Bleak House*: On Dividing the Responsibility of Knowing." *Bleak House: Charles Dickens.* Ed. Jeremy Tambling. New York: St. Martin's Press, 1998. 163–182.

James, P. D. *Death of an Expert Witness.* New York: Charles Scribner's Sons, 1977.

Jameson, Frederic. "Postmodernism, or the Cultural Logic of Late Capitalism." *New Left Review* 146 (July–August 1984): 53–92.

Kaplan, Cora. "The Thorn Birds: Fiction, Fantasy, Femininity." *Formations of Fantasy.* Eds. Victor Burgin, James Donald, and Cora Kaplan. London: Methuen, 1986. 142–166.

Kaplan, Fred. *Dickens: A Biography.* New York: William Morrow, 1988.

Keats, John. *Selected Poems and Letters.* Ed. Douglas Bush. Boston: Houghton Mifflin, 1959.

Keily, Robert. "Plotting and Scheming: The Design of Design in *Our Mutual Friend.*" *Dickens Studies Annual: Essays on Victorian Fiction* 12 (1983): 267–283.

Kendrick, Walter M. "The Sensationalism of *The Woman in White.*" *Wilkie Collins: Contemporary Critical Essays.* Ed. Lyn Pykett. London: Macmillan, 1998. 70–87.

Kucich, John. "Dickens' Fantastic Rhetoric: The Semantics of Reality and Unreality in *Our Mutual Friend*." *Dickens Studies Annual: Essays on Victorian Fiction* 14 (1985): 167–189.

Lacan, Jacques. Écrits. Trans. Alan Sheridan. New York: W. W. Norton, 1977.

Lacan, Jacques. *Four Fundamental Concepts of Psycho-analysis*. Trans. Alan Sheridan. New York: W. W. Norton, 1978.

Laplanche, Jean. *Life and Death in Psychoanalysis*. Trans. Jeffrey Mehlman. Baltimore: Johns Hopkins University Press, 1985.

Lewis, Matthew. *The Monk*. Oxford: Oxford University Press, 1998.

Litvak, Joseph. *Caught in the Act: Theatricality in the Nineteenth-Century Novel*. Berkeley: University of California Press, 1992.

Loesberg, Jonathan. "The Ideology of Narrative Form in Sensation Fiction." *Representations* 13 (Winter, 1986): 115–138.

MacKay, Carol Hanbery. "The Encapsulated Romantic: John Harmon and the Boundaries of Victorian Soliloquy." *Dickens Studies Annual: Essays in Victorian Fiction* 18 (1989): 255–276.

Malone, Cynthia Northcutt. " 'Flight and Pursuit': Fugitive Identity in *Bleak House*." *Dickens Studies Annual* 19 (1990): 107–124.

Marnie. Dir. Alfred Hitchcock, Universal, 1964.

Marx, Karl. "The Eighteenth Brumaire of Louis Bonaparte." *Selected Writings of Karl Marx*. Indianapolis: Hackett, 1994. 187–208.

Miller, D. A. *Narrative and its Discontents: Problems of Closure in the Traditional Novel*. Princeton: Princeton University Press, 1981.

Miller, D. A. "Cage aux Folles: Sensation and Gender in Wilkie Collins's *The Woman in White*." *Representations* 14 (1986): 107–136.

Miller, D. A. "Discipline in Different Voices: Bureaucracy, Police, Family, and *Bleak House*." Ed. Steven Connor. *Charles Dickens*. London: Longman, 1996. 136–150.

Miller, D. A. "From roman policier to roman-police: Wilkie Collins's *The Moonstone*." *Wilkie Collins: Contemporary Critical Essays*. Ed. Lyn Pykett. London: Macmillan, 1998. 197–220.

Miller, J. Hillis. "Dickens's *Bleak House*." Ed. Steven Connor. *Charles Dickens*. London: Longman, 1996. 60–75.

Mishra, Vijay. *The Gothic Sublime*. Albany: State University of New York Press, 1984.

Mitchell, Juliet and Rose, Jacqueline. *Feminine Sexuality: Jacques Lacan and the école freudienne*. New York: W. W. Norton, 1982.

Modleski, Tania. *The Woman Who Knew Too Much: Hitchcock and Feminist Theory*. New York: Routledge, 1989.

Morris, David B. "Gothic Sublimity." *New Literary History* 16 (1985): 299–319.

Mulvey, Laura. "Visual Pleasure and Narrative Cinema." *Issues in Feminist Film Criticism*. Ed. Patricia Erens. Bloomington: Indiana University Press, 1990. 28–40.

Napier, Elizabeth R. *The Failure of Gothic: Problems of Disjunction in Eighteenth Century Literary Form*. Oxford: Clarendon, 1987.

O'Donnell, Patrick. " 'A Speeches of Chaff': Ventriloquy and Expression in *Our Mutual Friend.*" *Dickens Studies Annual: Essays in Victorian Fiction* 19 (1990): 247–279.

Petrie, Graham. "Dickens, Godard, and the Film Today." *The Yale Review.* Vol. LXIV, No. 2 (1975): 185–201.

Poe, Edgar Allan. "The Philosophy of Composition." *The Complete Poems and Stories of Edgar Allan Poe, Volume II.* New York: Alfred A. Knopf, 1946. 978–987.

Poe, Edgar Allan. "The Fall of the House of Usher." *The Murders in the Rue Morgue and Other Stories.* Köln: Könemann, 1995. 63–85.

Poe, Edgar Allan. "The Purloined Letter." *The Murders in the Rue Morgue and Other Stories.* Köln: Könemann, 1995. 279–301.

Psycho. Dir. Alfred Hitchcock, Paramount, 1960.

Punter, David. *The Literature of Terror.* London: Longman, 1980.

Punter, David and Glennis, Byron, Eds. *Spectral Readings: Towards a Gothic Geography.* Basingstoke: Macmillan, 1999.

Punter, David and Glennis, Byron, Eds. *The Gothic.* Oxford: Blackwell, 2004.

Pykett, Lyn, Ed. Wilkie Collins: *Contemporary Critical Essays.* Basingstoke: Macmillan, 1998.

Rear Window. Dir. Alfred Hitchcock, Paramount, 1954.

Robbins, Ruth and Wolfreys, Julian, Eds. *Victorian Gothic: Literary and Cultural Manifestations in the Nineteenth Century.* New York: Palgrave, 2000.

Royle, Nicholas. "*Our Mutual Friend.*" *Dickens Refigured: Bodies, desires and other histories.* Ed. John Schad. Manchester: Manchester University Press, 1996. 39–54.

Ruskin, John. "Of Queen's Gardens." *Sesame and Lilies. The Works of John Ruskin.* London: George Allen, 1905. 109–144.

Sedgwick, Eve Kosofsky. *The Coherence of Gothic Conventions.* New York: Methuen, 1980.

Shaffer, Lawrence. "Obsessed with *Vertigo.*" *The Massachusetts Review,* Vol. 25, No. 3 (Autumn 1984): 383–397.

Shelley, Mary. *Frankenstein.* London: Penguin, 2003.

Silverman, Kaja. "Fragments of a Fashionable Discourse." *On Fashion.* Eds. Shari Benstock and Suzanne Ferris. New Brunswick: Rutgers University Press, 1994. 183–196.

Simon, William. Lecture on *Psycho.* New York University, May 15, 2001.

Smith, Andrew. *Gothic Radicalism: Literature, Philosophy and Psychoanalysis in the Nineteenth Century.* New York: St. Martin's Press, 2000.

Sophocles. *Oedipus Rex.* Trans. Dudley Fitts and Robert Fitzgerald. New York: Harcourt, 1977.

Stevenson, Robert Louis. *Strange Case of Dr. Jekyll and Mr. Hyde.* New York: W. W. Norton, 2003.

Tambling, Jeremy. "Prison-Bound: Dickens and Foucault." *Essays in Criticism* 36 (January 1986): 11–31.

Taylor, Jenny Bourne. *In the Secret theatre of Home: Wilkie Collins, sensation narrative, and nineteenth-century psychology.* London: Routledge, 1998.

Thomas, Deborah A. "In the Meantime: Dickens's Concern with Doubling and Secret Guilt between *A Tale of Two Cities* and *Great Expectations*." *Dickens Quarterly* 3 (June 1986): 84–89.

Todorov, Tzvetan. *The Poetics of Prose*. Trans. Richard Howard. Ithaca: Cornell University Press, 1977.

Van Boheemen-Saaf, Christine. " 'The Universe Makes an Indifferent Parent': *Bleak House* and the Victorian Family Romance." *Bleak House: Charles Dickens*. Ed. Jermey Tambling. New York: St. Martin's Press, 1998. 54–64.

Vertigo. Dir. Alfred Hitchcock. Paramount, 1958.

Vinken, Barbara. "Temples of Delight: Consuming Consumption in Emile Zola's *Au bonheur des dames*." *Spectacles of Realism: Body, Gender, Genre*. Eds. Margaret Cohen and Christopher Prendergast. Minneapolis: University of Minnesota Press, 1995. 247–267.

Weiskel, Thomas. *The Romantic Sublime: Studies in the Structure and Psychology of Transcendence*. Baltimore: Johns Hopkins University Press, 1976.

West, Ann. "The Concept of the Fantastic in *Vertigo*." *Hitchcock's Rereleased Films: From Rope to Vertigo*. Ed. Walter Raubicheck and Walter Srebnick. Detroit: Wayne State University Press, 1998. 163–174.

White, Hayden. "The Value of Narrativity in the Representation of Reality." *On Narrative*. Ed. W. J. T. Mitchell. Chicago and London: The University of Chicago Press, 1981. 1–23.

Wilde, Oscar. *The Picture of Dorian Gray*. Ontario: Broadview, 1998.

Wolfreys, Julian. *Victorian Hauntings: Spectrality, Gothic, the Uncanny, and Literature*. New York: Palgrave, 2002.

Wordsworth, William. *The Prelude*. New Haven: Yale University Press, 1971.

Zola, Émile. *The Ladies' Paradise*. Berkeley: University of California Press, 1992.

INDEX

aberrant states of mind, 7
absence, 7, 125
  of narrative, as death, 27, 70,
    114, 157
Ackroyd, Peter, 134, 147, 148, 157,
  173n.24
Adams, Parveen, 99
adornment, 96, 97
aesthetics of artifice, 135–6
after writing, 1, 9, 64–7, 130, 132,
  144, 157
alienation, 134, 136–7, 143
ambiguity, 50, 79, 91, 149, 159
  about origins, 128–9
ambivalence, 49
  celebration of, 131
  feminist reading of double, 55–6
  gender and, 91, 109, 111, 160
  male encounter with female as,
    and sublime, 17
  mother and, 55
  narrative, and walking, 150, 152
  uncanny and, 49
angel in the house, 3, 5, 51, 57
anonymous narrator, 44–6, 49, 50,
  55–7
Arabian Nights, The, 27, 75, 146
army of the dead, 149, 151–2
Auden, W.H., 165n.19
autobiography, 69–70, 123–5

Bakhtin, M.M., 77, 119, 171n.1
  Dialogic Imagination, The, 104
Barthes, Roland, 103–5, 107, 170n.1
Baudelaire, Charles, 148, 173
  Painter of Modern Life, The,
    95–97, 153–4

beauty of gothic, 148–50, 152
beginning at ending, 123, 131
Bellour, 170
bildüngsroman, 49, 123, 129
binary opposition, 7, 16, 33, 38, 55,
  91, 92, 116
Blain, Virginia, 166n.2
blank
  at core of identity, 125
  rationality reduces woman
    to, 32
  see also cipher; silence
blank page, 31, 39, 66
body
  in cinema, as ghostly presence, 6
  inhabited by parade of selves, 86
  in pieces (*corps morcélé*), 68
body of woman
  contradictions and, 31
  degeneration figured onto, 89
  department store founded on, 10,
    82–3, 88–90, 92
  fears projected onto, 38
  male anxieties about, 2
  male gaze and, 94
  mastering, through narrative, 50
  ownership of, 3
  transferal of symptoms onto, 37,
    104–6, 108, 110–11
  uncanny and, 52
  see also female body
Bowlby, Rachel, 169n.1
Brantlinger, Patrick, 164n.9, 165
Brontë, Charlotte
  Villette, 8, 35, 73, 115
Brooks, Peter, 69, 73–5, 169n.1,
  171n.2, 172

burial
    of dead man, and multiplot, 63
    of female voice, 15
    of repressed desires, 150
    of stories, 10–11, 20–1, 139
    of woman, and obsessive
        description, 81–2, 95
    see also live burial
buried ending, 131
buried manuscript, 3, 14–15,
    17–20, 133, 138
buried mystery, 69
buried narrative, 14–15, 24, 27,
    75–9, 155, 159
buried question of masculinity, 107
buried secrets, 23, 137, 140
Buss, Robert William
    "Dickens's Dream" (painting), 85
Butler, Judith, 170n.11

capitalism, 5, 62, 83, 84, 88–9, 96
Carroll, Noel, 170n.1
Castle, Terry
    "Phantasmagoria," 44
castration anxiety, 51, 92, 107
Chaney, David, 169
channeling, idleness and, 155
character
    critique of, 71
    department store and, 85–7
    gothic apparatus to shadow, 150–1
    history and melodrama and,
        136–8
    multiplot directed away from, 127
    obsessive interplay between
        narrators and, 154–5
    poetical, 153
chiaroscuro, 108
cinema, 6, 10, 160
    department store and, 82
    identity and, 101, 126
    multiple voices and, 104
    railroad and, 86
cipher, 25, 31, 39
city, 147–54, 149
    poetic, 149, 153

closure, avoidance of, 44, 66–7,
    74–5, 100, 105, 107, 131,
    144–5
    see also ending
clothing or dress, 87, 92–3, 96–7,
    111–12, 151–2
Coleridge, Samuel Taylor, 139
    "Ancient Mariner, The," 139
Collins, Wilkie, 1, 138, 156
    Frozen Deep, The, 134, 144,
        172n.11
    Haunted Hotel, The, 1, 8, 13–21
    Law and the Lady, The, 32, 38–9
    Woman in White, The, 1, 8,
        16–17, 21–41
commemoration, 143, 145
commercialism, 98
commodity, love plot as, 100
consumerism, 81–2, 87, 89
contradictions, 26, 29–31, 40,
    79, 87
control and mastery
    anxiety and, 33–4
    language of, 92
    looking and, 106–7
    of narrative, 107, 111–12, 114
copy or replica, 2, 3, 9, 29, 57, 82,
    103, 122, 151
Cornell, Drucilla, 169–70n.9
corpse, 16–18, 20
    narration and, 9, 62–71, 76
    narration over women's, 30
    obsession with, 123
    of woman, department store and,
        9–10, 82–3, 88–9
    see also dead body
creativity, death and, 149–50, 154
creator, 3, 130, 134, 143, 149
crime, 67, 69, 71, 75–6
    of detective, 25–6, 31
    against family, 141
    return to scene of, 115
    telling of one's story and, 122
criminal, entering mind of, 27
crisis
    in identity, 110

in interpretation, and woman's
        identity, 33
    in narrative, 23
    in origins, 160
    in reason, 34
    in vision, 107, 112
Crosby, Christina, 135
Crystal Palace, 84
Cummings, Katherine, 166n.2
Cvetkovich, Ann, 164n.5, 165n.17

Dacre, Charlotte
    Zofloya, 15
Darwin, Charles, 1, 4, 5, 11, 14–15,
        37, 45, 57, 64–5, 125–6,
        128–30, 134, 147, 160
    On the Origin of Species, 4, 37, 45,
        57, 134, 149
dead
    appropriating speech of, as
        linguistic mystery, 77
    coming to life, 125, 149–56
    consorting with, 55
    continual resurfacing of, 63
    department store as locus for, 82
    images of, 67
    see also corpse; ghosts; resurrection;
        return of the dead
dead/alive, 8, 53–4, 117, 122–3,
        144–5, 157
dead body, 68–70
    origins in, 65
    of woman, 30, 82, 88–9
dead-end, 114, 120
deanimation and reanimation,
        119–20
death
    absence of narrative as, 65,
        71, 114
    ambivalent view of, 129
    beauty of imagination and,
        148–50
    double as harbinger of, 153
    exuberance of, 152
    female body embodies, 82
    first person narration and, 77

idleness as, 154, 155
life story about, 123
love and, 116–17
lurking, 135
multiplot to avoid, 43, 66–7, 71,
        73, 75, 78–9, 123, 146
narration to surmount, 130,
        142–5, 156, 158
obsession with, 65, 109, 111,
        113–14, 123, 153, 157
of representation, 116
restaging, to resurrect narration,
        10–11, 154
silence as, 27
specter of, and guises, 114–15
symbolic, 31–2
death drive or instinct, 72–3, 79,
        108, 110–11, 113–14
death in life
    Darwin's metaphor for, 5
    home and, 127
decapitation, 136, 139
decay, 89, 121, 129, 148–9
defacements, 67–75
delay or postponement, 69,
        73–4, 103
De Man, Paul de
    "Autobiography as
        De-facement," 87
department store, 5–6, 9–10, 81–98
De Rougement, Denis, 171n.7
Derrida, 144, 166n.2
desire, 6–7, 10
    for artifice or fake, 96–7, 101
    for dead woman, 103
    department store and, 83–4,
        86–7, 92–5, 100
    dialectically working of, 67
    displaced, for woman, 83
    for fantasy image, 87
    female, repression of, 89, 116–17
    for image of painting, 102–3
    law and, 138
    for lost feminine, 92–7, 99–100
    narration and, 69–70, 73–5, 78
    for story of own making, 31

detection, 22–6, 37, 41, 45
  see also logical detection
detective, 25–7, 37, 39, 59–60,
    106–7, 112, 165
detective story, 22–3, 27, 28, 31–5,
    37, 104, 117
detour, 73–5, 78–9
diabolic, 154
dialogue, 27, 143
  melodrama substituted for, 141
  with readers, 132–3, 146, 158
Dickens, Charles, 10–11
  Bleak House, 1, 9, 43–60, 120
  "Bridal Chamber, The,"
    154–6
  David Copperfield, 37, 44,
    64, 120
  Dombey and Son, 146
  Great Expectations, 1, 2, 5, 7, 11,
    47–8, 50–1, 62, 64, 73,
    119–33, 144, 148
  journalistic writing, 145–58
  *Lazy Tour of Two Idle Apprentices,
    The*, 1, 2, 146, 154
  Mystery of Edwin Drood, 157
  "Night Walks," 148–52
  Oliver Twist, 37, 45
  Our Mutual Friend, 1, 9, 61–79,
    101, 130; Postscript in Lieu
    of Preface, 1, 9, 64–7, 130,
    144, 157
  public readings, 85–6, 130, 133,
    146, 157
  Tale of Two Cities, A, 1, 2,
    133–45, 148
  "Travelling Abroad," 152
  Uncommercial Traveller, The
    (Dickens), 1, 2, 146–53
difference, 46, 49, 52, 55–6, 111
disease, 54, 56, 59, 60
  uncontained woman and, 17
disembodiment, 139, 142–5
disfigurement, 63, 67, 70, 76,
    78–9
  see also defacement
disguise, 38–9, 71, 72, 97

disjunction
  history and, 138
  between self and representation,
    160
displacement, 7, 78, 104–7, 113,
    122–3, 126–7
display, 9, 89, 97–8
distinctions, obliteration of, 55–6
Doane, Mary Ann, 91
doll, 47, 52–3, 87–8
domestic, 1, 3–5, 7–9, 30, 49,
    62–3, 88, 140, 147
double ending, 2, 11, 131–3,
    144, 146
double geography of advent of
    capitalism, 89
double narration, 22, 43, 44,
    46–50, 55–6, 160
doubleness
  novelist and melodramatist and,
    133, 136
  woman surrounded by, 10
double reading of Victorian
    fiction, 159
double reflections, 37
doubles, 22, 48, 55–6, 83, 103–4,
    121–4, 131, 136–7, 142,
    150–1, 153, 160
doubling, 55, 102, 109, 119, 139,
    143, 152
  gothic identity and, 101, 160
dreams, 36, 112–13, 150
dummy or model, 82, 86–8, 93, 97
  see also doll
dynamism, 145, 150

embedded stories, 9, 15, 24, 27, 40,
    88–9, 104, 133–4, 138, 141
embodiment, 134, 137, 143–5,
    151–2
ending, 43, 60
  avoidance of, 46, 65–7, 73–5,
    144, 148, 153, 157
  beginning at, 123, 131
  desire for, challenged, 20–1
  desire for happy, 83, 100

desire for, and plot, 73–4
lack of, 158, 160, 161
merging of voices at, 142–5
see also closure; double ending;
non-closure
energy, 154–6
enervation, 124
"entangled bank," 4, 64–5, 125,
128, 149
epitaph, 125
epithet, 71, 75, 78
eternal return, 142
evolution, 130, 145, 147, 149
excessiveness, 32, 124–5, 136
identity and, 160–1
see also obsessive description

fabricated image, 97
fabrication, 103
face, 48, 54, 58–60
of dead, 18–19, 67–71, 78
giving, to thing, 87
hidden, 47
manufactured images of, 62
of mother, 54–5, 60
removal of, 136
trying on new, 152
fairy tale, 88, 129, 136, 154
fake or counterfeit, 102
falling, 105, 106, 107, 112–13
false identities, 22, 64, 75
family secrets, 138–41
fantasy image, 83, 95–7, 99
fashion, 96
fecundity, 149
Felman, Shoshana, 171n.5
Felski, Rita, 169
female body, 2–3, 10, 50, 82–3
female desire, 89, 116–17
female voice, 1, 8–9, 15, 13–22, 41,
44–55, 58
feminine or female
castration anxiety and, 51–2
department store as site of, 82
hermeneutic code and, 105
home as site of, 128

male fascination and fear of,
16–17
within male, haunting by,
111–13
male supremacy and desire
for, 92
power of masculine "I" and, 94
unconscious and, 94
feminine identity
misrepresentation of, 29
obscured, returns to haunt, 117
Victorian representation of, 63
feminine sublime, 17
feminist reading of double, 55–6
fetish, 7, 92, 110
figuration, 63
figure of woman, 159
contingencies mapped onto, 37
fabrication of new, 86, 88–90
gothic excess and, 32
haunts in many guises, 8, 21
as problematic entity, 3
secrets coded in, 23
terror of falling and, 105,
107–8, 113
as unknowable, 40–1, 117
first person narration, 3, 48–9,
61–4, 68, 69, 71, 75–9,
119–21, 123–4, 132, 136–7
fixity, 38, 40, 105
flaneur, 81–2, 84, 147–8
fog filter, 102, 108, 111
Forster, John, 148, 173n.22
Foucault, Michel, 7
Madness and Civilization, 34
found manuscripts, 3
see also buried manuscripts
fragmentation, 6–7, 18, 47, 67, 68,
75, 129, 142
corpse and, 68
double and, 153
face of mother and, 54
history and, 138
spectacle and, 84–5
France, 9, 81, 83, 84, 90
French Revolution, 133, 134

Freud, Sigmund, 32, 46, 79,
94, 109
Beyond the Pleasure Principle,
72–3, 75, 105, 171n.10
Five Lectures on Psychoanalysis
(Freud), 159–60
Interpretation of Dreams,
The, 106
"Moses of Michelangelo,
The," 23
"Uncanny, The," 4, 33, 46,
49, 51–2, 55, 138, 143,
150, 153
Fuss, Diana, 170n.11

Garrett, Peter, 167n.8
gaze
face and, 54, 67–9, 76
male, 94
self seen through, 85
terror and death and, 116
see also look; seeing
gender, 1–2, 4
ambivalence about, 91, 109,
111–12
binary modes and, 7–8
denial of categorical, 46, 129
fall into, 111
identity and, 92–3, 103, 113
instability of, home and, 128–9
phantoms of, 7, 82, 101, 113
photograph and film and, 160
seeing and, 106
gender relations, 90–1, 110–11, 116
gentleman, shifting meaning of, 129
ghostly feminine, 13–21
ghostly figure, 151
ghostly presence, 6–7, 22, 43–4,
134, 139
ghostly remainder, 34, 89
ghostly or spectral effects
double ending and, 132
double narrative and, 22, 43–4
film as, 10, 102, 108, 160
gothic novel as, 7
identity and, 126, 161

layers of meaning and, 5
psychology and, 150–2
repetition and history and, 143
unlocatable voice and, 145
ghost(s) or specter
bodily form as, 86
confronting, by narrating one's
story, 120, 122–3
Dickens's imaginative vitality and,
2, 11, 50, 142, 148–9, 152–3
Dickens the writer as, 146, 158
female voice and, 13, 159
history as, 135, 137–8
home and, 4–5, 156, 159
indeterminacy of origins and,
3–4, 160
as leftover or excess, 7–8, 35
memory of what has been buried
and, 160–1
multiple, 10, 102, 107, 113, 117
nun as, 30, 115
returns and, 145, 160–1
self as, 125, 131–2
time, 135–6
ghost's walk, 11, 44, 51, 56–7,
60, 145
see also walking
God, disappearance of, 130–1, 134
gothic
attempts to contain, 36
city and, transformed into
poetic, 153
corpse of representation and, 89
cultural horror and, 2–3
Darwin's text as, 4
Dickens's obsession with, and
resurrection, 146–50, 152
difficulty getting story told in, 15
motif of live burial in, 15
oppression and, 105
power of, to disrupt rational,
32–4
presentation of character and, 136
see also Victorian gothic novel;
and specific aspects and
techniques

gothic death, 19
gothic excess, 7
gothic identity, 101, 160–1
gothic narration and, 1–2, 7,
　119–20, 160–1
gothic plot, 18, 23, 34–5
grave, 113
　gaze of woman and, 34
　home and, 127
　narration from, 30, 66, 69, 71,
　　120–4, 131–2, 143
　unfinished tomb and, 158
grave inscriptions, 32, 66, 67, 75,
　121, 123–4
gravestone, 114, 128
graveyard, 158
Griffith, D.W., 173n.18
Grosz, Elizabeth, 94

haunted space
　department store as, 82, 83
　home or house as, 51, 53–4,
　　156, 159
haunting
　Bleak House and, 43, 46,
　　48, 55
　"Bridal Chamber" and, 154
　Dickens, the writer, and, 146–8,
　　152–3
　Great Expectations and, 120, 121,
　　123, 130–1
　Haunted Hotel and, 8, 14–15, 17
　Our Mutual Friend and, 75
　Tale of Two Cities, 134–5,
　　138–40, 144
　Vertigo and, 102, 107–8, 110–13,
　　116–17
　Victorian novel and, 1–3,
　　159–60
　Woman in White and, 23–4, 34
Heath, Stephen, 169n.8
Heller, Tamar, 163n.2, 166n.25
Hennelly, Mark M., Jr., 164
hermeneutic code, 103–7
historical novel, 138–9
history, 134–41, 143, 145

Hitchcock, Alfred, 2
　Birds, The, 105
　Marnie, 105
　Psycho, 105, 106, 114
　Rear Window, 105
　Vertigo, 1, 2, 6, 10, 101–17
Hoffman, E.T.A.
　"Sandman, The," 24, 51–3, 87–8
Hollander, Anne, 93
Hollington, Michael, 172–73
home, 1, 3–5, 8, 49–52, 55, 60,
　109, 124–5, 127–9, 132, 135,
　138–40, 156, 159
homelessness, 128, 132, 147,
　150–2, 158–60
house
　encased in, 141
　ruined, 124, 126–7
　see also haunted space
Hughes, Winifred, 164n.13
Hutter, A.D., 164n.7, 165n.15,
　166n.26
Hutter, Albert, 168
hysteria, linguistic, 50
hysteric, 20–1, 34, 46, 105,
　132, 160

"I"
　anxiety about narrating, 66–72,
　　75–9
　kaleidoscopic, 153
　that must be heard, 144
idealized image, 111
　of mother, 54, 95
　of self, 47, 54, 68, 84–5
　of women, 27, 96–7
identification
　with Other, 99
　with woman, 106–7, 110–13
identity(ies)
　corpse and, 62–5, 70–1, 76
　crisis of, 20
　desire for fantasy image and,
　　83–7
　disguise and, 38
　dispersion of, 125

identity—*continued*
  dynamics of repression and delay
    and, 69
  figure of woman haunts Victorian
    ideas about, 159
  first person narration and, 47, 64,
    77, 78
  fixity of, critiqued, 36–8, 40
  gothic vs. logical, 26
  illusion of masculine power
    and, 112
  imposter and, 53
  instability of eye and, 102
  limits of representation in
    forming, 62
  multiplot and, 70–2, 126–7
  mystery at core of, 28, 41, 125
  nun and, 35
  obsession with stories of, 72
  overlapping and, 104, 113
  performative or display view of,
    82–7
  secret of, 22–3
  shifting and transferable, 54, 55,
    83–4, 86–8, 101, 126
  technology and, 9–10, 81
  terror and, 126–7, 131
  time and space and, 6, 153
  uncanny, 62
  understanding of, outside
    narrative, 40
  visual projection and, 102–3
  wandering and, 151
  see also gothic identity; woman's
    identity
image(s)
  of desire, 94, 102–3, 113
  instability of, 10, 103
  piling up of, 82–3, 91–2
  self as, and spectacle, 85
  shifting and linked, 147
image of woman, 93–5, 99–100,
  104, 106
imagination, 150–2, 159
impersonation, 126
in-between genders, 129

in-between space, 20, 60, 86,
  119–20, 123, 143–5, 153–4
indeterminacy, 4, 7
instability, 35, 45, 102
interiority, 5, 137
irrational, 33, 38, 40–1

Jaffe, Audrey, 166n.2
James, Henry, 138
Jameson, Frederic, 163n.1
James, P.D.
  Death of an Expert Witness, 28
jouissance, 32, 74

kaleidoscopic eye, 148, 153
Kaplan, Cora, 170n.15
Kaplan, Fred, 173n.21
Keats, John, 153
Keily, Robert, 168n.16
Kendrick, Walter M., 165n.20
knowledge and knowing, 25, 27,
  28, 40, 43, 117, 136, 140, 158
known and unknown, 49
Kucich, John, 168n.11

labyrinth or maze, 23–4, 63, 64, 71,
  82–3, 95, 103, 146, 148, 160
Lacan, Jacques, 47, 54, 68, 71,
  83–6, 88, 93–4, 167–8,
  170n.14
lack, 7, 91–2
  of dialogue, in family story, 141
  of identity of corpse, 70–1,
    75, 78
  see also absence; blank; cipher
language
  crisis in, 20
  disembodiment of, 144
  self and, 121–2
  shadows of, 128
  sublime and, 17
  uncanny and, 33
LaPlanche, Jean, 171n.10
law, 26–8, 31, 32, 34, 38, 40, 45,
  60, 138
  of the father, 112

layering, 11, 23, 45, 46, 102, 108, 113, 119, 122, 126, 129, 141, 145, 155, 160
see also superimposition
leakage, 43, 102
legitimacy, 60, 138
Lewis, Matthew
Monk, The, 15, 30, 115
life
affirmation of, and connection with death, 148–50, 154–6
images of, in consumer goods, 82
inability to contain, 73–4
recalled to, 134, 144–5, 146–7, 154
see also dead/alive; death in life; resurrection
life instincts, 72–3, 79
linguistic mystery, 76–7
linguistic ruin, 50
Litvak, Joseph, 169n.4
live burial, 2–8
Collins and, 13, 15, 19–22, 24–5, 30, 34
Dickens and, 50, 56, 61–3, 67–75, 119, 123, 127, 134, 138–9, 141, 143, 148, 156–7
Hitchcock and, 102–3, 105, 109
Zola and, 82, 88
Loesberg, Jonathan, 165n.16, 166n.23
logical detection, 10, 23, 25–6, 31–2, 34, 39
London, 37–8, 45, 46, 133, 138, 139–41, 146–50, 153
look and looking
control and, 106
at corpse, 67–8, 70
at woman, 15–16, 30, 94
see also gaze; seeing
lost, getting, 125, 150
love, 83, 87, 97–100, 104, 140–1
and death, 108, 110–13, 115–17
Lukacher, Ned, 173n.20

machine or mechanized self, 3, 6, 123
MacKay, Carol Hanbery, 168
madness, 34, 36–7, 113, 150–1, 155–7
Malone, Cynthia Northcutt, 166n.2
Man from Somewhere (or Nowhere), 68, 70, 73–6, 78
marriage, 31–2, 99, 156
Marx, Karl
"Eighteenth Brumaire of Louis Bonaparte, The," 141
masculine and feminine
ambivalence between, 90–4, 104, 116, 160
anxieties about gender and, 2
joining of, 128–9
masculine identity, 37, 55
collapse of, 104
fear projected onto woman and, 107–8, 110
law and, 40
Matrimonial Causes Act of 1857, 172n.13
meaning
inability to resolve, 103–4
multiplicity of, 74–5, 129, 131, 160
Medusa figure, 16
melodrama, 133, 135–8, 141–2, 145
memento mori, 92, 108
memorialization, 30, 32, 67, 109
Miller, D.A., 164–5, 168n.9
Miller, J. Hillis, 166n.1
mirror, 59–60, 124–5
ghosts in, 120
other in, 78
pantomime in front of, 137–8
remnant of self in, 54
wandering and, 147–8
mirror image, 36–7
desire and, 102–3
double and, 137–8
idealized identity and, 47–8
inability to interpret, 113
nun as, 116

mirroring
    of woman and falling, 110
mirror stage, 47, 54, 68, 84–6, 94
missing part or lacuna, 22, 63,
    65, 76
mistaken identity, 69, 70, 75
Mitchell and Rose, 170n.13
Modleski, Tania, 170–71n.4
monster, 3, 47
morgue, 152, 153
Morris, David B., 46
mother, 54–5, 60, 93–5
    male as maternal figure, 128–9
mourning, 125, 129
multiple voices or stories, 14, 20,
    22–5, 27–9, 104, 145, 149,
    156, 160–1
    see also embedded stories
multiplot novel
    Collins and, 22
    Dickens and, 2, 9–11, 46, 61,
        63–64, 67–75, 78–9, 125–7,
        130–2, 146–7
    Dickens and psychology and,
        150–1
    gothic narration and, 1–2, 7,
        119–20, 160–1
Mulvey, Laura, 91, 114, 171n.9
    "Visual Pleasure and Narrative
        Cinema," 91
murder, 40, 63, 64, 66–7, 69–70,
    75–7, 156
mutability, 35, 128–9
mystery, 40, 138, 140
    of human personality, 38, 150
    of "I," 76
    woman as, 32, 35, 36

Narcissus, 111
narration or narrative
    to avoid or overcome death, 11,
        27, 66–7, 70, 75, 78–9, 114,
        156, 158
    blocked, 20–1, 34, 138
    to compensate for unease, 133
    compulsive, 130, 155–6

conjunction between psychological
    dynamics and, 7
dead-alive space and, 53–4, 144
diabolic and, 154
difficulties of telling and, 15,
    18–19, 63, 102
disguise and, 38
face and, 48, 69
failure of female, 20
female and, 57–9
forward and backward, 107,
    109, 123
ghost and, 18, 21, 131
from grave, 30, 66, 69, 71,
    120–4, 131–2, 143
identity and, 69
imposed by male narrator, 28,
    32, 40
inexhaustibility of, 73, 150
innovations in, by Dickens, 134
love and, 117
memorialization and, 114
multiple origins and, 125
new, arises out of decay, 129
novel as survival of fittest, 1
perpetual death of, 19–21
reported, 24
resurrection and, 27, 70, 130,
    133, 142, 144, 146, 148,
    157, 159–61
retrospective, 120–1, 123, 132
ruins and, 19–21
sentence as basic grammar of,
    105, 107
transgression and, 47
voice of author and, 43, 66
wandering and, 147–8
woman and, 39–40, 114
wordless, 21–41
    see also anonymous narrator;
        double narration; first person
        narration; gothic narration;
        multiple voices or stories
narrator
    characters vie to be, 156
    masquerade and, 38–9

non-closure, 105, 160
nothingness, 48
Novak, Kim, 116
nun, 30, 35, 115–17

obituary, 66, 69
object
    of desire, 93, 95, 97–9
    of gaze, 84–5
    as stand-in for woman, 91–7
obsession, 7
    with classification, 4
    with death, 70, 113, 146
    with eyes, 110
    with ghosts, 9
    with narrating, 15, 65, 66, 79,
        130, 132–4, 155–6
    with order, 4
    with past, 110
    with reading the female,
        15–16
obsessive description, 81, 82–3,
    91–2, 124–5
O'Donnell, Patrick, 167
Oedipus, 27
oppression, 39–40, 88, 105,
    140, 141
order, 4–5, 26, 40–1, 63,
    105, 140
original trauma, 107–8, 111
origins, 57, 103
    double at place of, 48
    history and, 135
    leading away from, 63–5
    multiple and undefinable,
        3, 19, 43–6, 55, 70,
        125–6, 128–31,
        133, 147
    quest for, 24–5, 37, 49
    return to, 61, 131
    of species, 4, 160
    uncanny as space without, 50
    Victorian obsession with, 1,
        3–4, 159
    of woman, 3–4, 33
other, 36, 55, 68, 78–9, 99, 160

parent, lack of benevolent, 130, 132
Paris, 133, 138, 140, 141, 150,
    152–3
paternity, 128
patriarchal culture, 91, 92, 94
performance, 85, 97
personification, 87–8
Petrie, Graham, 173n.18
Phiz, 48
photograph, 6, 85, 160
"pleasures of the chase," 74
plenitude, 67, 150
plot
    drive toward end, 73–4, 143
    multiplot and, 1
    repetition and, 75
    wandering and, 150
    see also embedded stories;
        multiplot novel; narration
Poe, Edgar Allan
    Fall of the House of Usher,
        The, 148
    Man of the Crowd, The, 153–4
    "Philosophy of Composition,
        The," 108
    "Purloined Letter, The," 27
poetic, city as, 153
Poole, Adrian, 167n.3
portrait or painting, 56, 102–3,
    108, 113, 114
    see also copy or replica
Powell and Pressburger
    Black Narcissus (film), 116–17
power
    home and, 140
    knowledge and, 25
    of phallus, 107
    rests on sham, 112
    woman invested with, 92
    workers and masters and, 141
powerlessness, 111–12
presence and absence, 6, 10
prison, 23, 134, 140, 141, 143
prison escape, 77
progress, 82, 137
projection, 102, 152

prophetic voice, 143–5
prostitute, 52
psychoanalysis, 23
psychology
  detection and, 26
  dynamic of gothic and, 160
  of mind, in Dickens, 150–1
  new reality of, 7
Punter, David, 34, 45
puzzlement, 137
  see also riddle
Pykett, Lyn, 164n.3

quiescence, 72–3

railroads, 5, 6, 64, 86
rational, 21, 23, 27–8, 32–4, 36,
  40, 62, 137–8
reading
  face of dead, 69
  identity, 161
  woman, 21, 23, 29–30, 36, 40,
    94–6
real, return of, 102
realism, 22, 23, 34–5, 87, 119
reanimation, 63, 125
rebirth, 10–11, 111, 134, 142, 146,
  148, 152, 156, 158
repetition (compulsion to repeat),
  49, 59, 75–6, 105, 107,
  109–11, 114–15, 131, 161
representation
  death of, 105, 116
  drowning in, 62–5
  face as, 54
  as fakery, 29
  identity and, 70–3
  nun and, 35
  reanimation and, 63
  retelling and, 66
  self and, 152, 160
  woman and, 34–6, 83, 86
repression, 2, 7–8, 11, 50, 62,
  69–70, 75, 107, 109–11, 132,
  140, 142, 157
  of woman's desire, 116–17

resurrection, 2, 8, 43, 132–4,
  141–6, 148–9, 153, 154, 156
return(s)
  to childhood, 4, 47, 120
  from dead, 1–2, 4–7, 11, 19–20,
    22, 56, 67, 82, 101, 102,
    105, 111, 120, 138, 148–50,
    155–7, 161
  of ghost of feminine, 159
  ghostly, 160
  history and, 137
  home, 50–52, 109, 125, 128,
    156, 159
  of past upon the present, 160
  of repressed, 11, 13, 58, 83, 89,
    100, 116–17, 150
  to site of feminine, 49, 50–2, 128
  telling story entails, 55
  to traumatic event, 143
  to womb, 143
revolution, 134, 139–41
riddle, self as, 72, 76
Ross, Kristin, 87
Royle, Nicholas, 167
ruin and ruination, 14, 19–21,
  34–5, 45, 46, 61, 82–3, 120–1,
  124–5, 128–9, 132
rupture, 138
Ruskin, John
  "Of Queen's Garden's," 128

sadomasochism, 110, 112
Sanders, Andrew, 142
Sartre, Jean-Paul, 69
scapegoat figure, 112
scars, 58
Scheherazade, 27, 46, 75, 146
Schelling, 51
scriptural word, narrative as
  replacement for, 134, 142–3
secret, 48
  bringing to light, 57, 58
  detective and, 22–3, 25–6, 107
  history and melodrama, 137
  home and, 136, 139–41, 156
  identity and, 24–5, 71

misunderstanding of "I," 71, 78
mother and, 60
revelation of, 141, 151, 156–57
woman's identity and, 19, 23, 36
Sedgwick, Eve Kosofsky, 163n1,
   167, 171n11
seduction, 74, 97–98
seeing and vision, 144
   crisis of, 10, 106, 107
   errors of perspective and,
      28–29, 35
   identity, 101–3
self
   alienation of, 136
   authorial, forced to wander, 152
   disjunction between
      representation and, 160
   dissolution of, 113
   dummy as prop of, 82
   encounters with, and missed
      connection, 151–52
   evasion and, 78–79, 137
   figuration, 70
   fragments of, and mirror, 84–85
   ghosts and, 125, 127, 131–32
   history and, 137–38
   idealized image and, 68
   identity and, 9
   image and representation and,
      62–63
   inability to find past, 121
   inability to own, 125
   interchangeable, 136
   lack of center and, 127
   language outside, 121
   moving picture of, in time, 85
   multiple, 126
   mysteries of, 76
   narration and representation,
      72, 78
   never ending, 152
   not locatable, 151
   as object of gaze, 62
   replacement of parent figure
      by, 130
   as riddle, 72, 76

secrets at heart of, 136
spectacle and, 81
technological, 62
Victorian model of, as
   inadequate, 63
sensation novel, 138
sentence, narrative and, 105,
   107, 116
Shaffer, Lawrence, 171n.6
Shelley, Mary
   Frankenstein, 3, 47, 68, 70, 126,
      131, 134, 139, 153, 160,
      172n.6
silence, 26–7, 41, 130, 138, 139
Silverman, Kaja, 169n.7
Sisyphus, 130
social gothic, 7
social order, 24, 31, 34, 38, 58
spectacle, 124, 160
   gory, 135–7, 139, 141
   identity and, 81, 83–9, 126
   love plot as, 97–9
   mirror stage and, 84–5
   wandering, of metropolis,
      147–8
spiral structure, 114
Stevenson, Robert L.
   Dr. Jekyll and Mr. Hyde, 153
Stewart, Garrett, 168n.14
Stewart, James, 106
storytelling
   desire and, 98
   grave and, 123
   obsession with, 72–4, 79
   see also embedded stories;
      narration
subjectivity, 72, 123, 156
sublime, 17, 33, 82–3, 95,
   142–3, 149
superimposition, 2, 8, 22, 44, 50,
   57, 63, 82, 106, 120, 136,
   145, 152–53
   identity and, 4, 126, 160
supernatural, 21, 101–2
survival of fittest, 8–9, 14–15
suspense mode, 103, 105

Tambling, Jeremy, 172n.4
taming of woman, 16, 21
Taylor, Jenny Bourne, 164n.6
technology, 5–6, 9–10, 62, 64, 82,
    86, 160
terror or horror
    beauty and, 150, 152
    blocked voice and, 138
    castration and, 107
    containment of, 15–16
    creating someone in one's own
        image, 122
    dead man or corpse and,
        63, 68
    difficulty getting story told and,
        15, 20
    disease and unruly woman, 17
    face of dead and, 18–19, 70
    falling, 105, 108, 110
    female narration and, 57–59
    ghost and, becomes life
        affirming, 148
    gothic and, 32–3
    history and melodrama and, 138
    home and, 50, 127–8, 140
    identity and, 113–15, 127
    lack of ending and, 20–1
    lack of parent figure and, 130
    language and, 117, 121–2, 131
    lessened by writing, 17–18
    live burial and, 65, 123, 143
    love and, 116
    multiple stories and, 132
    of nothingness, 115
    plurality of meaning and, 129
    reconciliation of dead with living
        and, 120
    replaced by exuberance, 11
    representation and, 53
    repressed, and narrative, 33–4
    revolution and family and, 136,
        140–1
    staged scenes of, 135
    telling of self and, 126
    uncanny and, 46, 103, 110

voice beyond consciousness, 43
    woman and, 30, 33, 37, 46,
        92, 106
third person narrator, 77, 78
    see also anonymous narrator
Thomas, Deborah A., 171n.3
time, 6, 84, 86, 115, 134–7,
    142–3, 145
Todorov, Tzvetan, 70, 114, 157,
    164n.8, 171n.8
trafficking in woman, 90–1
tramp, 151–2
transference, 113, 123
transgression, 21, 30, 47, 56–7,
    60, 116
triangle, 116
tripling, 110
truth, one vs. multiple, 27–8

uncanny, 160
    department store and, 82
    desire as, 6
    dialogue of plots and, 139
    domesticity haunted by, 62–3
    double and, 55
    ending on note of supposition
        and, 60
    feminine narrative voice and,
        20–1, 44–6, 48–54, 58
    feminine sublime and, 17–18
    home and, 49–51, 138–9, 159
    identity as, 62
    illegitimacy and, 60
    indeterminacy in representation
        and, 3
    layering and, 46
    live burial and, 143
    multiple origins and, 125
    multiplication of stories and, 71,
        103–4
    nun and, 115–17
    Postscript in Our Mutual Friend
        and, 65
    return to original home or womb
        and, 4

space and time and, 6, 54
space between life and death and,
123, 145
unresolvable contradiction
and, 109
woman and, 16, 30, 33, 50, 87,
109–10
unconscious, 40, 94
unease, 32–3, 56, 133
see also disease
unfinished story, 158
unruly woman, 16–17
unspeakable or unnamable, 15,
22–4, 33–4, 41, 68, 81, 117

Van Boheemen-Saaf, Christine,
166n.3
veil, 32, 48, 59, 116, 126
ventriloquating the self, 77, 114
vertigo shot, 2, 107, 109–11
Victorian gothic novel, 5–7, 11
double reading of, 159
ghost haunting in, as woman, 3
ghostly presences in, and
limitations of realism, 119
going home in, and site of
feminine, 3, 128
influence of Darwin on, 1
melodrama and, 136
phantom-like structure and, 7
see also gothic identity; gothic
narration; gothic plot; *and
specific aspects; authors; and
techniques*
Vinken, Barbara, 169n.6
vision, *see* seeing
voice(s)
blocked, 138
buried, 160
of dead, resurrection of, 142,
144–5
dispersal of, 64
at ending, 132
from grave, refuse to stop
talking, 132

without home, 145
of oppressed, 141
speaking, vs. narrative, 43
see also female voice; multiple
voices or stories

walking, 47, 84, 146–54, 156
see also ghost's walk
wandering, 2, 11, 22–4, 30, 44,
56, 57, 114, 125, 132,
146–52, 159
Weiskel, Thomas, 17
West, Ann, 171n.8
White, Hayden, 138, 172n.12
Wilde, Oscar
Picture of Dorian Gray, The, 7
window shopping, 5–6, 147
Wolfreys, Julian, 55
woman's identity,
department store and, 83–4,
88–9, 95–7
failure of logical detection to read,
23–9, 63
gothic plot and, 23, 33–8
irrational at core of, 31, 33, 41
marriage and, 31–2
nun and, 35
supernatural and, 101
woman's speech, as transgressive, 15
woman's stories, 8, 31
wordless narration and, 21–41
woman's writing, 18, 20–1
woman in white, 24, 26–8, 30,
32–4, 37
woman (women)
attempt to enclose, 26
cultural ways of seeing, 35
death and, 109, 116
department store items as stand-in
for, 81–3, 87–8, 91–2, 94–6
department story constructed on,
9–10
disguise and, 38–9
encounter with, and uncanny, 30,
33–4

woman—*continued*
  figurative live burial of, 3
  ghostly figure of, and desire, 7
  home and, 3–5
  identification with, 92, 111–12
  invisibility of, 24
  legal and social position of, 13,
    39–40
  love plot and, 100
  male detection and, 37
  male narrator vs., 36
  male in position of, 107–8,
    110–14, 117
  narrator, and ability to stay
    alive, 27
  object of gaze, 27
  origins of, 3–4, 37
  refiguring, 88
  supernatural and, 101
  threat of, 32
  transgressive figure, 30
  unconscious and, 32, 94
  see also body of woman; female
    body; figure of woman;
    image of woman; reading,
    woman
womb, 4, 129, 143
Wordworth, William
  Prelude, The, 37

Zola, Émile
  Ladies' Paradise, The, 1, 5, 9–10,
    81–101
zombie, 122, 157